Saskia Noort is a novelist and studied theatre and journalism two children and began her career by writing columns for *Marie Claire* and *Playboy*. Her first novel was *Back to the Coast*, a literary thriller and international bestseller now available for the first time in English. Her second thriller, *The Dinner Club*, was published in English by Bitter Lemon Press in 2007. Saskia Noort's novels have sold over a million copies in the Netherlands alone and have been translated into twelve languages.

**Also available by Saskia Noort**

*The Dinner Club*

# BACK TO THE COAST

## Saskia Noort

Translated from the Dutch
by Laura Vroomen

**BITTER LEMON PRESS**
**LONDON**

BITTER LEMON PRESS
First published in the United Kingdom in 2009 by
Bitter Lemon Press, 37 Arundel Gardens, London W11 2LW

www.bitterlemonpress.com
First published in Dutch as *Terug naar de kust* by
Ambo/Anthos uitgevers, Amsterdam, 2003

This edition has been published with the financial support of the
Foundation for the Production and Translation of Dutch Literature

Bitter Lemon Press gratefully acknowledges the financial
assistance of the Arts Council of England

A CIP record for this book is available from the British Library
ISBN 978-1-904738-37-4
Typeset by Alma Books Limited
Printed and bound by CPI Cox & Wyman, Reading, Berkshire

*For my children, Mathieu and Julia*

"Mum! Mummy! I can do it, look, I can stand on my head!"

Wolf's squeaky voice pulled me back ashore, out of the maelstrom of sadness and away from the pain in my empty womb. There he was, his flushed face upside down in the sand, his belly exposed and blue with the cold and his bare feet pointing up at the leaden sky. He fell over, laughed, jumped up again and threw me a cheeky look.

"Did you see me, Mum? Merel! Did you see that? I can do it too!"

Merel ignored her little brother and continued her search for shells for her necklace. Gingerly, with her toes pressed together, she walked into the shallow water. She had hitched her trouser legs up and her skinny legs were covered in gooseflesh.

"Mum, Merel's not looking!"

I was sitting on my jean jacket. With my arms wrapped around my knees, I swayed back and forth as gently as possible to ease the painful cramps. I looked at my children running around, playing with the sand and stopping to look at a dead jellyfish or a beautiful shell.

I had set off at seven o'clock this morning. My mind was made up. I had been carrying Geert's baby, but I wasn't in a position to raise another child on my own. I felt sick with hunger, but I couldn't eat a thing. My children were all I could think of: their tangled mass of hair, Wolf's eyes still heavy with sleep, Merel cuddling up to me in bed. They had been given a chance.

Geert would be furious. He wasn't exactly a good father, but he did love his son and my daughter and his love for this child would be unconditional too, even if he wouldn't be able to look after it. But it was out of the question. It was out of the question and it was about time I did the sensible thing. No interminable discussion, which would degenerate into a messy fight, with accusations flying, and end with Geert breaking down and me having to comfort him.

The baby had to go. And since it was my fault it had happened in the first place, I was the one who had to deal with the pain of saying goodbye. It wasn't something I could inflict on Geert. It was the right decision.

I thought of the Colombian mother I had seen on television once. Her tears at seeing a picture of the daughter she had been forced to give up for adoption. Her regret at depriving her eldest daughter of a little sister. Her hopes for a better life for her youngest. Not a day went by when she didn't pray to God that this little girl would one day come looking for her. Having to say goodbye to your child, even if you didn't know it, was the worst that could happen to a mother.

When it was over I went home, had a shower and went to bed. "Some paracetamol and a good night's sleep and you'll be fine," the gynaecologist had said. But the empty house was oppressive. The noticeboard with pictures of Merel and Wolf as babies. The toys scattered about. Children's bottoms in TV ads. All wordless reproaches. This mother had murdered her child. And now she was in bed. I was overcome with guilt. I had to get away. And as always when I felt that things were getting the better of me, I drove to the seaside, to the place where I was born, on the edge of the dunes. The sea breeze will blow all your worries away, my father used to say.

# 1

The letterbox rattled and the mail landed on the floor with a soft thud. I realized it must be after eleven. I had been staring at the rain for at least two hours, if not more. The ashtray was full of cigarette butts and my coffee had gone cold.

I hauled myself up and shuffled over to the door, where I picked up the damp pile of envelopes. Two letters from the taxman, a bank statement, a reminder for my six-monthly dental check-up and a postcard. A black-and-white photograph of cute pink baby feet. Tiny feet smelling of little white lambs and baby oil, tiny feet I wanted to kiss and cuddle, tiny feet I was mourning. What a horrible coincidence. My womb was still throbbing with pain.

It wouldn't hurt, the doctor had said. Perhaps the lower abdomen would be a little tender, a bit like a period, that's all. She was wrong. It had been five days now and I was still racked with pain.

I picked up the card with trembling fingers and caressed the crinkly toes, the delicate heels. I swallowed the tears that welled up and turned over the card.

Maria!
You're a viper. A slut. You murdered your child. You don't deserve to have children. You don't deserve to have a life.

I've been on your case for years. Someone ought to punish you, whore!

I'll be watching you.

I had to read the words three, four times before they sank in. Then I screamed. *What idiot would write this?* That very instant I knew who the culprit was. There was only one person furious enough to call me a viper and a slut; the only one who knew about my abortion: Geert. It was his child I had got rid of. I yanked open the front door, expecting to find him lurking behind it, grinning maliciously, but there was nobody except a miaowing cat.

The bastard. He had clearly lost it.

Still shaking with anger, I sloshed water into the percolator and scooped coffee into the filter. Some ended up on the worktop. I lit a cigarette and stared at the pathetic trickle of brown liquid dripping into the pot. This was just what I needed. After all the scenes, the struggle to detach myself from him, he had started stalking me. I looked outside at my rear neighbours' windows; I didn't know them and they always kept their curtains drawn. It had to be him.

This was a serious threat. Perhaps I ought to report it to the police. After all, he had called me a whore only four days ago. Ranting and raving, he had walked out after I had told him about the abortion. He was angry enough, no question about it. Was this his idea of getting even? I couldn't believe it. If Geert were to hurt anyone, it would be himself.

But who else knew about this? Who else had any reason to hate me this much?

I thought about that fight when I had come home with the children to find him sitting on the doorstep. I had felt too rotten to argue with him, too frail to come up with some

10

story about what was wrong with me. I simply blurted it out, even though I'd had every intention to hide it from him.

His face turned ashen. His initial thought was that I had got rid of some other guy's child. After I had finally managed to convince him that there was no other and it dawned on him that we were talking about his child, he became even more furious. "Why?" he had shouted. Surely it didn't make any difference whether we had two or three children?

"No, not to you!" I had yelled back. "But it does to me! I want to move on with my life. You're dragging me down with your depression and I can't take it any more. Another child will only make it worse. Can't you see that?"

The coffee was done. I poured it into Wolf's football mug and took a sip. I didn't know what to do. Call the police? No. That would be a bit much. I had to talk to Geert first. Today. I didn't care how angry and hurt he was, this time he had gone too far. I knew he would be sorry. He had written the card in a spiteful, drunken mood, last night, when he couldn't sleep.

Geert inched open the door with the dark-green, peeling paint and peered through a crack with bloodshot eyes. I was soaking wet and beside myself with rage.

"Open up, damn it, I'm drenched," I said and kicked the doorpost. Still half asleep, he fumbled to unhook the chain. "Easy," he mumbled and let me in.

Six years ago Geert and I had met at an audition for The Healers, a covers band. I had shuddered when I shook his strong, slender hand. It was that look in his big, deep-brown eyes that seemed to be crying out for love. With his head of thick, dark curls and his lanky frame he could have been mistaken for a gypsy.

Two hours later I was lying on Geert's mattress, drunk and madly in love, oblivious to the mess in his room and the fact that he had polished off a bottle of vodka in broad daylight. Three days later he moved in with me. My daughter Merel took no notice of him for the first few months. She had seen a couple of men come and go, including her father. But Geert stayed and eventually captured her heart as well. Together we had another child, Wolf.

He was wearing a drab T-shirt and boxer shorts. He scuttled ahead of me up the stairs, back into the warmth.

"Come on up," he said. "Let me put some warm clothes on."

I followed him and when I saw his skinny legs covered in gooseflesh I felt my anger give way to an intense sorrow.

Siebe, our drummer, had gone to Nepal for a couple of months to find himself. I had promised to water his plants, check his mail and feed his cat, Marvin. Siebe knew that Geert and I were going through a difficult patch, and when he handed over his keys he added that his flat could serve as a refuge. So now Geert was staying here and had left his stamp on the place by turning it into an utter shambles. The table was littered with empty beer bottles and a half-full bottle of wine, three overflowing ashtrays and a white carrier bag with the remnants of a Chinese take-away that Marvin was eating. Geert's bass guitar and a pile of sheet music were lying on a mattress he had dragged from the bedroom to the lounge. Familiar sounds emanated from the shower. He was still singing that tune I had heard him sing just about every morning for the past six years. *When I woke up this morning, you were on my mind.*

"Coffee?" Geert walked in with his long, wet hair dripping on his sweatshirt. I nodded and looked at him, at his anguished

12

face, and couldn't detect the merest hint of malice. We both lit a cigarette and tried to come up with something to say. I didn't dare mention the postcard. Geert went to the kitchen and returned with two steaming mugs and a bag of sugar under his arm. With trembling fingers I took the postcard out of my bag and put it in front of me on the table.

"What's this?" he muttered when he saw the picture. As he picked up the card and read the message he chewed his lower lip.

"What a fucked-up idiot…" There was a look of shock in his broken, weary eyes. I averted my gaze, because it hurt me to see him like this, in such a mess, alone. Sitting there all huddled up, he looked so vulnerable and crushed. I loathed myself. How could I suspect him of sending me something so revolting? This man I had loved for years and knew inside out. I had already robbed him of everything he loved and now I hurled this accusation at him. Then again, who else could it be? It must have been him. The thought of a stranger, some psychopath, targeting me was a thousand times worse.

"Surely you don't… You don't think I wrote this?"

Geert got up and flung the card on the table. He peered at me through screwed-up eyes and blew out his cigarette smoke in angry puffs.

"That's insane! Look at me! Be honest… Damn! Just how unhinged do you think I am? Do you really think I would want to frighten you?"

I got up as well and put my hand on his arm. He shrugged it off.

"I can't believe it, Maria! What a mess! As if things weren't bad enough. Now here you are… accusing me, as if I'm some kind of psycho. As if dumping me and getting rid of our child wasn't enough!"

He kicked a cushion across the room and shook his head, something he always did when his emotions got the better of him. He didn't want me to see his pain. I rubbed my eyes to force back the tears and bit the inside of my cheek.

"That's not fair, Geert. Are you surprised that you came to mind when I saw that postcard? After all our fights! You hurled an iron at my head the other day! You yelled that I'd be really sorry…"

"What did you expect? You threw me out of the house! We hit a bit of a bad patch and bam, I'm sent packing. As if our relationship didn't mean a thing. And then you let slip that you had our child aborted…"

He lay down on his mattress with his hands under his head and closed his eyes. His eyelids trembled.

"It wasn't quite like that. I didn't send you packing. You wanted to leave because I said I couldn't handle your problems. Because I said I wanted a life. I couldn't take it any more… And yet you didn't do a thing. You preferred to keep wallowing in your depression."

I walked over to the window, sat down on the window sill and rested my cheek against the cold glass. I looked at the grey sky that had been hanging over the city for months.

"Admit it. You were losing it. Completely messed up. I couldn't help you any more."

He rolled onto his side, wrapped his arms around his knees and buried his head in the mattress. He groaned as if in pain.

"You need to seek professional help. I can't help you. It may be selfish, but I just don't know what to do with these dark moods of yours. It's hard to love someone who's always negative, who doesn't have any lust for life. We can't bring another child into this situation, can't you see that? You need to get yourself back on track. And I've got my own life to live…"

"Ah, I see, so this is about you. You dumped me because I cramped your style. And while you were at it, you got rid of my child as well."

"Stop it, Geert. I asked you to seek help. I begged you to stop drinking. And you kept promising. You said you'd have therapy… During the past year I was there for you day and night. But it didn't make the slightest bit of difference! Things only got worse."

Geert stood up. He rubbed his face, ran his hands through his hair and all of a sudden I found him so outrageously beautiful again that the tears welled up once more. I let them flow freely this time. He looked upset.

"I love you, Maria. I would never, ever hurt you, whatever you do to me. I didn't write that postcard."

"But… who else would write a thing like that?"

"An unhinged fan, I don't know… Perhaps one of those anti-abortion freaks who spotted you at the clinic. You should take this to the police."

I shuddered. This wasn't what I wanted to hear. It was slowly sinking in. Someone was targeting me. Someone wanted me to be afraid.

"Perhaps it's all quite harmless," Geert sighed, "a one-off prank. But I'd report it if I were you. Anyway, if there's a problem, you can call me any time."

I got up and walked to the table. My hand trembled as I picked up the postcard and slipped it back into my bag. I took my coat from the back of the chair and put it on. I wanted to say something to ease the tension between us, but I didn't know what. Whatever we had shared was gone and I felt I was the one to blame. For a moment I couldn't remember why I had ended our relationship. Why I had opted for an abortion. All I knew was that I was being punished for these decisions – had I not taken them, I wouldn't be carrying a postcard from some madman in my bag. I slung my bag over my shoulder and knocked over a cup of coffee.

"Shit." I dropped to my knees to pick up the broken pieces, but found I didn't have the strength any more. Geert bent down and put his arm around me.

"Maria, I don't want us to be like this." He pressed his nose in my neck. "I want you back. I want my family back. I want to protect you…" He draped himself around me, like a tired, battered boxer. I breathed in his freshly washed hair and shaving soap, his familiar smell. He kissed me with his full, dry lips and licked the tears from my nose, while his hands slid down eagerly, fumbling for my bra fastener.

"I don't think that's a good idea," I said in a croaky voice. He kissed me again, licked my lips and burrowed his head against my breasts.

"I just want to lie next to you for a while. Feel your body."

We lay on his mattress for another half-hour. Then I got up to collect the children from school.

# 2

I was late. Except for a couple of older children, the school-yard was deserted. Wolf and Merel were waiting hand in hand by the gate. Wolf was chewing his blue scarf, lost to the world, while Merel stood fidgeting and scanning the street with a dark look in her eyes. Instead of cheering up when she spotted me, she only got angrier. She came marching over to me, dragging Wolf with her.

"Where were you?" she scolded. "I was going to play at Zoë's house and Zoë's mother waited for ages, but then she said: 'I've had enough, you can come over tomorrow.' So now I haven't got anyone to play with!"

She kicked my bike, clambered onto the luggage carrier in a huff and sat down with her arms tightly folded across her chest.

My angry little girl. While I apologized profusely, Wolf stood there with his arms up in the air, yelling "Mummy, kiss!" Snot ran down his red, chapped chin and his hands were cold and wet, but he couldn't care less. Wolf was always happy. It never ceased to amaze me that two children, born from the same womb, could be so completely different.

I often felt guilty towards Merel. Guilty over the fact that she had such a negative self-image. Steve, her father, had left us a year after she was born and she seemed to live in constant fear that one day I might leave her too.

Merel wanted the kind of life her girlfriends lived. Zoë, Sterre and Sophie had mothers who worked part-time or didn't work at all and fathers who came home in the evening and earned lots of money. They lived in respectable houses with immaculate kitchens, the kind where you had to take off your shoes and the mothers started preparing dinner at half-past four in the afternoon. She wanted a "normal" life. She would flare up whenever I started singing or dancing while doing the washing-up. "Oh please, stop it! You're always trying to be sexy," she would yell, before doing an over-the-top impression of me and stalking off. One time she poured all of our wine down the toilet and threw our cigarettes into the compost bin. Merel was an anxious child. She often had trouble falling asleep, because she would be fretting: about me dying of lung cancer, having a car crash or falling in love with another man and splitting up with Geert. Those were the kinds of things she saw on television and she had more faith in television than in me.

Like all mothers I only wanted the best for my children, but somehow I never managed to get organized. I wanted a proper family, but tended to fall for men with whom you couldn't have a normal family life. I wanted a stable, ordinary life and a regular income, an efficient, well-run household, but I was too impulsive, too lazy and too chaotic. One minute I would be on my way to the supermarket with the children, with a shopping list in my bag, and the next I would find myself in the pub with a colleague. A toasted sandwich and tomato soup for the children, and a burger and a pint for me. Fuck it, I would think, you only live once. I am happy and healthy and I want to cherish this moment. This is the message I want to pass on to my children: life is one big adventure and every day brings something new, something exciting, provided you are open to it. At such moments I would be filled with this wonderful sense of freedom and happiness and I would feel proud and glad to be different from my parents and to be living my life with so much more passion. I was giving my children much more than my parents had ever given me. What had they ever gained from all their hard work, their bitter, dogged drudgery? Nothing. Both had died young. After a life full of psychoses and depressions my mother had topped herself, while my father had died of a heart attack five years later. They ate healthily, went to bed on time and were faithful to one another. They didn't smoke or drink. They confessed their paltry sins in church. My parents. I never had the impression they were happy with me and my sister. Or with one another.

We cycled home. Wolf in front, belting out a song about gnomes on toadstools, Merel sulking on the luggage carrier. I asked them about school and told them in my perkiest voice that we would be stopping at the bakery for some fresh bread and that they could pick a treat.

"M&Ms?"

18

"No, a pastry or something. A croissant or a scone…"

Merel insisted on a Twix, Wolf wanted a breadstick.

"What's for dinner tonight, Mum?"

"Pea soup, with bacon and bread. Yummy."

"Yuck!!!"

I buried my nose in Wolf's hair, which smelled of hay, hunched over the wheel and pedalled furiously. Merel rested her head against my back.

When we got home I put the groceries away and made tea. Merel did her piano exercises, while Wolf played with his Lego, and if it hadn't been for that horrible postcard in my bag I would have enjoyed this homely scene. In Geert's arms I had been convinced of his innocence, but now my misgivings resurfaced. After all, that postcard had driven me right back into his arms. On the other hand, I couldn't imagine him getting out a typewriter and writing something so malicious. In my head, I worked my way down a list of friends and acquaintances, but halfway through I realized it was pointless. My friends were all musicians. They had better things to do than threaten me. I wasn't in anyone's way, I was just some insignificant singer leading a perfectly ordinary life. Relatives? Hardly any. Just my sister Ans and an ancient, demented aunt. When I spoke to Ans, about once a week, we both pretended to have some kind of bond. No, let's face it, Geert was the only one who had any reason to hate me.

Unless it was a stranger. A stranger who knew what nobody else knew: that I'd had my child aborted. Perhaps one of those anti-abortion activists. Someone who had spotted me at the clinic and followed me home. My name was on the door and in the phonebook. Not so long ago Dorine,

19

background singer with The Healers, had advised me to go ex-directory and to have secure door and window locks fitted. Her mother had been robbed in her own home by a gang of criminals from the Balkans. These thugs had probably been watching the house for weeks and the minute Dorine's father nipped out they made their move. They would keep an eye on you at night, waiting for the right moment, when they would ring up and ask for the homeowner. If you replied in all innocence that he wasn't at home, then bingo. They would come round to rob and rape you, just like they did back home to all those women whose husbands were up in the mountains. "Those guys are tough as nails, a human life has absolutely no meaning to them," Dorine had said. "And they know that musicians are often paid cash in hand. They'll wait for you after a show, preferably on a Sunday night, when you've had two, sometimes even three gigs and lots of cash in the house. They'll threaten to shoot your kids if you go to the police. That's exactly what they did in Bosnia and Kosovo. Extort money from the women through their children. Things are getting pretty dangerous around here with all these war criminals on the loose."

The doorbell rang. I opened the door to find the neighbours' little girl, Eva, on the doorstep, wearing roller-blades and carrying a big, fat envelope. "This is for you," she said, shoving the envelope into my hands. Then she carefully made her way down the stone steps on her skates.

"Wait, Eva, where did you find this?" I asked, while Wolf clutched my leg and Merel yelled that she wanted to join Eva.

"My mother was worried that the kids in the street would nick it, so she took it home. It was on your doorstep." Merel squeezed past me with her scooter. I saw my name on the

20

envelope and felt my mouth go dry. "Confidential" it said in the upper left-hand corner. It had the same typeface as the postcard.

## 3

I was sitting on the toilet with my head in my hands. Wolf slammed his body against the door, whining that he wanted to get in. He couldn't understand why I had locked the door. But I couldn't face him right now. I was still shivering all over and might throw up again any minute. The pictures. The children must never, ever set eyes on them. Meanwhile Wolf had started screeching with anger.

"Mummy! I want a drink! What are you doing? Open up!"

I wanted to say something reassuring, but the words got stuck in my throat. I heard him run away, wailing.

The envelope contained a computer print-out with the text "Child killer" and some thirty images, downloaded from the Internet under the heading "Abortion Gallery". Pictures of three to four-month-old foetuses in the womb, floating safely in their amniotic fluid, followed by pictures of amniotic sacs, filled with foetuses, dangling from the big, masculine fingers of an abortion doctor.

*Freedom of Choice?* read the caption underneath a picture of a pair of forceps holding a severed baby's head the size of a fist, its tiny face contorted by fear and pain. Embryos, foetuses and nearly full-grown babies cut into pieces on bloodstained sheets, next to big forceps and scissors, in bin bags. Severed little arms, legs and heads. Discarded children. Rubbish.

My stomach seemed to be turning itself inside out. I had tried to block these kinds of images, tried to suppress them by rationalizing the intervention, by saying that it was better for this child not to be born. That it wasn't a child yet, only a cluster of cells, without feelings, without consciousness. And besides, I thought, if I get the abortion over and done with without anyone knowing, it will be like it never even happened. I will carry on as normal. But that was all nonsense.

"Do you know what really bugs me?" Geert had asked, with that suspicious look that appeared on his face whenever he was angry with me and tried to find some way of hurting me or putting me down. "That you keep falling pregnant. Merel, accident. Wolf, oops, mistake. And now this. Are you backward or something? I'm beginning to realize just how stupid you are. I thought you were taking the pill?"

I merely shook my head, because I couldn't be bothered to defend myself. He wouldn't listen anyway. And perhaps he was right.

The fact was, I had become pregnant because Geert couldn't sleep. For the past six months, he hadn't slept a wink at night. Moaning, cursing and sometimes even crying, he would get up again night after night. He would sit downstairs for hours on end, smoking, listening to music or strumming his guitar. His insomnia brought him to the brink of despair. Nothing helped. He would down bottles of whisky in a bid to get drowsy, but only ended up getting more irate. Sleeping pills would wear off after two or three hours. I was at a complete loss. He lay beside me blubbering, begging for sleep and I did everything I could to comfort him. I made him hot milk with rum, rolled joints, caressed him and sang songs. Then suddenly he would fly into a rage and claim

I was going to leave him. He would grab hold of my hips, put his head in my lap and cling to me like a baby monkey to its mother. I had sex with him as a consolation. And to have some peace and quiet myself. Geert would often not fall asleep until the children turned up at our bedside, having been woken up by their alarm clocks. After I had taken them to school, I would go back to bed. Gradually my body clock got confused as well. Sometimes I would take the pill as late as five o'clock in the afternoon, sometimes first thing in the morning at half-past nine. When my period was three days late, I could already tell from my breasts. They were heavy and sore. I knew right away that this child couldn't be born. And that we couldn't carry on like this.

The pictures had hit home. The instant I saw the bloody, maimed, dead babies, my womb contracted and my stomach turned. "Oh my God, oh my God," I gasped, while trying to breathe normally. I kneeled among the pictures, with my head over the toilet bowl, afraid to get up and see those slaughtered babies again. Whoever sent me this had to be out of his mind.

Trembling and with my head averted, I gathered them up and stuffed them back in the envelope. I retched every time I caught a glimpse. A baby boy, with his legs pulled up, his tiny fists in front of his mouth and his little head in a puddle of blood, was lying on a dirty sheet, next to a pair of surgical scissors that were as big as he was. It had been different in my case, I tried to reassure myself. I had been at a very early stage. I'd had a suction curettage. It was still minuscule. Just tissue. Not a child.

After I cleaned the toilet, I put some logs and newspapers in the fire basket in the backyard, lit it and flung the ghastly pictures into the flames. Within seconds the images of the dead foetuses shrivelled up and faded, caught fire and went up in smoke. I lit a cigarette to get rid of the taste of vomit, threw some more logs and newspapers into the basket and stared at the flames.

"Wolf, Wolf, Mum is making a fire, hurry!" Merel's excited voice rang out from the hallway and jolted me out of my gloomy thoughts. She ran out of the house and started throwing twigs onto the fire.

"Why are you making a fire in winter, Mum?"

"I wanted some heat. And since we don't have a fireplace, I thought: hey, why not build a nice little fire outside."

Merel came over, put her arms around me and rested her head against my belly.

"I think it's beautiful, Mum. And cosy."

I stroked her unruly black curls, forcing myself to enjoy this brief intimate moment. Such spontaneous hugs were rare.

Wolf ran towards us, his bare feet slapping on the floorboards like a pair of flippers.

"Wow, fire!" he yelled. He came bouncing over to us, wrapped his little arms around my legs and laughed.

"Got you, Mum, you're in the sandwich. You're the sausage!"

I lifted him up and tickled his chubby belly until he was choking with laughter.

"You know, Mum?..." Merel began, calmly throwing more leaves, twigs and bits of cardboard into the fire.

"What is it?"

"Stijn's father died."

"Oh no, that's awful. Is he the father who was really ill?"

"Yeah. We're all making a painting for Stijn."

"That's very sweet of you. Was Stijn in school today?"

"Just for a bit. He was quiet, but he didn't cry. I gave him my Milky Way. I told him you get used to not having a dad and that another one will come along. But then the teacher said: you only have one real father."

We didn't say anything.

4

The last time I saw Merel's father was when he was escorted out of my house by two police officers after kicking in our kitchen door. I had asked him where he had been that night and that wasn't the kind of question you put to Steve. He came and went as the mood took him, and did as he pleased, even though we had a daughter and we were living together. If we were on the road with the band, he would have one of his mates take me home after the gig. He himself would stick around: to drink, jam, play cards or screw. I knew, even though he never said a word. Nervous girls would call me at home, asking for Steve. Blonde chicks would be at the front at every gig, pressing up against the stage and shaking their tits, waving their hands in the air and throwing him horny looks. They would toss teddy bears with little notes onto the stage. And Steve didn't want to disappoint his fans.

For five long years I was addicted to him. Addicted to his smooth, black body and his rich, warm voice. When he laughed, everybody laughed; when he danced, everybody danced. I adored him, this man who had saved me from my dull, stifling nest and who had introduced me to the world of music. He discovered I could sing and urged me to develop my talent, and thanks to him I came to believe that my dream could come true: that I could escape the parochial dump in which I had grown up.

As my manager and lover, Steve took care of everything. One day he would love me passionately and the next he would pretend I didn't exist. In the end, my complete and utter dependence on him reduced me to a jealous and skinny nervous wreck. Always suspicious and scared that one day he would swap me for someone else, always trying to please and seduce him. But on stage my love, my adoration for him had an electrifying effect. Nobody could sing those lyrics about infidelity, desperate love and fear of abandonment better than I could. I really meant what I sang and I could move the crowd to tears. On stage Steve was mine and mine alone, despite all those irritating little sluts sweating at his feet. I took great pleasure in making them feel just how insignificant and dull they really were.

I first saw him in the Cell, a pub in Bergen, the neighbouring village and a marginally more exciting place. He was performing with his band The Sex Machine. I practically lived in that pub, where the proprietors turned a blind eye to people smoking joints and the loudspeakers still reverberated with Jimi Hendrix and the Stones. It took me five minutes to walk from school to the Cell, five minutes to another world, a free world. That's where I would go to escape who I was, the daughter of guesthouse manager Cor Vos and his loopy wife Petra. That's where I would hang at the bar with much older men, smoking Lebanese Red, because I didn't want to go home. At home I ate wholesome meals with my taciturn family, did my homework like a good girl and was little more than a stranger to my parents. In the Cell I danced with drug dealers and coke fiends claiming to be musicians, poets and artists. Men who promised to initiate me into their artistic world, a vibrant world without rules. I genuinely believed that that's where it all happened, that the Cell was the beginning, the birthplace of art and music, where writers, artists and musicians got their inspiration. That's where I wanted to be, where I would find someone who would take me to the city, to other countries, who would introduce me to that big, mysterious world of the bohemians.

Steve Thomas, or "the Dutch Otis" as he liked to call himself, was my hero. His voice was dark and raw, sensitive and intense, alternating between sobs, screams and whispers, and I hung on his every word. Whenever he played the Cell, I was right at the front. His band The Sex Machine played classic soul: covers of Otis Redding, Marvin Gaye, Wilson Pickett and James Brown. I had never been into this kind of music as an adolescent, but after seeing Steve, soul records were all I bought. I wrote down what he sang and bought it the following day. I cleaned rooms in the guesthouse so I could buy albums and songbooks in the nearby town of Alkmaar. I wanted to know all the lyrics and spent ages practising in my room with headphones on. I would stand in front of the mirror pretending to duet with Steve.

One night, after another performance in the Cell, which I had spent singing and dancing at his feet, with tears streaming down my cheeks during 'I've Been Loving You Too Long', he came up to me. I was waiting at the bar when he suddenly leaned over me. I could smell the coconut oil on his head, the whisky he had just had and his leather trousers, and tried to think of something interesting to say, but my throat seized up and all that came out was a pathetic little squeak. Steve kissed my hand and asked me to come along to Ecstasy, a disco in Alkmaar. Finally he had noticed me.

That very same night he kissed me, aggressive and gentle at the same time, caressed my face with his thumb and said, in English: "*I love you, baby. You sexy, naughty girl.*" Steve liked to speak English, even though he was as Dutch as I was. Never

27

before had a kiss left such an impression on me. His lips were hungry and strong and left mine throbbing and tingling. I felt like I was floating, like I was a flower bursting open. He had noticed me, wanted to get to know me, had actually chosen me from among all those other girls.

After that night I never wanted to go home again. Six months later we were living together in Amsterdam and I was singing in his band.

A couple of years later he disappeared from my life as abruptly as he had entered it. The neighbours called the police when Steve was having another one of his tantrums, and two officers came to pick him up for a bit of a "cool down". Merel cried and trembled in my arms like a scared little puppy. Steve went along, laughing, with his hands in the air: "Hey man, everything's cool, you know." When he kissed us he whispered in my ear: "I hope for your sake that it wasn't you who called them." Merel started crying again.

I stayed up all night, waiting. I had decided to end our relationship. I had finally plucked up the courage to ask him to leave. The police were on my side. I could do it. But Steve didn't come back. He never did. He had disappeared off the face of the earth. His friends, his band mates, none of them had seen or spoken to him. An hour after they had picked him up at my place, the police had released him again. He had his passport and credit card with him. A month later I started receiving statements from American Express. He had blown ten thousand guilders on a hotel room, a bespoke suit, three Ray-Bans, fifteen visits to the Blue Note, an acoustic guitar and a pair of cowboy boots.

His belongings were still in my loft: three boxes full of clothes, books, photographs and CDs. I knew that sooner or later he would turn up on my doorstep again.

# 5

Nobody said a word on the bus to Leiden, on our way to Minerva student society. None of us was looking forward to a venue full of drunk, beer-tossing frat boys, but they paid well and had been loyal fans for years. We had a special repertoire for these students: lots of golden oldies, but no sexy outfits, it would only get them worked up. We had to keep them occupied, get them clapping and screaming along, because the second they got bored we ran the risk of being jeered.

Geert avoided any kind of contact with me. He put his discman on and sat slumped in his chair with his eyes closed. The others stared gloomily at the rain or slept off the previous night's hangover. Charles, our trumpet player, was at the wheel and got all worked up about the traffic. Dorine, Ellen and I dozed on the back seat. I thought about my children, whom I had left at home in the care of our fifteen-year-old babysitter. I had warned her not to answer the door and to let the answering machine take all calls. When I checked to see if all the windows were closed, she looked surprised and asked if anything was wrong. I instantly regretted my hysterical behaviour. The last thing I wanted was to scare the living daylights out of my babysitter.

I knew from experience how a failing relationship between band members could lead to a band's demise. We had been together for six years now, travelling four to six nights a week from one dead-end town to the next, from discos here to sports centres there. We had always shared our successes and failures, but the problems Geert and I were having now were off-limits to the band. I had promised Geert not to mention his depression to anyone and I didn't want any of them to know about my abortion. I dreaded their disapproval, the endless debates that would only fuel my own doubts.

Performing and rehearsing were a great way of escaping my everyday life in Amsterdam, where everybody was trying to be somebody. On stage, *I* was somebody, a star, a singer captivating the crowd. Performing together was a kind of drug that aroused a euphoric, almost religious love for music in me. No other form of art packs such a punch. Only music can comfort, cheer or cut your soul like a knife.

As a rule, this sense of euphoria wouldn't wear off until I arrived home in the middle of the night to find the babysitter asleep on the sofa, surrounded by piles of toys, empty crisp bags and half-full glasses of cola. I would be overcome by fatigue and feel drained: I earned a pittance working evenings, without any prospects, and abandoned my children just to indulge my vain hopes of becoming a star. But I couldn't help it. I had to sing, even though I knew that my big break would never come, that I was part of the big army of second-rate musicians playing other people's songs at country fairs and corporate events.

The venue of the Leiden student society was packed with guys in blazers and ties and posh girls wearing university sweatshirts. The students swayed under a blanket of grey cigar smoke, reeking of beer and sweat, jostling each other, whistling and chanting impatiently for the band to come on. I stood fidgeting in the wings, waiting for a signal from Martin, our band leader and lead singer. He joined me, just as tense as I was.

"Listen," Martin said without looking at me, tugging at the tails of his purple jacket. "That bullshit between you and Geert is your business and you'd better make sure your performance doesn't suffer. I don't want to lose you, but if I see things aren't working, and you're provoking or avoiding each other, one of you will have to go. I told Geert exactly the same thing."

The band struck up the first few chords and I didn't get a chance to respond. Martin put on his black Ray-Bans, raised his hand and ran to meet the whistling crowd. *We're so glad to see so many of you lovely people here tonight…*

Dorine, Ellen and I joined in. *Everybody needs somebody, everybody needs somebody, to love.* Deafening screams. I was a horny, blonde bitch. Nothing mattered now, except this humping, thumping orgy of soul.

Three encores later we were sitting in a storage room turned dressing room, drinking beer and jabbering away like footballers after a winning match. We had steamrollered these frat boys. Martin was still so pumped up he couldn't sit still and carried on dancing with his fists clenched.

"Oh man, we were good. Yes, yes! They went wild. I'm going to meet that crowd and do one of those Minerva bitches."

"No way, man. I'm not going to hang out with those conservative tossers. We'll grab a quick drink back in Amsterdam."

When Geert took off his white shirt I noticed that he was even skinnier than he had been a few weeks ago. The rest of the band agreed with him. None of us fancied joining this boisterous, binge-drinking crowd. I also wanted to get away as quickly as possible. I had just started removing my make-up, when there was a knock on the door. A hoarse, posh voice asking for Maria Vos. I turned round and saw a young man, the sleeve of his jacket hanging by a thread, his necktie askew. Martin laughed.

"Hey, Maria, a fan. Frederik-Willem von Wankenstein has a present for you. A dildo with the Minerva coat of arms!"

The twit blushed; Dorine and Ellen were in stitches. He was carrying a parcel the size of a shoebox, wrapped in gold-coloured paper with a red ribbon.

"A courier dropped this off for you," the young man stammered. He thrust the parcel into my hands and hurried away. There was something heavy inside that slid around when I tilted the box. My hands started shaking. I was pretty certain who had sent me this.

"Come on, open it!" Martin said. Dorine complained: I was the lucky one again, she never received gifts from fans. I said I preferred to open it at home. Or not at all. I pushed the box away and looked at Geert, who frowned back at me. Before I could stop her, Dorine snatched the parcel from the table. She shook it.

"It's not fragile," she laughed. She put her ear to the box. "It's not ticking either."

Ellen smelled it and winced. She stopped laughing. "Ugh! It stinks. It's really foul!"

Dorine dropped the box and looked at me. "Jesus, what could it be?"

Martin picked it up.

"Stop bullshitting, for God's sake."

He ripped off the paper, lifted the lid and flung the box away. He looked horrified.

"Ugh… Bloody hell. It's an animal! A dead animal!"

He ran out, white as a sheet, a hand in front of his mouth. On the floor lay a big, dead, stinking rat with a note around its neck.

"A muskrat," muttered Charles, who leaned over the dead creature in an attempt to read the note that had been tied around its bloody neck with a red satin ribbon.

"Does anyone have a pair of scissors, or a nail file?"

"Sod off, Charles," Geert said. "We're not touching that creature. It could have all sorts of diseases. We should call the police. And call that guy back in."

Dorine put her arm around me and handed me a glass of

gin and a cigarette. My head was spinning, as if I were high up in a Ferris wheel, looking down. I didn't know what to do. It began to dawn on me that this wouldn't just go away. He even knew where and when I was performing. It would only get worse. I took a swig of gin and the stuff seared my tongue and throat, an excellent antidote to the putrid stench in my nose. The smell of alcohol cleared my head a little.

"I'd like to be alone for a minute," I said. Five faces stared at me in astonishment.

"Shall we get rid of that creature first?" Geert asked. He used the lid to try and push the rat back into the box.

"No, it's all right, leave it."

"Would you like me to stay? You can't just sit here all by yourself."

"Geert, please leave me alone, will you!?"

The others left the room.

"I'm going to find that guy. And I'm going to call the police, whether you like it or not," he said, jabbing his index finger in the air. He certainly seemed to relish the role of hero.

As soon as everybody had gone and I'd had some liquid courage, I dropped to my knees beside the rat. The creature gave off a rancid odour of decay that made me gag again. But I had to read the note before the others came back. Oddly enough I felt ashamed that someone hated me with such intensity. Apparently hate mail was just as intimate and private as a love letter.

With a handkerchief pressed to my mouth and gagging, I tried to untie the ribbon around its neck without touching the animal itself. When I finally succeeded, I picked up the piece of paper with a tissue.

You're a rat.
Rats breed like rabbits

33

Down in the sewer.
I'm the rat catcher.
With a single blow I'll smash your skull
And the world will have lost another slut.

# 6

Geert insisted on coming back home with me. Only he had read the note. He had been beside himself, while I just sat there, whimpering with fear. I won't leave you and the children alone, he had yelled, which only added to my problems. Geert had used my vulnerability to wheedle his way back into my life, and although I didn't want him back, I certainly didn't want to be alone tonight. Our roles had been reversed: this time I was the bawling nervous wreck getting pissed, while he was the one trying to comfort me.

I managed to pull myself together after two shots of Southern Comfort. Geert had lit some candles and joss sticks, turned up the heating and tidied up the kitchen. Both of us were better at taking care of others than looking after ourselves.

The rotten stench that seemed to be clinging to my hair and clothes was slowly dispersed by the smell of incense and cigarettes. But I still felt dirty, defiled, violated almost, by the threatening note and the comparison between me and the stinking, dead rat.

Geert sat down next to me and filled my glass for a third time. He opened himself a bottle of beer with his lighter. The crown cap fell on the floor but he showed no intention of picking it up. Over the past few years I had picked up thousands of crown caps. And just as many times I had asked Geert to please break this annoying habit. The carelessness with which he tossed his rubbish on the floor infuriated me.

"Pick it up, Geert!"

"Relax, Maria. Come, give me your hand."

"Why?"

"Because whenever you're stressed or unhappy your hands are cold as ice. I want to warm them."

"Piss off. I don't fancy your kitchen-sink psychology right now."

He leaned back in his chair again and started rolling a cigarette. His hands were trembling.

"You should go to the police, Maria. Personally, I think this is just a nutter who gets a kick out of scaring you. But what if..."

He stopped and pulled deeply on his cigarette. He looked away and that familiar, sad expression appeared on his face. He took a swig of beer, lowered his eyes and sighed.

"What are you trying to say?"

"Well... I remember reading somewhere that most stalkers are people you know. Perhaps not very well, but they're often closer than you think. And this one... He knows you had an abortion. He knows where and when we play... Think carefully, who have you been in contact with in the past few months? I mean, perhaps it's someone you rejected in the pub. Or perhaps a neighbour who's got the hots for you... Or a one-night stand..."

"Or an ex bent on revenge."

"Jesus, Maria, we've been there. Besides, if you really believed that, I wouldn't be sitting here."

I swirled the ice cubes in my glass.

"I know I should go to the police, but I dread telling them about this business."

My head was buzzing with a thousand questions, but the alcohol had befuddled my brain and I was starting to slur my speech. I wanted to sleep, but I also wanted some answers.

I wanted to stop thinking, but I also wanted to remain alert.

"Why don't you go to bed, I'll stay down here. You need to rest, Maria."

As I got to my feet I wobbled and started sobbing.

"Why me? Why does someone hate me so much he sends me dead rats?"

Geert put his long arms around me and helped me up the stairs.

"What about you?" I cried. "You need to get some sleep too."

"You know I can't sleep," Geert said.

After he had laid me down on the bed, I fell into a troubled sleep. I dreamed about Steve fucking my sister and about rats crawling from my mother's grave.

7

The bedroom door creaked, waking me up. Merel tiptoed towards my bed, lifted the duvet and crawled under the covers. She kept wriggling until her buttocks were comfortably ensconced against my belly. Then she pulled up her knees, stuck her thumb in her mouth and fell asleep again. Every morning around six she came to my bed. As soon as she had cuddled up against me, I didn't want to go back to sleep. I would stroke her soft, warm back and bury my nose in her neck. She smelled of warm milk and also vaguely of her father. Her face was still completely relaxed. Beautiful hazelnut-brown lips, eyelashes that looked like two shiny black fans, her long dark curls draped across the pillow and in her hands a sad-eyed, threadbare rabbit, its floppy ear wrapped around her nose. Not a single morning went by when I wasn't touched by her beauty and astonished by the fact that I had given birth to her, that she had come out of my white body.

I was already four months along when I discovered that she had nestled in my womb. It was September and we were touring Europe with The Sex Machine: Germany, Austria, Italy, France, travelling from one festival to another. I felt exhausted and run-down and blamed my overdue period on the tour and the stress.

But when, after two weeks at home, I was still knackered and constantly running to the loo, I decided to go and see a doctor. He took blood and urine samples and ten minutes later called me back into the surgery.

"You're pregnant," he said, and I burst out crying. He offered me a tissue and asked if these were tears of joy or misery. "I don't know," I snivelled.

Steve was over the moon. He swept me up in his arms and roared with laughter, and then went out on the town to celebrate. He came back at half-past five in the morning. Singing. *That you're having my baby, what a wonderful way to say how much you love me…*

I had spent the night counting back. The doctor estimated that I was about sixteen weeks gone. Sixteen weeks ago. The Queen's birthday festivities in the Hague. We had gone on stage at midnight and played until around two o'clock. Afterwards we had hit the bars and ended up having sex on the bus. I didn't get round to taking the pill until I got home later that day, after we finished playing on a barge in front of the Palace pub in Amsterdam. Dumb, dumb, dumb. I didn't want a child. I was twenty and hungry for fame. A baby didn't fit the picture. And despite his enthusiasm, Steve was definitely not cut out to be a father.

\* \* \*

In a bookshop I had a look at a guide called *A Thousand Questions about Pregnancy* and saw that the child in my womb was already the size of an orange with two small arms and legs. Steve wanted this child, although he would never take care of it. I wanted Steve. And fame. What was I to do now, with a baby in my belly? Before long, performing would be out of the question. There was simply no place for a pregnant woman in The Sex Machine stage show, alongside the Dutch Otis. Steve would be only too happy to find a replacement. She would be travelling on the bus, touring the country and getting changed right in front of him. She would be hanging out with him after shows and, in due course, go to bed with him.

Which is exactly what happened. I grew bigger and bigger while Steve's absences grew more frequent, on the pretext of having to earn a crust for his young family. His mother stepped in to fill his place. She cooked for me, brought baby clothes and presents and urged Steve to shield me from the wickedness of the musician's nocturnal life. When I was seven months pregnant, he no longer wanted me on stage. He wanted me to go to bed early and eat for two.

My replacement was called Suzy. She was a head taller than me, and bigger, with huge breasts. I thought her voice wasn't as good as mine. It lacked pain and anger and she had no feeling for soul. But when they were on stage together, the chemistry between her and Steve was plain for all to see. "It's all show, honey. You know the score," he would reassure me.

The moment my daughter lay blue and slimy on my belly, after she had been pulled out of my body with a vacuum extractor, I loved her more than I ever thought possible. I couldn't keep my eyes off her and marvelled at her tiny body, her little mouth searching for my breast and drinking greedily. Here at last was someone who really needed me and who loved me unconditionally. It felt as if she had always been there, inside me, and I immediately recognized her as my daughter. I had a child, a little girl, and when she looked at me with her bright black eyes I knew her name was Merel, my very own blackbird.

Geert knocked on the door before he came in with Wolf riding piggyback. "Wake up, girls," he said. "I've got coffee and croissants downstairs."

Merel jumped up. I stayed put with my eyes closed. I had a hangover and knew my head would start throbbing the minute I got up. Southern Comfort and two packets of cigarettes. The image of the dead rat. Geert who had re-entered my life.

The children dashed downstairs and Geert sat down beside me.

"Did you sleep well?" His brown curly hair was a mess and his face was yellowish grey. He smelled of rolling tobacco.

"You didn't, by the looks of it," I replied.

"Come on, get up. I tidied up downstairs."

"Sure, in a minute. You go ahead."

He left and I hauled myself out of bed. All my muscles were sore. Croissants. The mere thought made my stomach turn. I wanted Geert to leave. I wanted to read the paper in my pyjamas, have fun with Wolf and Merel and pretend everything was fine. So far he hadn't mentioned the police, but I knew he would as soon as I'd had my first cup of coffee. I didn't want to go. I didn't have fond memories of the fuzz.

I wanted to do what I always did in times of trouble: hide until it was all over. Or run away. I had lost count of the number of times when, as a child, I had wandered along the beach until long after sundown, pretending I would never go back. I would play with sand and shells, build a hut and imagine it was my home. I would stay out until my mother had calmed down and had gone to bed. Or I would hide under the kitchen table, behind the tablecloth with the red cherries, with my arms clasping my knees. They never found me there.

But the police did. I still remember their black leather boots and the white trouser legs of the male nurses who had come to collect my mother. Her shrieks and the doctor's soothing voice. The police officer who lured me from under the table, claiming everything would be just fine and I needn't be afraid. How could I not be afraid, with my father's blood dripping onto the linoleum? My mother had hit him over the head with an ashtray. I saw her being taken away, scratching and biting her blue floral nightgown spattered with blood.

Geert cleared the breakfast table. I hadn't touched my plate.

"I asked Rini to look after the children for a bit." He poured me another cup of coffee. "So we can go to the police."

"We?" I asked, both surprised and annoyed. "Why would you come along? Why are you suddenly running the show around here?"

"I'm only trying to help. And I don't want you to be on your own. Besides, I'm a witness too, remember."

"Listen. I promised to go to the police and I will. On my own. It was very sweet of you to stay with me last night, but I'll be fine."

"There happens to be a son of mine around here, remember. And a little girl I love to bits. I don't want anything to happen to you guys."

40

"Oh, I see. Protecting us is your new goal in life!"

He sat down opposite me. "What's the point of fighting? Why not accept my help? Why insist on doing everything on your own? And run the risk of someone killing you? Or harming the children?"

"I'm afraid you just don't cut it as a hero. I don't want you to come along. I don't want to have to worry about you. I don't want to encourage the children into thinking we might get back together. I don't want to encourage you."

Geert got up and put on his coat. He walked to the door.

"Fine, whatever you say. I'm off. Bloody cow."

He slammed the door shut. I felt bad about being so blunt, but I had no choice. I had to reject his offer of help. He got on my nerves. I liked him better in his guise as a depressive, dependent creature than as my saviour, since I suspected he was merely playing a role.


# 8


The police station smelled of sweat, a sharp, rancid odour that pervaded the entire waiting room. The receptionist had sent me to this seedy little room and promised that a police officer would come and collect me shortly. She even asked if I preferred a female officer. I didn't really care.

I sat down on one of the plastic bucket seats, two places down from a fat, bald man, who kept nodding off. The body odour was his. I didn't feel at ease here, alone with this snoring bloke and stared at by dozens of faces on pale pink posters. The faces of missing children and wanted criminals. Rewards for information. I seemed to have landed in some crime series and it was strange to think that someone whose head belonged on one of these posters was harassing me, and that I too might end up as a poor black-and-white photocopy on one of the walls of this dingy, stuffy room.

I wondered what the fat man was doing here. He wasn't a suspect, or he wouldn't be sitting here. Having said that, everybody who turned up at reception was sent through to this room. Perhaps he was a murderer who had come to turn himself in.

Apparently it was OK to reek of alcohol and sweat in this place, but you weren't allowed to smoke. As I walked out I could feel a pair of eyes in my back. "Someone will be with you in a minute!" the receptionist called after me in a broad Amsterdam accent. She must have thought I was doing a runner. To be honest, it did cross my mind.

I heard a man calling out my name and the receptionist replying. "Yup, she's still here. She's outside, smoking." The police officer, a good five years younger than myself, stuck his head round the glass door and asked me to follow him. I dropped my cigarette, crushed it underfoot and followed him and his shaven, blotchy neck. It was almost comical to see him walk ahead of me: handcuffs on the left of his narrow arse, an enormous handgun on the right, no shoulders to speak of under his blue shirt. He had taken the recruitment slogan – "This uniform suits us all" – rather literally. I couldn't imagine him taking an aggressive junkie into custody and yet he strutted down these corridors like Arnold Schwarzenegger himself.

We entered a simply furnished office where Johan Wittebrood, as he introduced himself, offered me a comfortable chair and asked if I wanted coffee or tea. He excused himself and went to fetch the coffee. Officers walked up and down the corridor, laughing and talking. I tried to catch what they were saying, on the assumption that they were all discussing exciting cases. Meanwhile I grew more and more nervous.

"Well, Ms Vos, tell me. What brings you to the police?"

Wittebrood leaned back casually, cradling his coffee cup. I stirred my watery coffee with a plastic swizzle stick.

"Someone's threatening me. That is to say, I'm being harassed…"

"I see. And do you have any idea who this person might be?"

"No. I've no idea."

"What kind of threats?"

"I get letters. And yesterday he sent me a stinking, dead rat. I've brought the letters with me. Not the rat, obviously."

A nervous, squeaky sound escaped my throat and I felt acutely embarrassed. I took the letters from my bag and put them on the table.

"So you're only receiving letters? No phone calls? No unsolicited visits to the house?"

"No."

Wittebrood had a cursory look at the papers on the table. "Ms Vos, we've got a problem. Intimidation is an offence, but writing threatening letters is not. You may experience this letter as a threat to your person, but it isn't. You'd be amazed to know how many people send or receive nasty letters. We can't investigate every single one of those cases. The people who write these letters very rarely carry out their threats."

I was beginning to get angry.

"Mr Wittebrood, I'm not really interested in what most letter writers do or don't do. I just know that this man is up to something. I'm a single mother with two small children… Perhaps if you read the letters, you'd see that I've got every reason to be afraid."

He picked up the letters and skimmed through them.

"Yes. Horrible stuff. I understand why you're upset…" He looked at me with great sympathy. He must have been a good student at the police academy. "…but I'm afraid we can't do anything. We can't open an investigation until you've actually been injured or physically threatened."

"Can't you have the letters fingerprinted?"

He smiled politely.

"No, that would be a complete waste of time. Do you have any idea how many people have handled these letters… The sorting office, the postman, you, perhaps your friends and family…"

"They didn't arrive in the post. He put them through my letterbox himself."

"Let's see now… Have you recently ended a relationship by any chance?"

"That's got nothing to do with it. It's not my ex."

"We find that virtually all cases involve ex-lovers threatening their former partner. Sometimes anonymously. Some even remain on friendly terms with their ex yet still send her the most perverse threats."

I thought of Geert. Surely he couldn't be that cunning and sick?

"I was thinking… I sing in a band, you know. It could be a deranged fan. Or someone who saw me at the abortion clinic and then followed me home… An anti-abortion activist."

That smile again. "This is not the US. There is no anti-abortion terrorism in the Netherlands. I believe you ought to have a think about those around you. Ex-lovers, someone you fell out with, some guy you took home after a few drinks, raising false expectations…"

"I haven't fallen out with anyone. And that includes my ex. And I haven't taken any guys home with me."

"Perhaps another ex-lover? Cast your mind back."

"My other ex lives in the US."

"Are you still in touch with him?"

"No."

I felt sad and drained. As I sat there talking, I realized just how stupid it all sounded. Of course the police couldn't help me. I got to my feet.

"I realize, Mr Wittebrood, that I'm barking up the wrong tree here and that I ought to sit back and wait until I've actually been raped or assaulted." I took my coat and stuffed the letters back into my bag.

"I'm really sorry that we can't be of more help, Ms Vos. But do let us know if any more letters arrive or anything else crops up."

I smiled. "Thank you for your help and have a nice day."

"Wait! Let me take your details. That way, if you come back, you won't have to tell the whole story again."

I fled the station. The fat man was gone, but his odour lingered. It was raining again. I didn't care any more. I got on my bike and felt the cold air through my thin cotton coat. I clenched my fists. "Don't cry, don't cry," I whispered to myself. I didn't want to be a victim. And even though the rain pelted my face and soaked my thighs and back, I got warmer and warmer. Now I knew I was on my own.

9

I cycled flat out, across Surinameplein and onto Overtoom, and cursed the city. The traffic chaos, the cars blocking the cycle path, the pedestrians crossing the road with scant regard for their life, all these obstacles slowing me down. All I wanted to do was cycle until my legs ached.

I think best while I am cycling. On my bike I can mull over the big dilemmas I find myself facing time and time again. While cycling I had decided to terminate my pregnancy. And to end my relationship with Geert. Only on my bike did I dare to think of my dead parents, did I have the ability to maintain enough distance from unpleasant memories and raw emotions.

I turned into Vondelpark where, despite the foul weather, it wasn't much calmer. I realized I was afraid to go home. It was absurd that he could get away with this, that the police couldn't take any action against such maniacs until it was too late. As a rule they never act on their threats, that was more or less what the police officer had said. As a rule, sure. But what if I were the exception to the rule? Lost in thought, I cycled into a skater, and while I stammered my apologies, he called me a bloody whore and fucking bitch. He kicked my bike and would have hit me had I not made off as quickly as I could. What had got into all these people?

I cycled on, completely worked up and ignoring the stitches in my side. Perhaps I ought to leave Amsterdam. Sell my house and settle in a village, where people didn't lose their cool at the drop of a hat and where a psychopath wouldn't be swallowed up by the masses. But I had escaped just such a village twelve years ago and not without reason.

My thoughts were interrupted by a noise. I heard a bike approaching. Its chain skipped and judging by the sound this individual was cycling faster than me. I pedalled harder, doing what I always do when I get the paranoid feeling that someone is following me: accelerate. I hated being overtaken. The individual behind me accelerated as well and in that instant I realized he really was chasing me. Fear paralysed my muscles and my throat seized up so I could hardly breathe. It was him. He was following me. I cycled faster and faster, wheezing like an asthma sufferer, my blood tearing through my veins and my eyes desperately scanning for people I could stop and ask for help, but suddenly the park seemed deserted.

I fell when someone put a big, strong hand in the back of my neck. His heavy, spicy aftershave, combined with a familiar coconut smell, was so overpowering it made me sneeze.

I hit the wet asphalt with a heavy thud. I had to stop myself from running away into the shrubbery, and I recoiled when he tried to help me up. My trousers were ripped and my knee was throbbing. I looked up… into Steve's face.

"Jesus! I was frightened out of…" I hauled myself up and brushed the mud off my clothes.

Steve was beaming. "I'm so sorry! I didn't mean to frighten you, baby!" He couldn't stop laughing.

There I was in Vondelpark, soaking wet, with my hair plastered to my face, mascara probably down to my chin, opposite a bald black man roaring with laughter. His smooth skull was beaded with raindrops and his glasses were all steamed up. Steve hadn't aged a bit, even though he must have been pushing forty. He was wearing a khaki raincoat, a grey suit and a pair of smart, shiny Italian brogues. Very much the Steve I used to know. Vain and full of himself, passionate about suits, silk scarves and starched white shirts. The Steve who groomed himself to the point of obsession with all kinds of creams, lotions and nice scents. "Your body is your temple, you know."

In between fits of laughter he gasped for air. "Man, you were fast! I'm out of practice, you know! I saw you from a distance and said to myself: hey Steve, there she is, let's go man."

And off he went again, bent over his wheel, shaking his head with laughter. I laughed a little sheepishly and looked at passers-by who also burst out laughing. "Oh man, you're still hot, you know! Jesus, it's been ages. Come on, let's have a drink!" He put his big hand on mine and my cheeks flushed.

Vertigo was warm, smoky and packed with people sheltering from the rain. Damp coats were drying on chairs, people were shaking out umbrellas and everyone was moaning about the recent spell of foul weather. I popped into the Ladies to recover from this rather unexpected encounter. I looked in the mirror and touched up my mascara, put some red lipstick on and cursed my tired face. Under the harsh, cold strip-lighting I suddenly bore an uncanny resemblance to my mother. She looked at me with contempt. I pressed my cold hands against my temples and pulled my skin taut. The crease running from my left nostril down to my chin disappeared. My mother had had two such creases, left and right. It must have been lack of sleep.

I dried my hair under the hand-dryer, pinned it back up, took a deep breath and walked back into the pub. Steve had found a table and sat back in his chair, confidently surveying the place. As soon as he saw me, he started smiling again. He got up and pulled back a chair for me. I sat down awkwardly. I felt a sharp, throbbing pain behind my eyes, the kind of pain caused by too little sleep and too much booze.

Steve pushed a steaming double espresso towards me and chuckled. He spread his arms and groaned: "Oh, it's so good to be back in Amsterdam. I really missed this place. And you! Fancy running into you! You look great, you know! And how's my little Merel? You must tell me everything!"

I tried to sip my espresso without trembling.

"Does she take after me?"

"No. In actual fact, she's the exact opposite of you. Thoughtful and serious. Quite introverted. And she's doing really well at school."

"Does she ever mention me?"

"Jesus, Steve, what do you think? You left when she was one... No, she never talks about you."

I lit a cigarette. He immediately started waving the smoke away with big, exaggerated gestures.

"You ought to quit! You should take good care of yourself! My daughter needs you, you know!"

The old exasperation reared its head again. As if he hadn't been away for six years but for a mere two days.

"I can tell you've been in the US. What brings you back to this neck of the woods?"

Steve threw his hands in the air and started talking at the top of his voice. "I just couldn't hack it any more. The music scene in New York is poisoned, you know. Drugs, money, weirdoes. Not chilled. I was in this band, a good one, professional guys, but we were playing five sessions a night, six nights a week. And then we had to pass round the hat. Even if we'd brought the house down, we'd still only make six hundred dollars between the six of us. Man, it was impossible! It's an expensive place to live, you know. And those guys, one after the other, they all started doing dope. Just to keep going. One night I thought to myself: any longer and you'll either end up in the gutter or with a knife in your back. And because I didn't have a green card, I couldn't work as a session musician. I thought to myself: Steve, it's time to go back to your roots. You're forty, it's not happening. No

American dream for me. *It's over. Wake up!*" He whacked the table. I jumped up and giggled nervously.

"What about you? What have you been up to these past couple of years? I saw you, you know. You were good! As sexy as ever. And your voice has more character. More depth. Shame you're in such a shit band."

"We're not a shit band, Steve."

"But Martin and Geert are dickheads."

"Why d'you say that? You don't even know them!"

"I sure know Martin! He hates my guts because he's worried I'll poach his musicians. He's scared shitless now that I'm back. I went to Minerva to have a look at you girls. Ellen invited me. She wants to join my band, you know. I wanted to pop in after the show, say hello, but then Geert completely flipped his lid! You should have heard him, yelling that I ought to stay away from you! That seeing me was the last thing you needed. He started shoving me and then Martin asked me to leave, or he would 'have me removed'. Huh?! Have me removed!"

*Geert hadn't told me this.*

"I only wanted to have a chat with you. About my little Merel. I often thought about her when I was alone in bed in New York."

"Alone in bed? You? Yeah right. And if you thought about her that often, why didn't you send her a postcard every now and then?"

Steve took off his glasses and rubbed his eyes. Then he took my hand and caressed my fingers with his thumb. It felt as if he wasn't caressing my fingers, but my belly.

"I don't know. Things were really hectic. I just didn't get round to it. And then there were times when I thought: perhaps it's better not to get in touch, better for her to forget all about me. I know I'm a bad father."

50

"Poor you."

"But now I'm back! Let's fix a date. I'd love to see her."

I ordered a Southern Comfort, Steve a vodka-and-orange. I needed the warm glow of the sweet whisky, something to stop my head from spinning. I thought of Geert, who hadn't said anything about his fight with Steve. Meanwhile he blithely carried on talking about New York and meeting Roberta Flack. He asked again to see Merel, but I was reluctant to commit to anything. I didn't want my daughter to be abandoned again. And let's face it, it was bound to happen. Steve was unreliable, unless we were talking about his career or sex. And I had the sneaky suspicion that he was more interested in the latter than in a second chance at being a father.

The whisky didn't help me relax. Quite the opposite: I felt under constant threat. Every single man in the pub seemed suspicious to me. Someone was keeping an eye on me, watching me, hatching plans to bump me off. As I looked at Steve gesticulating wildly while telling me about his life in New York, it occurred to me that it was quite a coincidence that he had reappeared at this moment in time.

## 10

My house was a mess, even though Geert had tidied up in his own inimitable way. There was a big, neat pile of washing-up on the worktop, while the play area was littered with crayons, half-finished drawings, Lego and Merel's My Little Ponies. The kitchen cabinets were open, the curtains were still drawn and the place smelled of sour milk and stale beer.

"This place is such a tip," I muttered, not knowing where to start, what to do or in what order to tackle things. I was

tired and edgy and I wanted to do everything at once
– sleep and clean the place, open and close the curtains,
flee and fight. It was too much, I had too much on my
plate. I was standing up to my ankles in rubbish, literally,
yet I had to protect my children. There was no food in
the house, but it was raining and I was afraid to go to the
supermarket.

I walked to the back door and pulled the curtains aside. My
eyes fell on a crate of beer, two broken children's bikes, an
old buggy, two boxes full of empty bottles and the blackened
fire basket. Then I looked up at the balconies and windows
of the houses at the back. One of my neighbours was
playing the Red Hot Chili Peppers at full blast. He walked
past the window, naked, with a towel over his shoulders,
and lowered the blinds. I used to while away hours like
this, a cigarette in one hand and a glass of wine in the
other, spying on my neighbours, who believed themselves
unobserved. Now I realized that others were doing exactly
the same thing. My life, too, was under scrutiny.

A big clean-up. That was it. I would put everything back
in order. Get both my head and my home straightened
out. I opened the windows, slipped into some comfortable
shoes and put on Ann Peebles. *I can't stand the rain, against my
window, bringin' back sweet memories…*

I filled a bucket with water, added a generous squirt of
all-purpose cleaner and plunged my hands into the soapy
water. The worktop, the cabinets, the cooker, the cooker
hood – I scrubbed and rubbed away all the coffee and
grease stains, pulled a roll of bin bags out of the cupboard,
tore off a bag and started filling it with all the rubbish
on the floor. Felt-tip pens without caps, colouring books
covered in scribbles, old newspapers and magazines, dolls

without limbs, cars without wheels, broken hair-clips, crown caps, pistachio shells, a mouldy orange, egg cartons, separate gloves and socks, empty cigarette packets.

I filled four bin bags with rubbish while I hollered along to the music. Meanwhile I got more and more angry. I wouldn't give in so easily. I wouldn't be robbed of everything that was dear to me, give up my freedom because someone had issues with the way I lived my life. Damn it! I rolled up my sleeves, refilled the bucket, wrung out the cloth and started scrubbing the floor.

Steve was allowed to see Merel, but he could forget about formal visiting rights. He couldn't just step in and out of her life. He was her father, but only in a biological sense. I squirted a liberal amount of bleach in the sink and inhaled the swimming pool smell as if the chemicals might disinfect my head as well. My hands had become all wrinkly from the warm water. I vigorously scrubbed the brown deposits from the sink and the tap, and scoured the tiles until they were gleaming white again. When I stood up and stepped back to see the effects of my hard work, I felt dizzy. I wobbled and only just made it to a chair.

I sat down with my head in my hands. For an instant I questioned my sanity. Perhaps I was going mad and none of this was really happening. Perhaps I was turning into my mother, who had been convinced that my father was trying to kill her. All of a sudden I doubted everything. What was it that the psychiatrist had said to my father, back when my mother had been admitted? "Your wife has genuine fears for her life. To us, her psychosis is a sign of delusion, but to her these delusions are real. There is no point denying them, it won't make her feel any better."

I didn't want to go mad. I wasn't going mad. What was happening to me was real. Geert had seen it, that police officer had seen it. All I needed was a good night's sleep and I would feel much better.

I woke with a start. Someone was fumbling at the door. Someone was calling me. It had gone dark and rain pelted the windows.

"Mum, Mum, open the door! We can't get in!" I jumped up, switched on the light and took the door off the latch. I couldn't remember putting it on the latch. Merel and Wolf charged in and kicked off their muddy boots. Rini, my neighbour, followed them in. She wiped her feet and looked around with a smile on her face.

"Wow, you went mental in here!" she said, as she took off her coat. "Those kids were completely manic, love! I said to Guus: I think there's a storm brewing!"

She rattled on while she walked into the kitchen and sat down.

"Glass of wine?" I asked, hoping she would say no.

"Just the one, thanks. I'm off to yoga later. Do you mind?" She picked up my packet of cigarettes and pulled one out. "I'm sorry, I owe you a packet. But I just have to cheat once in a while."

She and her husband Guus had quit smoking together three months ago, and were at each other's throats by now.

"Hey listen, you never tell me anything..." She threw me a sly look, shook her head and inhaled deeply. She blew out the smoke with a hiss, reminding me of an angry school teacher waiting for an answer.

"What do you mean?"

"Well, Geert moving out, for example."

I removed the seal from a bottle of red wine and twisted the corkscrew into the cork. Rini watched me closely, dying for some gossip.

"I haven't had the chance… things have been really hectic lately, and I just didn't fancy telling anyone."

"Oh Maria, I'm so sorry. And the kids. They're so upset. Merel told me. She just blurted it out…"

She leaned back, ready to hear the rest of the story.

"Rini, I can't talk about it yet."

"Is he seeing someone else?"

She wouldn't let go. She had dug her claws in and wouldn't rest before she had extracted at least one juicy piece of gossip. I owed her that much for the babysitting.

"No, it's not that. It's complicated. We just didn't get on any more."

The children came running down the stairs, Wolf jumped on my lap and Merel put her arms around my neck. "Dear, dear Mummy…" Wolf planted about a dozen kisses on my cheek and flashed me his sweetest smile. "Can we have some crisps while we're watching telly?"

"All right then. They're in the cupboard. But don't spill any on my bed, OK?"

Rini waited until the children were out of earshot before she continued her grilling.

"What do you mean? How come you didn't get on?"

"You know how it goes… All we did was argue and in the end it just became too much. He'd become more of a burden than a help to me. We'd reached the end of the road, that's all." The rest was none of her bloody business.

"Are you playing around by any chance?"

"No, what on earth makes you think that?"

"I know it's none of my business, but there was this guy on your doorstep the other day, claiming to be your brother-in-law…"

My brother-in-law? Martin? I hadn't seen him for months. What was he doing here? I vaguely remembered a message on my voicemail, a couple of weeks ago. He had wanted to speak to me. I had thought to myself: probably something to do with money – as my accountant Martin took care of all that – he'll call me back.

"Did you talk to him?"

"Yes. You weren't in and I happened to be passing. He was sitting on your doorstep. I asked if I could help and he said he was waiting for you, that he was your brother-in-law. He seemed a little peculiar. I told him you'd probably be home late. He was gone soon after that."

"What do you mean peculiar? What was he like?"

"Just, you know, weird. Very nervous. Tense. He wanted to know if I could let him in, said he'd forgotten the key, that you wouldn't mind. So I said: do you think I'm stupid or what? No way. Anyone can claim to be your brother-in-law."

This was very odd. What did he want? Why hadn't he left a note, or given me a call?

Rini was right, I wasn't even sure if this man was my brother-in-law. Martin wasn't a nervous kind of guy and he would never just turn up on my doorstep. He would certainly not waste his precious time hanging around waiting for me. Unless something was wrong, but then I would have heard.

"Yup, Maria, the guys are queuing up on your doorstep."

Rini laughed and poured us both some more wine. "I should be so lucky! And tell me, who's the black guy who dropped you off this afternoon?"

"That's Merel's father, Steve."

"Never! So he's crawled back out of the woodwork, has he? Wow. Now what? Is he after custody or something?"

"No, there's no way he'd get it. He never acknowledged her. But he wants to see her…"

"Good grief! The poor girl. These guys think they can just step in and out of her life as they please. Arseholes, that's

56

what they are, the lot of them. Mind you, mine's not much better. You won't believe what he got up to today…"

This brought Rini to her favourite subject, her husband, Guus the Dickhead. She smoked five cigarettes and finished the bottle of wine before staggering off to her yoga class. After she had left, I ordered two pizzas for me and the children. We ate them in bed, watching television. We saw *America's Funniest Home Videos* and *Idols*. Merel said I should enter the talent show. I would become rich and famous. They nodded off beside me, with the pizza boxes still on their laps. I tiptoed out of the bedroom for a nightcap and a cigarette. Downstairs I checked the windows, drew the curtains and locked the doors. I left all the lights on. And still I felt unsafe. I was well and truly on my own. For the first time in ages I longed for a mother – someone I could call and who would reassure me.

While I was looking at the street from the kitchen window, my feet turned to ice and my hands became numb with cold. I was afraid to go to sleep. I could call my sister. I should call my sister. But there was too much between us, we were both so stuck in our roles that I knew that if I talked to her I would only feel worse afterwards. Tomorrow, that's when I would call her. Ask her what Martin was after. I had to go to sleep now. Somehow or other. From behind the coat stand in the hallway I retrieved an old golf club that Geert had once given to me for protection and climbed the stairs.

11

I was having a strange dream. My mother sat by my bed and smiled at me sweetly. She laid her warm, dry hand on my forehead, stroked my hair, brushed a few strands from my face and took my hand. "Sweetheart," she said, "you have such beautiful children." On my belly lay a baby. He was asleep and sucking his thumb. My mother leaned over us to see his little head and caressed him very gently with her finger.

"May I hold him for a moment?" she asked, but I wouldn't let her.

I held the child in a protective embrace and pressed his soft body against mine. "I can't, you know that," I cried. "I can't give you my child. He's all I have. He's my family. You ruin everything."

She grabbed my baby anyway and I couldn't stop her. I didn't have the strength. I lay there paralysed, while she snatched the baby from my hands. I looked down at my gaping belly. She had ripped both my child and my heart out of my body and made off with them. I wanted to scream, but no sound came out. Warm blood sloshed from my belly, down my legs.

Wolf's sobs woke me up. He had wet the bed.

"I couldn't help it, Mum, I woke up and before I knew it…"

"Don't worry, Wolfie, it's OK," I comforted him. I held him and rubbed my cheek against his.

"Mum, stop pinching me!" He squirmed out of my embrace and got out of bed. I followed him. My head was heavy, as if there were cobble-stones rather than brains underneath my skull, pressing against my eyes. My belly still felt sore and empty.

Drowsy, Wolf walked out into the dark corridor. Hadn't I left all the lights on? I felt a tight knot of anxiety in the pit of my stomach. "Wolf!" I yelled in a panic. "Wolf, wait! Stay here! I'll get you a clean sheet and a pair of pyjamas."

The shock made him cry even harder.

Merel woke up as well. "Shut up!" she muttered and turned over. When she felt the wet patch beside her she jumped out of bed and swore.

"Stop being so bloody angry, Merel!" Wolf screeched. "I couldn't help it!"

"You're such a baby, Wolf. Still wetting the bed! Ugh!"

I took their hands. "Let's not argue now. I want you to stay here while I get some clean sheets. And then we'll all go back to bed."

Merel tore herself free. "I'm going back to my own bed!"

"No! Stay here!" I took her by shoulder and held her tight.

Merel rubbed her eyes and looked at me in that contemptuous way I knew so well. "Calm down, will you!"

I held her, on the verge of panic. There couldn't be anyone in the corridor. It was probably nothing. But I was afraid to let go. We had to stick together. "Please," I said. "Merel, Wolf, I'm feeling a bit sad. Let's change the sheets together and go back to bed, OK. The three of us, nice and snug…" A very solemn-looking Wolf took my hand and said: "OK, Mum." Merel frowned, but sat down on the bed anyway.

My heart was pounding as I walked out onto the landing and took some bedding and a clean pair of pyjamas out of the wardrobe. I tried to remember whether I had left the lights on or not. After I had changed the sheets and all three of us were back in bed, quiet but wide awake, I realized things couldn't go on like this. I shouldn't let myself be carried away like this, and certainly not in front of the children. Perhaps we ought to go away and stay with someone for a while. But where could we go? And what about work? No work, no money. I had sunk my entire inheritance into this house and that meant I couldn't put bread on the table.

We had better wait a bit. Perhaps this bizarre situation would resolve itself. Perhaps it was all just a sick joke and whoever was responsible had found another target. I closed my eyes and wrapped myself around Wolf's warm body. My mother's face reappeared, looking at me fondly. I couldn't remember her ever looking at me like that.

The doorbell woke us. It was still dark outside, so it had to be very early. When the buzzer was pressed again I hurried downstairs. Halfway down, it occurred to me that it was really rather odd to have someone at the door at this time of day. I tiptoed down the stairs, into the kitchen, and carefully lifted the curtain a little. On the doorstep was a man in a dark suit, his face obscured by a big, black umbrella. Just the thing for Steve, I thought to myself, to appear on our doorstep in the middle of the night, but then I spotted the big, black Mercedes behind him. This looked familiar. The man in black come to collect a body.

He had come to the wrong address. I had no choice but to open the door and give him directions. Then again, I didn't know that many people in my street.

Upstairs, I heard Merel calling.

"What is it, Mum? Who's there?" I heard her bare feet on the stairs.

"Nobody, honey, stay there. I'll be up in a minute. Go back to bed."

The man seemed shocked to see me when I flung open the door. "Good morning, madam, allow me to introduce myself. My name is Gerard de Korte. Please accept my heartfelt condolences…" He held out his hand.

"I'm afraid you've got the wrong address, sir. Nobody has died here. Who are you looking for? Perhaps I can help."

The man seemed to flinch under his black hat. Raindrops

fell from his umbrella, while I shivered with cold in my dressing gown. "Oh. But this is Vondelkerkstraat 13, is it not? Are you Mrs Maria Sophia Vos?"

"Yes, that's me…"

I rubbed my frozen hands and sensed something terrible was about to happen.

"Would you mind if I came in for a moment?"

I stepped aside to let him pass. He folded his umbrella, shook it and left it to drip against the outside wall. Shaking his head, he followed me into the kitchen.

"I don't understand," he said softly, "I'm awfully sorry, but we received notification that Mrs Maria Sophia Vos had passed away at this address."

My legs were tingling with cold. Sitting opposite me with his slicked-back grey hair and his oversized glasses, the man looked ill at ease. He didn't have a script for this eventuality: the deceased turning out to be alive.

The doorbell rang again. The man excused himself and got up to open the door for a plump woman who, like him, was dressed in black and who carried a suitcase in her right hand. I overheard her shocked reaction and then they both walked into my kitchen. The woman put her hand on my shoulder. "I'm terribly sorry, Ms Vos. A dreadful misunderstanding. My name is Nelly de Wijn. May I use your phone, please?" she asked in a soothing tone.

Rini barged in, completely beside herself. She threw her arms up in the air and wailed: "Oh no, oh no!" Her shrieking brought me back down to earth.

"Nobody's dead, Rini. It's just a sick joke. Or a mistake, that's possible too. Some mix-up…"

By now the children had also made their way down to the kitchen in their pyjamas, Wolf clutching his toy rabbit and hiding behind Merel. Rini ushered them back up again.

Gerard de Korte took a notebook from his black briefcase. He opened it, almost afraid to look me in the eye. "At 5.30 we received a phone call from your locum family doctor, a certain Van der Horst, to inform us that you had died. He was filling in for Doctor Zwaanswijk. Is that your family doctor?"

I nodded. "But I don't know any Van der Horst."

"My colleague is investigating the matter as we speak. You were born on 15 April 1971 in Bergen, is that right?"

"Yes."

"And your mother is Petra Vos?"

"Yes. But she died when I was seventeen."

"I see. Doctor Van der Horst said he was calling on behalf of Mrs Petra Vos, your mother."

"He? Doctor Van der Horst is a man?"

De Korte looked at his colleague. She shook her head. "I'll need to check with the switchboard operator. I can't say so with absolute certainty…"

I tried to light a cigarette, but my hand shook so violently that I couldn't get my lighter to work. De Korte took a golden lighter from his coat pocket and produced a modest little flame. I offered to make coffee and he said he could do with some. I wanted to do something, keep busy, concentrate on measuring out the right amount of coffee.

"I've got a mobile number for Doctor Van der Horst. We usually double-check the numbers by returning the call. But here it says the line was constantly engaged. We also had difficulties reaching the out-of-hours service."

Mrs De Wijn returned to the kitchen and put the phone back. Rini came down again. "What the heck, Maria. I almost had a heart attack, honest, I thought one of you had died." She picked up a cloth, rinsed it under the tap and began to wipe down the worktop. "Go on, sit down, I'll take care of the coffee." She pushed me back towards the two black crows, who were sitting at my table with their hands folded.

"Ms Vos, it looks as if someone has tried to play a terrible joke on you," Nelly de Wijn began. "I called the control room and it turns out there is no doctor by the name of Van der Horst. And the operator was fairly certain she'd had a man on the line…"

De Korte continued: "We are dreadfully sorry. This has never happened before. I must admit that we made a mistake. We obviously failed to check the report. Normally we wait for a death certificate. Mrs De Wijn, why did we not follow our usual procedure?" Rini put four mugs of steaming hot coffee on the table, a jug of milk and a bowl of sugar cubes.

"The doctor claimed he'd already faxed it. I'm baffled. Our operator said the doctor had asked us to come here as quickly as possible, because the mother of the deceased was extremely distraught. You see, we're better at dealing with grieving relatives than a family doctor…"

"What cause of death did this so-called doctor cite?" I asked De Korte.

"Cardiac arrest. He said you'd been a heart patient…"

"Jesus." Rini took a cigarette from my packet. De Korte had his golden lighter at the ready again. "What an idiot. Why would anyone do that?"

Mrs De Wijn got up; her colleague followed suit. She extended her hand, thanked me for the coffee and urged me to call the police. They too would report it. De Korte handed me his card and then they left.

He was coming closer. He wanted me to feel it: his presence, his hatred, his power. I had to think now. It had all started with my abortion. Who was angry about it? Geert. Who else

63

knew about it? My family doctor. Did he have any reason to threaten me? No. Was it a coincidence that all this was happening now that Steve was back? Maybe. Did he have any reason to do this to me? I couldn't imagine it.

## 12

Rini helped the children get dressed and while she made them sandwiches I combed through my memories for a clue, a piece of evidence. Fear had wrapped itself around my heart so tightly that I couldn't think straight. I jumped when Rini put her hands on my shoulders.

"Listen. We'd better call the police now, don't you think?"

I shook my head. "I don't know. I've already been there. There's nothing they can do."

"What do you mean, you've already been there? What else happened?"

I told her about the letters, my abortion, the pictures. I just talked and talked and talked and no longer worried about her response.

"My God, that's absolutely awful!" She put a hand to her mouth. "You must tell the police. Even if there's nothing they can do, they need to know. And you must change all the locks and get a new phone number! Can't you go away for a while?"

"I thought about it. But where? Besides, I need to work, I need to make a living, otherwise things will just go from bad to worse."

"You can't perform any more. You're such an easy target on stage. That guy could easily be in the audience…"

"Are you saying I should give in? Stop doing what I enjoy most?"

"Yes, Maria. I'm afraid you have no choice. You've got two children... You can't afford to play the hero. And about the money... I thought you made enough doing voice-overs for commercials. Why not go to your sister's for a while?"

"Oh please! Besides, what about the children? They have to go to school... And how long am I supposed to stay away? Do you think he'll just disappear again?"

"All that matters now is your safety and that of the children. That's your responsibility. You're the only one they have. God, I dread to think what would happen if you were... Where would they go?"

So far I had pushed all such thoughts out of my head. What would happen if he did get his hands on me? I hadn't made any arrangements for them. Their fathers? That would be a disaster.

"If I died they'd go to my sister. I guess."

I would die and abandon my children, leaving them nothing but two incompetent fathers and an aunt they barely knew. How come I had never given this any serious thought? Because I just lived from day to day, that's why. It was quite unbearable to think of them as orphans. I gasped for air as if I had just been kicked in the stomach. Rini gave me a hug. "Don't worry, love, we're not going to let it happen, you hear me?"

Wittebrood phoned to say that there was nothing he could do, except make a note of what had happened. "I'm afraid this prankster has a rather macabre sense of humour, Ms Vos." He said he would discuss the case with his superior, but at this point he didn't really know how best to proceed. "Since there's still no real threat, we cannot give it any priority."

When I started sobbing Wittebrood was clearly stumped. "I'm really very sorry, madam, that there's nothing else we can do to help. If you had any idea who was doing this to you, we could go and talk to him, or get an injunction. It's extremely frustrating, I know, but the legislation in this area is still quite patchy. It looks as if whoever is harassing you is quite astute. He knows exactly how far he can go. And judging by the way he managed to talk the undertakers into coming to your house, he can be extremely persuasive. Are you renting your home?"

"What's that got to do with it? No, I bought it."

"Some landlords will go to extremes to get rid of tenants. Or neighbours. Do you get on with the other people in your street?"

"Are you telling me that someone is trying to drive me out of my house?"

"I'm afraid it happens. However, personally I believe it's something in the private sphere. Or, as you suggested, an obsessed fan. As a singer you obviously attract a good deal of attention."

My mind wandered. My stomach grumbled. I hadn't eaten a thing. I didn't have an appetite either, but I had to have something, because I could no longer think straight. I finished the conversation with Wittebrood and walked back to the kitchen.

At my kitchen table Rini raised her eyebrows. I shook my head.

"They're powerless. I think they want a body before they'll start an investigation."

She flew into a rage. "I can't believe it! That's outrageous!" I wanted her to leave. I wanted to have breakfast, read the paper and then get some fresh air with the children.

"We'll keep an eye out, Guus and I. It'll be fine, trust me. And don't worry about the kids. You can count on us. Even in the worst-case scenario. We could make arrangements if you like."

"What?"

"If worse comes to worst…" She flapped her hands about. "We're prepared to be guardians. Look after them. So they won't have to leave school, they can stay right here in the street…"

"It hasn't come to that yet. I don't even want to think about it!"

"You have to, love. We all do. It's part and parcel of parenting."

I shouldn't be clinging to Rini like this. She was my neighbour and our children played together, but she wasn't a friend, nor would she ever be. I already regretted confiding in her, telling her everything. I knew she couldn't wait to dissect my problems with her friends. Rini was the kind of person who would bully you into revealing all kinds of intimacies, without any respect for personal space. She had me where she wanted me and it would be difficult to re-establish some distance again. Characters like Rini were impossible to shake off except by picking a terrible fight with them.

What should I do? Deep down I knew. I had to leave. I wasn't safe here. I couldn't afford to pretend everything was fine and just carry on with my life. Merel and Wolf needed me. I had to flee and take them with me – for the rest of my life if necessary. There was only one place where we could hide, at least for now. It filled me with dread, the thought of going back with my tail between my legs, back to the house that held so many bad memories, back to the sister who still saw me as a silly little girl. But I had no choice. No matter how awkward our relationship was, she was the only one I could really trust.

## 13

By the time I was born, Ans was already earning her first pocket money by doing odd jobs around the guesthouse. She had twigged early on that there was only one way of attracting our parents' attention: pitching in. Rising at five in the morning to prepare breakfast, laying the tables in the evening before going to bed and folding towels and cutting vegetables after school. Non-stop drudgery from Easter until the end of September. Repairing punctures, sweeping the steps, scouring the shower cubicles with bleach, folding napkins, polishing tableware, baking bread, stripping and making beds, peeling bucket-loads of potatoes and sleeping in the barn, because in summer our rooms would be rented out to the guests. Holiday-makers. Men with long hair and women in colourful, strappy dresses. They sunbathed and laughed at their children, who played in the warm sand until the sun had sunk into the sea, and who got ice cream afterwards.

My mother hardly ever laughed. She never ran onto the dunes with us to look at the setting sun. She was always busy, her hands raw from washing, scrubbing and peeling. She hated the guests, the trendy city folk, the children running up and down the corridors and the sand that found its way into every nook and cranny.

It was different for my father. He had grown up in the guesthouse, he loved the sea and the beach and he enjoyed regaling the guests with his stories about stranded Russian cargo ships and whales. Guesthouse Duinzicht meant the world to him and it drove my mother insane.

When he died, five years after my mother's suicide, Ans said she would like to stay in Duinzicht. She loved the beach and couldn't imagine living in a terraced house. By then she had a job as a social worker, with a daily commute to Alkmaar where she witnessed quite enough misery. She could do without city life. She started looking for an accountant to settle the inheritance as equitably as possible and ended up hiring Martin Bijlsma. He advised her to buy me out of Duinzicht and so it happened that, shortly after Steve left, I had enough money to buy my little house on Vondelkerkstraat.

It looked as if the Duinzicht girls had come good. Ans started dating Martin, I met Geert, we were both in love and finally free from our parents' suffering. That first year after my father's death we were closer than ever. Some weekends Ans and Martin would babysit Merel, we would go out for dinner in Amsterdam occasionally and they even came to see us when we played a war memorial concert in Vondelpark. I felt I was finally getting to know my sister. She had become a friend almost and this filled me with childlike glee. Until, that is, she started meddling, quite subtly at first, criticizing the way I raised Merel, made a living and shacked up with Geert. Her response, when I told her I was pregnant again, was disparaging: No, I'm sorry, I really can't be pleased for you. You can't even handle one child. You're out every night. What were you thinking? As if there aren't enough unhappy children in this world. I see them every day. We had a blazing row and our newly blossoming friendship cooled and slumped to its old level: one phone call a week and the odd courtesy visit. From then on we both did our utmost to avoid any real conversation.

I had filled three large bags with clothes, two with children's books, dolls and other toys, and together with three pairs of shoes and three pairs of boots, winter coats and a box with paperwork, I crammed them into the boot of my rusty white Golf. Then I rang the school to tell them that until further notice the children wouldn't be able to attend. The head teacher made a real fuss, until I told him that "extremely threatening circumstances" were forcing me to take this step. I had to fax him a police statement as well as a forwarding address so he could send us homework. I told the children that we were taking a short holiday with Aunt Ans, at which Wolf whooped with joy but Merel just looked surprised and worried.

"But what about school?" she asked.

"Your teacher will send homework for us to do. So in a way I'll be your teacher," I replied.

Merel snorted with derision and shrugged. "A recipe for disaster." She sat down in the back, sulking, next to Wolf, who sat enthroned in his child's seat with a big smile on his face and immediately started begging for sweets.

I closed the car door, switched on the ignition with trembling hands and promptly drowned the engine. "Are we going away because of that man who was at the door this morning? The one who thought you were dead?" Merel had crossed her arms and frowned at me in the rear-view mirror. I muttered something and for the first time in my life lit a cigarette in the car in front of my children.

By the time we emerged at the other end of the Wijker Tunnel I had calmed down a bit. As I drove further and further from the threats it felt like a burden was being lifted from my shoulders. But they were instantly replaced by new worries. What would Ans think of this imposition? And Martin? I could only hope that Ans wouldn't start patronizing me straight away, but would give me a bit of space. I needed it. To clear my head.

I wound down my window. The salty sea air blew into the car. "Can you smell it, kids? We're not far from the beach!"

Merel said nothing, she was still sulking, but Wolf yelled that it smelled of chips with mayonnaise. We were in for a heavy downpour, as the sky over Bergen was virtually black. I switched the radio on. Ilse DeLange sang: *It's a world of hurt. Nothing works, it's a lonely little planet made of dust and dirt.*

Bergen aan Zee looked dull and deserted. The souvenir shops and cafeterias were closed. It was blustery and it rained salt water. Duinzicht perched lonely and forlorn atop the dune, looking like it might collapse into the sea at any moment. I parked my car and stayed put. All of a sudden this whole venture seemed utterly pointless. My sister would be at work and wouldn't come home until early evening. She would be shocked to find me and the children on her doorstep, invading her quiet, humdrum life with Martin. And then what? What was I supposed to do with myself and the children in this cheerless, draughty dump? Ans and I would be at each others' throats within an hour.

"Mum? Are we going to stay in the car for much longer?" Merel asked.

Wolf tried to squeeze out of his seat. "Look, it's Aunt Ans!" he yelled. I turned round and saw my sister, her long blonde hair blowing about her face. She walked towards us with her head held down and her dressing gown pulled tightly around her throat against the howling wind.

14

Merel and Wolf raced across the dunes to see the pounding waves, their animated voices drowned out by the whistling wind. I tried to call them back, but they could no longer hear me. Ans and I air-kissed, but not before she had expressed her surprise at our unexpected visit.

"Leave them to it," Ans said. "They're safe. They'll be back when they've let off steam." But I couldn't let the children out of my sight. The thundering wind and sea sounded too threatening, so I ran out after them, shouting down the waves, and found them at the back of the house, caked in sand and chortling with pleasure.

Oh my God, sand, I thought, and began dusting down their clothes and hair like a woman possessed.

"No sand in the house!"

I could still hear my mother yelling it as she came charging at us, grim-faced and armed with a hand brush to give us a thorough brushing down, or a good hiding if she was in a bad mood.

Ans didn't mind a bit of sand, as long as we left our shoes on the doormat, and so it was in our socks that we entered the living room, the room that fifteen years ago had been the dining room. Ans and Martin had erased all traces of the guesthouse and had turned Duinzicht into a beach-front villa, a veritable yuppie palace with acres of wood, leather and linen.

My sister said she would make us some cappuccino, hot chocolate for the children, and insisted I sit in the black leather chair by the fireplace. Her chair. She and Martin each had their own armchair, private seats they were so attached to that nobody else was allowed to sit in them. Guests had to sit on the sofa. The fact that I was allowed to sit in her chair was a huge privilege.

Something about Ans puzzled me. She didn't seem her usual, indomitable self. The way she walked around the house, so fragile and anguished, wearing that tatty old dressing gown, and with her hair all greasy and dishevelled. The fact that she wasn't at work. Her pleasure at our unexpected visit. Normally she hated surprises.

The children switched on the television and familiar Cartoon Network sounds broke the awkward silence. Ans came in with a large tray full of cups and a plate of biscuits, put it on the glass coffee table and sat down in Martin's chair. She cradled her cappuccino cup in her hands. For a moment she closed her eyes and breathed in the aroma of the coffee. Her complexion was dull and yellowish and her nose sported a bright red pimple. She had let herself go.

"Right," she said. "I wouldn't mind a cigarette now."

Something was wrong, no doubt about it. Ans had given up smoking years ago.

I offered her a cigarette and took one myself. Suddenly I no longer had the heart to tell her why I was here.

"So tell me. To what do I owe this surprise visit?"

I felt like a child on Santa's lap. Perhaps I could tell her we happened to have the day off and fancied a trip to the sea.

Wolf jumped between us, grabbed a fistful of biscuits and curled up on my lap. It was remarkable to see my children's lack of inhibition.

"You should ask first," I said to him. He looked imploringly at Ans, who nodded and smiled.

"I thought we were going to stay here, Mum?" Ans threw me a surprised look.

"I see, well, that's the first I've heard of it."

"Please, Mum, we can stay, can't we?" His chin started quivering and, just as he was about to start bawling, my sister said that of course he could stay. We could all stay. It went without saying. Her little sister and her nephew and niece were always welcome. In fact, she was sorry we didn't come and visit more often.

Reassured and with his mouth full of biscuits, Wolf turned back to the television. Ans dropped her voice to a whisper and asked me what on earth was going on.

"I fled my home, more or less. On a bit of a whim. I had to get away and I couldn't think of anywhere else…"

"What do you mean, you had to get away? Is Geert giving you grief?"

"I'm being stalked by a psychopath. Someone's been sending me threatening letters, really sick stuff… Saying he wants to smash my skull… The other day, after a gig, I received a dead rat. And this morning an undertaker turned up to collect my corpse. Someone had phoned him on behalf of Mother to say I had died of a cardiac arrest. I made a snap decision to leave…"

I didn't want to cry, break down in front of Ans. She leaned over and put her hand on my knee. "Jesus, Maria! That's awful. You must be absolutely terrified! Have you told the police?"

"Of course. But there's nothing they can do until he's committed an actual offence… And in a place like Amsterdam, with my line of work, where would they start? They told me that ninety per cent of these cases involve an ex-lover…"

"And what does Geert say about all this?"

"We split up."

"Oh. So he's one of those ex-lovers…"

"He's taking it really hard. But I can't imagine he's got anything to do with this. Geert may be a funny one, but threatening me…"

"You never know, Maria, you just never know. If there's one thing I learned in my job it's that people are capable of the most atrocious things when they feel rejected…"

She stared past me with dull, unfocused eyes. When she continued, it seemed as though she was talking to herself. "You must be careful. Feel free to stay here as long as necessary. The house is big enough."

74

"Anyway, how are you?" I asked. "Are you all right? I see you're smoking again…"

Ans flinched and looked away. She stared at the fire.

"No, I'm not all right," she said in a croaky whisper. She got up to take a log from the wood basket and placed it carefully against the other smouldering logs. Then she grabbed the poke and started prodding the fire until the flames flared up again. She swept up the ashes with the small brush that hung beside the fireplace.

"Martin has gone." She produced an odd, snorting sound. "Funny, isn't it? Now we're both on our own again."

"What do you mean, he's gone? Did he leave you?"

She sat down again and closed her eyes. She didn't want me to see her distress.

"I don't know where he is. We had a row and then he left, fuming. That was over a week ago now. I keep trying to call him on his mobile, but he won't answer…"

I remembered Rini saying that he had turned up on my doorstep.

"But what happened?"

"Oh you know…" She ran her hands through her greasy hair and blinked away her tears. She took another one of my cigarettes and I gave her a light. "Things hadn't been going well for a while. He… I couldn't get through to him any more. He'd set up his own business, converted the garage into an office and he'd just sit there all day long. He started talking about children. He wanted a proper family." A tear rolled down her cheek. She wiped it away with her sleeve.

"Oh, I love working with children, don't get me wrong, but to actually have some of my own… I'm finally in control of my life. I'm happy with the way things are."

"So he wanted a child, what's the big deal?"

"That wasn't the only problem. We just couldn't relate any more. Oh, never mind." She got up again and slammed the coffee cups down on the tray.

"Please, Ans, stop it. Where did he go?"

"I don't know. I hope he's lying low somewhere, mulling things over. I called the police to check if he'd had an accident. I suspect he's gone to France, to that bloody house of his parents."

"So what about his parents? Perhaps they've heard from him…"

"His parents are dead. His mother died last year. That's when it all started, suddenly he wanted a child. He thought we were a sad, lonely couple. Those were his words." She walked over to the children, who were staring at the screen like a pair of zombies.

"Do you like this show?" she asked. Wolf took his thumb out of his mouth to answer. "Oh yeah, *Dragonball Z*. It's cool! That's Goku, he's got super powers!" Merel said she was bored.

"You know what? I've got an idea. I'm going to get changed and then we'll go to the beach to watch the storm and have chips. What do you say? It will give your mother a chance to unpack and have a bit of a rest…"

Ans looked at me. It was fine with me. Great in fact. Perhaps I would have a nap, I was shattered. Merel preferred to stay with me, but Wolf jumped up and ran after my sister.

# 15

Ans' bathroom looked as if nobody had ever set foot in it, let alone had a bath. There wasn't a tube of day cream or a bottle of bath foam to be seen, no used towels or washcloths, not even a toothbrush.

"Wow," Merel whispered, as she gently traced her finger along the edge of the round bath. "What an amazing bathroom! Aunt Ans must be loaded!"

"Aunt Ans is super-tidy, that's what she is," I replied, while I tried to find us some towels and bath foam. Behind a sliding mirror we discovered not only some fluffy, pastel-blue bath towels, but also a big selection of tubes and jars, all of the same brand. It must be a full-time job keeping this place so pristine, I thought to myself, as I picked up a silver-plated, filigree box and buried my nose in the lavender pot-pourri. Merel turned on the tap. Steam filled the turquoise space. We undressed without a word. Merel carefully folded her clothes, impressed by my sister's orderliness. The mirrors steamed up and I drew a large heart with an arrow. I first wrote my own name in the moisture and then on the other side those of Merel and Wolf. "Now it's your turn," I said to Merel, who produced a neat little flower.

"This one's for you, Mum," she laughed. We dipped our hands in the water to check if it wasn't too hot and slipped into the comforting, warm bath.

Merel gathered up all the foam, covered her face and chest with it and made herself a pair of breasts and a beard. Then she showed me how long she could stay under water. I realized we had never had a bath together like this. Leisurely. In fact, we had only been on holiday once. I was always preoccupied with other people. With the band, with Geert, with odd jobs or with finding babysitters for the children.

I loved them more than I had ever loved a man, and yet I could never give them my full attention. I was too restless, too self-centred. To be honest, I had exploited the fact that I had children. I had used it as an excuse for my failed career. I had never really thought about it, but here, in the bathtub with my daughter, it suddenly dawned on me. Down the pub

I would often pride myself on having it all: a fun job, two small children, what more could I possibly want. My family came first. But that was a lie. Music came first. When they were ill, I would take them to Rini's, because the show had to go on. After all these years I was still hoping that one night there would be someone in the audience who would discover me and make me a star. It never happened. In fact, the older I got, the less likely it was I would ever get my big break. It had nothing to do with being a mother. I simply wasn't good enough. And while I had been giving it my all night after night, desperate for fame and recognition, I had been spotted by some dangerous maniac. The truth is, I had put myself at his mercy. Had I made other choices, none of this would have happened.

"Mum, why are we here?" Merel asked, while she tried to catch a spot of foam with her toe.

I didn't know what to say. Should I tell her the truth and burden her with my fears? I didn't want her to worry about me, as I knew from experience how hard that could be. But I didn't want to lie to her either. Merel was a smart girl. She might pick up on something. Besides, I also wanted her to be on her guard. I pulled her slippery, skinny body close to me. She put her head on my shoulder and stroked my arm with long, brown fingers that had become all wrinkly in the bath.

"I need to get away from the city for a while. Someone's angry with me. But the police are after him and as soon as they've caught him, we're going back to our own house."

Merel looked at me in shock. "Why would someone be angry with you? Is it that creepy man from this morning?"

"No, that gentleman had made a mistake. But there's another man who doesn't like me singing and dancing on stage."

"Jesus, how bloody stupid is that! Perhaps he's just jealous, because you can do something he can't. You remember when Zoë called me names because of my curls and you told me that she was just jealous because she didn't have any herself? I reckon that's his problem."

I kissed her on the forehead. "Yes, perhaps you're right."

"But why should the police catch him? Is he bad?"

"Well, I guess you could say that. He sends me nasty letters. But the police will protect us. So there's no need to be scared. Just don't talk to strangers."

"I never do."

"And keep an eye on your little brother."

"I always do."

"And please don't tell him anything. There's no need to frighten him. He's only little."

Merel pulled her most serious face and nodded. "Shall I show you again how long I can stay under water? You have to count!" She took a deep breath of air, pinched her nose and disappeared under the foam.

All rosy and warm and wrapped in bath towels, we mounted the stairs to the third floor, to the "guestroom". This is where our bedrooms used to be. Two Spartan cubicles, in which we weren't allowed to stick or pin anything to the walls, because they were rented out in summer. The guests would get a proper duvet, with jolly red-and-white check covers, and a pretty tablecloth. We had to make do with musty blankets I was allergic to, which meant I spent the whole winter snuffling.

Ans used to wet the bed, much to our mother's despair. She covered the mattress in plastic and thought Ans would get over it if she didn't change the sheets. Ans would often slip into my bed in the middle of the night, crying and stinking of urine. We would lie awake for hours, dreading the morning, when our mother would discover the wet sheets. "I'm going to air them," she would screech, "so everyone can see that this big twelve-year-old girl still wets the bed!"

Ans had turned our two little rooms into one big, bright space. It now had a French balcony, a large, antique cast-iron bed and a sitting area by the window. On the bed lay a duvet with lilac flowers, while the curtains and tablecloth had a matching pattern. On the wall hung the pieces of embroidery that Ans and I had done when we were little. When I showed Merel the violets and roses I had embroidered she dismissed them as "naff". "I can't believe you liked doing that," she said, and I explained to her that we hadn't been allowed to watch television. She couldn't imagine it. We threw ourselves on the bed. My blood seemed sluggish and I could no longer keep my eyes open. We slipped under the duvet and fell asleep together.

## 16

I woke up not knowing where I was. Outside it was dusky and still blustery. The wind howled around the house. Inside it was dead quiet. Merel was no longer beside me.

I sat up. I felt as if someone had hit me over the head with a mallet. There was a dull, throbbing ache behind my eyes and I had trouble opening them. I must have slept for at least four hours. Let me get this straight. I was at my sister's. In Duinzicht, in Bergen aan Zee. I was being threatened. I should have been in Utrecht now, playing with the band.

Feeling unsteady, I got out of bed and put my feet on the smooth, cold floor. I shivered. Where was the light switch? I groped along the wall until I found it. There were flowers on the table and our clothes lay neatly folded in the wardrobe. My sister had obviously put them all away and I never even noticed. I must have been virtually comatose.

I put on a pair of sports socks, my old grey jogging pants and my Healers sweatshirt and left the bedroom. Downstairs I heard the children's excited voices.

In the kitchen Wolf stood on a stool, with his sleeves rolled up and his hands in a big white bowl. He was covered in flour and grinning from ear to ear. Merel was dicing a bell pepper on a large cutting board, her tongue sticking out and her head wrapped in a tea towel. Ans stood in front of her gigantic stainless steel cooking range, stirring a pan.

The kitchen also looked like it was never used, not even to fry an egg. Except for an espresso machine, the large black granite worktop was bare.

"Mummy, you're awake!" Wolf exclaimed. "We're making pizza. For you! Aunt Ans says I can make the dough and Merel is allowed to use a knife!"

"Glass of wine?" Ans asked. "Sit down, please. I have some lovely Pinot Grigio."

She put the glass in front of me, slid an ashtray in my direction and handed me a bowl of olives.

"We went to the beach and there was this massive heap of foam and I was allowed to wade right through! Aunt Ans washed my trousers. And then we had chips. With fish. What's it called again?" Wolf looked at my sister.

"Cod."

"Oh yeah, cod. With sauce. And cola."

Merel had finished the bell pepper and turned her attention to the mushrooms. She brushed them and started slicing them thinly. "And I woke up, but you just slept and slept and slept. So I went downstairs. Aunt Ans made me a toasted sandwich."

"Right, that's the tomato sauce done. Now we'll have to wait for the dough to rise and then we can put the toppings on the pizza." Ans wiped her hands on her apron, took the bottle of wine and poured herself a glass.

"You can watch TV if you like."

The children ran out of the kitchen and Ans sat down opposite me.

"Did you sleep well?"

I nodded.

"Have you noticed? I put your things in the wardrobe, but you didn't wake up."

I impaled an olive on a cocktail stick with a small shell at the end. "It's odd, I usually can't sleep during the day. I only end up fretting and feeling guilty."

"You obviously need it after all that stress. Now that you're safe, your body has to refuel. Go ahead, give in to it. I enjoy hanging out with the kids. I never really had a chance to get to know them properly."

"It looks like you've got them under your thumb."

"You know what it's like, the thrill of the new."

"At home they never lift a finger. Whenever I ask them to lay the table or help with the dishes all hell breaks loose. They start yelling and arguing with one another."

"Your children are adorable. You should be proud of them."

I blushed and had to stop myself from divulging their less adorable features.

"Merel is a little anxious, but I guess that's to be expected."

"What do you mean, that's to be expected?"

"Well, she's been through a lot, wouldn't you say? She's seen two fathers come and go. And I don't know if it was such a good idea to tell her about those letters…"

"I had to, Ans. She's eight. She wanted to know why we'd left Amsterdam so suddenly. I don't want to lie to her. And besides, I want her to be careful…"

"I'm not sure if an eight-year-old can handle that kind of responsibility. And Merel feels extremely responsible. For you and for her little brother. What you told her has frightened her a great deal. She said she's afraid to leave you alone."

I had messed up yet again.

"What was I to do? Merel's not stupid, she knows perfectly well that we didn't just leave for the heck of it."

"The only thing that matters now is that she feels safe again. You must tell her that you're not afraid. You should never show fear in front of your children."

"I know that…"

I took a deep breath and started to have serious doubts about myself.

"Maria…" She put her hand on mine. "It's not the end of the world! I can see why you told her. Besides, it's easy for me to say, they're not my children…"

I withdrew my hand. "Exactly! So leave the child-rearing to me. I'm doing my best, OK? And all this pedagogical bullshit… I know it's your job, but if you had some yourself, you'd be surprised. It's not quite as simple as all those books would have you believe. Children ask the most awkward questions, ones that even you can't answer. It's not like it was in our day, when all mother had to do was blink and we'd do her bidding. My children always answer back. And they refuse to do as they're told. They're cheeky and never stop arguing. I get really fed up sometimes!"

"Let's not argue. It'll be all right. Don't worry. Come on, let's make some pizza."

Ans called the children. I wanted to get up as well, but I was shaking too much and my legs were wobbly. I was such a lightweight. I retched and only just made it to the toilet, where, hanging over the eucalyptus-scented bowl, I puked my guts out. I seemed to be spitting out every last ounce of strength. The sour white wine burned in my throat.

Of course Ans was right. I had to keep my children out of this. But why tell her that I found parenting such a challenge? What was that about? She irritated me, that's all. That whole jolly auntie act, larking about in the kitchen. It hurt me to see how much the children were enjoying it. How they lapped up her attention. Attention I ought to be paying them.

# 17

We ate pizza and listened to Wolf rattling on about *Dragonball Z*. It made no sense whatsoever, but I enjoyed listening to him, hearing his high-pitched voice and watching his face. It wouldn't be long before Wolf lost that cute toddler chubbiness. His face would become thinner and his milk teeth would be replaced by adult teeth. But right now his cheeks were still so round and soft and rosy, I wanted to take a bite out of them. His ears glowed, thrilled at having our full attention. Merel began to get annoyed, stuck her fingers in her ears and started singing, louder and louder, to drown out his babbling. It made him so angry he started stammering and lashed out. I was just in time to stop Merel from whacking him back, and sent her to her room. Then I pulled Wolf onto my lap and told him he must never, ever hit anyone, no matter how angry he was. It would be better to punch a cushion, or to just walk away.

Throughout this scene, Ans didn't say a word. She had obviously decided not to interfere in my parenting trials and tribulations. And yet I didn't feel comfortable with *Big Sister* watching me. My sermon to Wolf had been meant for her ears. As if I was sitting an oral exam to prove I had the pedagogical know-how to deal with my angry child. Had I been at home, I would have joined the shouting match.

I took them to bed, told them a story of my own invention and went through our entire "*Love you, little Eskimo*" ritual. – As soon as they were both in bed, freshly bathed, I would hug each of them in turn and rub noses with them, whispering, "*Love you, little Eskimo*." We would finish with our kissing contest: whoever managed to give the most kisses without catching their breath would win. – When we were done I wanted to get some fresh air. I didn't fancy joining Ans in the living room right now. However hard she tried to make me feel at home, the atmosphere was charged. There was a tension between us that had always been there and that would never dissolve.

After Ans' birth, my mother had spent five years trying everything she could to conceive a second child. Two miscarriages and a whole raft of hormone treatments later, she finally succeeded; I had nestled in her womb and she had to stay in bed for seven months. Ans grew up thinking that she wasn't good enough for my parents. However many tables she laid, napkins she folded and daisies she plucked, my mother's only concern was with her unborn child. But nothing would ever be enough for our mother. Even my birth didn't bring her the happiness and peace of mind she longed for. It was a son she wanted. He came along, three years after I was born. "My family is complete now," she had sighed when she came home from hospital, carrying a small bundle wrapped in a blue woollen blanket. Stephan died four months later. Cot death. The grief drove my mother literally insane. A year after his death she was admitted for the first time. She had put her head in the gas oven.

"I'm going out for a walk," I said to Ans, who had curled up in her black armchair by the fireplace. "Are you sure that's a good idea?" she called out after me, but I already had my coat on. I had to get out.

"I'll be right back. Don't worry, I'm safe here. I just want to get some fresh air."

I took my mobile from my bag, and no sooner had I switched it on than it started vibrating. "You have five voice-mail messages" it said on the display.

"*Life is calling*," I muttered and went outside.

The wind scoured my face and blew straight through my clothes. Great big waves smashed against the dark dunes and black clouds raced past the crescent moon. God, it all felt so threatening and familiar at the same time. I remembered what the winters in this godforsaken hole had been like for a sixteen-year-old bursting with untrammelled energy and inner turmoil. Those frightening concrete structures, the apartment blocks that were only occupied in summer, the bleak square that would fill with sand and water, the empty parking spaces. The sandy hollow at the back of our guesthouse that used to be overgrown with rosehip and bramble bushes was now clogged up with expensive new villas, the holiday homes of rich urbanites. Their thatched roofs and red brick walls rose up from the beach grass. They stood empty now.

I walked towards the square, past Neptune – a concrete, hexagonal building that looked like a colossal UFO and that had a restaurant on the ground floor. Perhaps I could have a drink in there. I sucked in the damp, cold sea air and thought of what my father used to say: the sea breeze will blow all your worries away. It hadn't worked for my mother.

Neptune was still open. The place was bright and warm and, save a few quiet elderly couples, completely deserted. Neptune looked like your archetypal beach hut: the walls were decorated with fishing nets, lifebuoys and photographs and paintings of shipwrecks, there were oil lamps over the tables, sand on the floor, the odd plastic palm tree to create the illusion of a much more exotic beach and a talking parrot at the entrance.

I sat down at a window table for four, and pushed aside the place mat with a picture of Bergen aan Zee in the nineteen-twenties. I threw my coat over the chair next to me. Then I fished my mobile out of my bag and dialled my voicemail.

Geert had left three messages. In the first he apologized gently for his abrupt departure. "*Maria, I'm worried about you, please get in touch.*"

His second message was more urgent. "*Where are you? Why aren't you at home? Why aren't you singing tonight? Shit. Call me.*"

His third message was downright furious. "*God damn it! I have a right to know where you and the children are!*"

Then I heard Steve's gravelly voice.

"*Hi, it's me. Steve. You know, it was really great seeing you again. When can I meet Merel? Please give me a call back, I want to discuss something.*"

The final caller hadn't left a message. I could hear pub noises, the hum of voices and a strange creaking sound. I switched my phone off again, not sure whether or not to call Geert. Of course he had a right to know where the children and I were, but something stopped me. I was afraid to trust him and that realization made me feel awfully sad.

"Maria?" A plump, blonde waitress stared at me. "You're Maria Vos, aren't you? From Duinzicht?" She smiled at me and then the penny dropped.

"Daphne? Daphne Wijker?"

"Wow, Maria! Lovely to see you again!" Daphne's neck got all blotchy with excitement. "It's been ages! Let me think… at least thirteen years, I reckon! How are you? Hang on, I'll get you something to drink first. What would you like?"

"I'll have a beer, thanks."

She rushed back to the bar, nearly jumping for joy at this surprise encounter on a cold and quiet night, amid the timid couples with nothing left to say to one another.

Daphne was the daughter of the local fishmonger and the same age as me. When we were young we used to play together on the square and cycle to school in Bergen. Later, in our teens, we would also cycle to Bergen town centre on Saturday nights, although once we got there we would go our separate ways. Daphne belonged to the "discos", a crowd that we, the "altos", who considered ourselves so different, despised. We smoked joints and drank Southern Comfort; they smoked Marlboros and drank Pisang Ambon and orange juice. Daphne and her bleach-blonde perm went to the local discotheque; I went to a gloomy music bar called the Cell. I could hardly wait to get out of this narrow-minded dump; she dreamed of becoming a hairdresser in the village.

Daphne came back with a beer and a glass of water. She sat down opposite me.

"I asked for a short break. The place is empty anyway. I'm covering for someone. So tell me, what are you up to these days?"

"I live in Amsterdam, with my son and daughter, and I sing in a band…"

Her mouth fell open and she let out a surprised little squeak.

"Really? You've got children? I never thought you were the type! And you sing in a band… That's what you used to dream of, right? Wow! What kind of band?"

"A soul band. The Healers. Old-school soul, with horns. Mostly covers."

"Oh wow. That's great. And where do you play?"

"Everywhere, you name it. Weddings, parties, corporate events, festivals. And what about you? How are you?"

"Well, not bad, actually. We live here, over in that new development. I had a baby last month, a little boy called Sam. And I'm married to Chris. You remember him? Chris van Buuren?"

"Chris, you mean that surfer?"

"That's right." Daphne giggled and blushed again. "He's a road worker now. He and Loek, I'm sure you remember him, they set up their own company. One for the Road. Isn't that a hoot? Officially I'm still on maternity leave, but my father took over this joint and he's short on staff." She got up. "Nice to see you again. How's your sister?"

"You probably know better than me. You're practically neighbours."

"I hardly ever see her. Chris does, he goes over there for the odd job. That husband of hers, Martin, I do catch the occasional glimpse of him. Is there anything wrong, is that why you're here?"

"No, no, everything's fine. I'm having a short break with the kids."

"Shouldn't they be in school?"

"Sure, but we had to get away for a bit. The youngest has bad asthma."

"Oh, I see." She nodded sympathetically. She looked round the restaurant but lingered by my table. "He's a funny one, don't you think? Martin, I mean."

"Why?"

"Well, you know, peculiar. A bit of a loner. He doesn't seem to know we exist, as if he's too good or something. And the other night, I was feeding Sam and looking out the window as I usually do. All of a sudden I saw him running past. That's to say, I saw someone running past. I went over to the window to get a better look and then I noticed it was him. In his underpants! I thought to myself: that house has got bad energy. It seems to affect everybody who lives there."

Suddenly she seemed to remember who she was talking to and the red blotches in her neck flared up again. "I don't mean you. Or your sister…"

"You mean my mother…"

"The other day my father said: all outsiders who move there seem to go mad. Your mother couldn't cope, and I get the impression Martin can't hack it either."

"That's far from 'everybody'. People here are always poking their noses in, because there's nothing else to do. That's the problem. Perhaps he and my sister had had a fight or they'd had too much to drink, or perhaps they were just having a bit of fun, chasing each other, I don't know…"

"In the rain?" Daphne threw me a quizzical, sceptical look, fluttered her mascara-laden eyelashes a couple of times and then screwed up her eyes and leaned towards me. "Just so you know. He wouldn't be the first… People from outside can't stand the wind and emptiness around here. Anyway, I'd better get back to work. Hang on, I'll give you my number, if you ever fancy a drink."

She scribbled her phone number on a beer mat and waddled off into the kitchen. Less than a day in this backward dump and already I felt exactly like I had done thirteen years ago. I was amazed that Ans could stick it among these narrow-minded, nosy people, who were still gossiping about us and everything that had happened.

The beer was on the house and Daphne's father came out of the kitchen briefly to say hello and shake my hand.

They smiled and waved when I left, but I could hear them thinking: why is she back?

## 18

When I came back, panting and soaking wet, Ans was still in her chair in the living room, with her legs tucked up. I went straight to the fireplace to warm my hands and I was about to start moaning about the weather when I noticed she was crying. Her chin was quivering, as were her lips, and tears trickled down the tip of her nose. I knew I ought to comfort her, but I couldn't bring myself to touch her.

"He called," she sobbed, and reached out her hand. I took it and squeezed it in some half-hearted gesture of support. She intertwined her fingers in mine, which were cold and wet.

"That bastard. That arsehole." She shook her head furiously. "I don't know. I just don't know what to do."

I sat down beside her on the stone floor, her hand still in mine, and in some strange way it felt good. Ans was leaning on me now. For once I was the strong one and she the victim.

"What did he say?"

"He's in Spain. In Madrid. He drove to Schiphol Airport and got on the first flight out. He had to get away. 'To straighten my head out.' I asked him how long he thought he would need. He didn't know. He only called to tell me not to worry. Then he said: 'Perhaps I won't come back at all.' 'But what about your customers?' I asked. They could eat shit for all he cared. I should take his files to ZHV – that's the company he used to work for."

She started crying again, slid down onto the floor beside me, and before I knew it she had draped herself around me, her head on my shoulder, her tears on my cheeks. I patted her hair and carefully put my arm around her bony shoulders. I don't think we had ever sat together like that before.

"I love him," she sobbed. "I miss him. He's the only one who ever loved me. Who understood me. How could this have happened?"

I didn't know what to say.

Ans wiped away her tears with her sleeve and sniffed. "That's quite enough blubbering… Damn. He wanted something different from life. That's all. End of story." She flailed her arms about and scrambled to her feet, still sniffing. Then she headed for the door. "Would you like a glass of red as well?"

I nodded and stared at the flames.

I was such a cow. For the first time in her life Ans really needed me, and here I was, completely tongue-tied and unable to reach out. Why could I not feel for her?

I really wish I could hug and comfort her, love her like you love a sister. I longed for reconciliation, for trust, for a real bond with my sister, the only person who had known me my entire life.

Without saying another word, we drank red wine and listened to the fire crackling. The intimacy between us had evaporated almost as quickly as it had appeared. The alcohol brought a warm glow to my cheeks and made me feel sentimental. Two women, abandoned by all and sundry, watching over one another and two gorgeous children, perched high atop a dune.

"I have to get on with my life," Ans said, and she raised her glass.

"We're not fit for love," I said. I lisped and stumbled over my words, which made me sound drunk.

"We're like those baby monkeys in medical experiments. They're raised by a surrogate mother, without love, so that when they grow up they can't give any love and reject their own children. The two of us don't know how to love. We never learned."

I felt dizzy and could no longer form a sentence. I wanted to say that I disagreed. I was capable of loving. Perhaps I wasn't the best mother in the world, but my love for Merel and Wolf was unconditional. And they knew it. I had loved and cared for Geert and put my own needs second. But the words wouldn't come out. My tongue was thick and limp and my lips felt numb. One minute the room was spinning before my eyes and the next everything went black. I heard my mother ranting and raving, heard her strike, the nauseating thud of iron on flesh and my father's weakening groans. But try as I might, I simply couldn't open my eyes.

# 19

My mother was the result of a brief affair between a resistance fighter who had gone into hiding and my grandmother, then a barmaid in a pub in Amsterdam's working-class neighbourhood De Pijp. She was born in 1943 in grandma's windowless little room above the pub, survived the cold and famine thanks to a caring neighbour, and after the War grew up in the bar, where she played among the regulars until at long last she was old enough to go to school and get out of grandma's way.

She excelled at school, to the great surprise of her mother, who was baffled by this skinny, earnest and introverted girl. My mother would shop, cook and clean the windowless little room before lying down on the bed to read. She never played with the other children in the street, nor did she ever set foot in the pub again, because she got exasperated by her mother and all those poor wretches who were after her. In turn, that solemn child with her stern, contemptuous gaze would put grandma on edge, especially during the holidays, so when my mother came down with bronchitis for the umpteenth time and the family doctor told grandma about Bio Recreation, she jumped at the chance. The doctor arranged for my mother to spend the summer in a holiday camp in Bergen aan Zee so she could recuperate in a healthy environment, in the company of other ailing children from the city.

But Bio Recreation wasn't a holiday camp: with its strict regime it was more like a penal colony. My mother's hands and feet were scrubbed until they were red and raw, her hair deloused with turpentine and her ears scraped clean. My mother, who had spent the past fifteen years alone with her books in grandma's gloomy little room, and who had learned to take care of herself, suddenly found herself sharing a dormitory with fifty other girls, sitting at a table with two hundred children and having to obey the cruel house mothers. They forced her to eat her porridge and whatever she threw up was scooped up off the floor and thrown back onto her plate. Every night she was weighed. Those who gained weight were rewarded, those who didn't had to stay another week.

The interminable walks; the daily beach activities in which she was the butt of jokes because she was no good at sports; the giggling and gossiping in the dormitory; the lack of peace and quiet – it was all one big nightmare.

Luckily she didn't stand out and she knew how to make herself invisible. One day, when she got behind during a walk in the woods, she noticed that nobody came to look for her.

More and more often she managed to escape the group activities without anyone noticing and would go and sit by herself in the dunes or by the sea, watching the seagulls and the people. Come five o'clock she would quietly fall in with her fellow sufferers for a dinner of mushy vegetables and stodgy meat.

Her favourite spot was a small bench with a view of the sea, on a dune close to the steps leading down to the beach. There was plenty to look at all day. In the morning the families would turn up, the parents laden with bags and chairs and parasols, prickly and angry with their children, who would run onto the beach, squealing with delight. You could set your watch by it: around five o'clock in the afternoon the exodus would begin. Everyone left at the same time, with sunburnt faces, prickly, angry and laden with stuff again, the children now reluctant and whining with fatigue.

The best moment on the bench came in the evening after eight o'clock, when she had managed to escape the evening programme and the deserted beach shimmered in the setting sun. That's when he emerged: the boy with the light-blue shirt hanging out of his breeches, the muscular arms and mane of blonde curls. His skin wasn't splotchy and sunburnt like hers, but golden brown. Barefoot and with a cigarette between his lips, he would haul deck chairs across the beach, line them all up again, pick up the litter dropped by tourists and then lean back in one of the chairs with a bottle of beer and stare at the sea. By this time my mother would be hurrying back to Bio, dreaming about watching the setting sun with him and not having to go anywhere.

The man with the deck chairs was my father. He was eighteen years old at the time and the only son of Piet and Annie Vos, the owners of guesthouse Duinzicht. In the

95

summer, Piet and Annie would lease a stretch of beach, sell chips and rent out deck chairs. Cor, my father, was in charge of rental and maintenance during his school holidays and spent the rest of his time chasing the daughters of German tourists staying at Duinzicht. Cor was a real beach bum, who was not averse to a bit of sand and salt and who would impress the girls by running down the dune and hurling his strong and tanned body straight into the sea.

That summer he had long since spotted my mother. That quiet, skinny, blonde girl with the hollow eyes, who would suddenly appear on the bench and disappear again a moment later, who was happy just to sit and stare for a bit. There was something tragic about her, the way she would sit there waiting, with her arms wrapped around her stomach, so lonely and mysterious. She intrigued him. He wanted to make her laugh, see her run onto the beach, watch her skinny arms get tanned and her blue eyes sparkle. He wanted to save her.

If only he had stayed well clear of her and had married Gisela, the daughter of a rich German beer brewer. If only he hadn't decided, one balmy summer evening, to sit down next to my mother on that bench. If only he had never told her about the phosphorescent sea, about his nocturnal camp fires – for it was all wasted on her. In the end, the sand, the sea and the raging wind would drive her insane and she would come to hate everything he held so dear. If only he had never fallen head over heels in love with this spindly-legged creature. If only he had never looked into her mournful blue eyes and mistaken her empty gaze for vulnerability.

If only my mother had been more self-confident. Then she wouldn't have plumped for a man from the coast. Then she wouldn't have married the very first boy to come along and she would have stayed with her books, alone, in a respectable flat in the city. She might have been lonely, but never as unhappy as she became in her marriage to my father.

But my parents fell in love and thought it was all that mattered. My mother swapped her windowless little room and her books for a room by the sea and initially took great pleasure in being adored. Nobody had ever really loved her and now she was being showered with love. She proved to be insatiable. It was never enough and she couldn't return any.

My father never stopped loving her. Even when she became psychotic, attacked him with a knife and hit him over the head with an ashtray, he still loved her. He loved her so much that he kept quiet about her illness for as long as he could, so nobody would come and take her away.


## 20


How much had I drunk? No more than four glasses of wine and yet I felt as if I had knocked back an entire bottle of whisky before hurling myself under a tram. All my muscles ached, my eyes stung, my mouth was dry and bitter and my stomach had tightened into a ball that pressed painfully against my midriff.

From the moment my sister had started talking about love, I couldn't remember a thing except for some vague nightmare about Mum attacking Dad. I heard a muted ringing somewhere far away and I reached for the alarm clock to switch it off. I checked the time. Half-past ten. It was that late? Shit! The children had gone. I stumbled out of bed, looking for the source of the ringing that suddenly stopped again. My mobile phone.

I found it in the inside pocket of my jean jacket. "Three missed calls" it said on the display. I was about to check who had tried to get in touch when the phone started vibrating. I answered it straight away.

"Hello?"

"Hello, Ms Vos, this is Johan Wittebrood, calling from the police station at Surinameplein. My word, you're difficult to get hold of… I'm glad I finally managed…"

"Has anything happened?" I cleared my throat and couldn't think of anything more sensible to say.

"Well, there's a problem… you've clearly not been informed yet, but uh… Your house burned down last night."

"What?"

I gasped for breath. My knees wobbled and I sank down on the bed.

"Yes, well, the kitchen is completely wrecked, and so is the first floor. The bedrooms suffered some smoke and water damage… We're now trying to ascertain the cause of the blaze."

"Oh my God…"

"The firemen risked their lives trying to rescue you, but discovered that you weren't at home. Your neighbour was convinced that you and the children were in bed. May I ask you where you are right now?"

"At my sister's…"

I fell back onto the bed and my head went all woozy. I couldn't believe it. It must have been him. I had escaped and this was his way of getting even. He had taken nearly everything from me.

"Ms Vos?"

"Just call me Maria, please."

"I'm very sorry. About your house, Mrs… I mean Maria. Are you well insured?"

"Yes, I think so. It was all taken care of when I bought the house."

I thought about my CD collection and gasped. My photo albums. Pictures of Merel and Wolf when they were babies. Pictures of myself, of my first gig. With Steve. Geert asleep. Me on my father's lap. The children's drawings. The sweet little rhyme Merel had given me for Mother's Day. All my demo tapes. My sheet music. My guitar. Wolf's football kit. The video of our first and only holiday on Crete, with Wolf and Merel a deep golden brown, Geert's beaming smile, Wolf with his plump bottom lugging a bucket full of sand. The painting of a lying nude, myself, done by a former boyfriend who was quite famous now. No amount of insurance money could ever reimburse me for the loss of these things. All my memories, all my children's memories of the first few years of their lives, all those precious little trinkets and toys, all gone. It had been really important to me to take pictures of them, while they were eating or taking a bath, playing in the park or sleeping, so I could show them later how much I loved them.

I only had a single picture of myself as a child, sitting on my father's lap beside the Christmas tree, taken by Grandma Annie. Three weeks later she died and nobody ever bothered to take our picture again.

Why was this bastard trying to destroy my past? And why had he chosen to destroy me, of all people? I couldn't understand, and this infuriated me. I had already had my share of misery. I simply didn't deserve this.

He was angry with me. Angry because I had simply vanished, furious because he didn't know where to. That is why he had set the place alight. Then again, that might be the most positive spin on things. Perhaps he had intended to send all three of us to our deaths. Perhaps we had narrowly escaped his funeral pyre.

"Maria, one of my colleagues would like to talk to you.

About the fire and the incident with the undertakers. And the threats of course. Could you come to the police station?"

"No. I refuse to set foot in the city again until that bastard's been found. Can't your colleague come to me?"

"If that's what you prefer. If you give me the address, he'll drop by this afternoon."

"May I ask why you're not coming yourself?"

"Because of the fire, the case will be transferred to another department. A criminal investigator is taking over. Perhaps you can give him the threatening letters…"

The letters. They were at home. In a drawer. In the kitchen. They had been destroyed. My only evidence had been reduced to ashes.


Wolf and Merel were drawing at the large kitchen table. Ans had made them a big plate of sandwiches and braided Merel's hair. On the worktop lay a note: "Have gone to work. I'm picking up my life again. Make yourself at home, see you tonight, x, your sister." So I was on my own today. I made myself a double espresso. I couldn't bear the thought of food. Now I faced the task of telling the children that our house was gone.

I lit a cigarette, inhaled and exhaled again noisily and then washed away the sharp taste of nicotine with a mouthful of scalding, bitter coffee. Merel pulled a face and waved the smoke away with her hands. "Tut, Mum, when are you going to quit those filthy cigarettes? You said you would!"

"Very soon, sweetheart. But not just yet." I sat down beside the children.

"Smoking kills, you know!" Wolf scolded, while he scribbled all over his sheet of paper with a pink crayon. "New crayons. Aunt Ans gave them to us. And paper."

"If you're smoking, we can have sweets," Merel said and dragged her chair to the kitchen cabinet, climbed it and took a bag of pink pig-shaped marshmallows from a tin full of boiled sweets and liquorice. I didn't have the heart to stop her.

"Listen," I began.

"Oh no, we're not having one of those 'special talks' again, are we?" Merel stuffed a pink marshmallow into her mouth and looked at me with mock-fatigue.

"No, I'm afraid I have some bad news." My eyes filled up when I looked at them.

"What is it, Mum?" Merel put her hand on mine and bit her lip. Wolf put down his crayon, ran round the table and sat down on my lap with his thumb in his mouth.

"Something terrible happened last night. Our house in Amsterdam burned down."

"Really? Was everything burnt?" Wolf's mouth fell open and his wet thumb slid out. Merel looked at me with big, startled eyes.

"My Lego too? And my Plasticine? And my *Dragonball Z* poster?"

"Shut up, Wolf, who cares! All you ever think about is yourself! Our house is gone. Our kitchen is gone and our bathroom, our beds and our money! Everything's gone up in flames!" Merel got up so abruptly she overturned her chair. She wanted to run away, but had no idea where to. She didn't have her own room here, no place under the stairs where she could hide, like she did at home when she was sad about something.

"We still have money. It's in the bank and the insurance people will give us more, so we can fix up our home again. But our things are gone. And we won't be able to go back for a while."

Merel kicked her chair. "Life's shit! This place is shit! The beach is shit and this house is shit! And these crayons are shit!" She flailed her arms about and swept the box of crayons off the table. I grabbed hold of her and pressed her against me. "And you're shit too!" she yelled, trying to get away. But I wouldn't let go of her and held her while the tears poured down my cheeks and Wolf kept listing everything that had gone up in flames. His *Pokémon* cards. Our board games. The *Star Wars* videos that Geert had given him and that they would watch together when he turned six. His rucksack. His dinosaur book. His skates. His new bike.

Merel broke down and started sobbing too. "It must have been that shit bastard, the one who's angry with you… And now we're homeless."

Wolf wriggled free and started picking up the crayons. "I'm going to draw our house. For you, Mum, so you won't forget what it looked like." With the tip of his tongue sticking out of his mouth, he started drawing.

21

Rini was in a real state and for the first five minutes on the phone could only cry.

"Oh, love… We were so scared. I was the first to notice… I said to Guus: I can smell something burning. He actually went downstairs to check the gas and the meter cupboard. I popped into the children's rooms to see if perhaps one of them was playing with a lighter. Nothing. We went back to bed. But I could still smell it. I even asked Guus if he'd had a sneaky smoke. So off he went again. He came back yelling that your kitchen was ablaze. The flames were sky-high! I dragged our girls out of bed and we ran out onto the street, still in our pyjamas. Called 112. Guus wanted to go in, because we thought you and the children were asleep. Thank

God the fire brigade arrived within five minutes. The whole street had come out to watch. Children were crying… They went up on one of those ladders and broke the windows… Jesus, I was scared. They're going to come out with three charred bodies, seriously, that's what I thought. I told Guus to take the children and leave. I thought: it'll be too much for them. But then those firemen came out yelling that the beds hadn't been slept in. I can't tell you how glad I was when I heard you weren't there, Maria. It doesn't bear thinking about…"

Her story made my skin crawl. I could picture the scene, the hysteria, Wolf and Merel's dead bodies in the arms of the firemen. I could imagine them waking up, gasping for breath and slowly suffocating. I could feel my own panic and mortal fear, dying a slow, painful death before I could reach my children. The flames might have devoured us. I could almost hear the screams of the children.

I didn't know what to say to Rini. I hadn't trusted her. She had feared for my life, firemen had risked their lives for me and my children, while I had been sleeping off my hangover, twenty-five miles away. And Rini wasn't even angry with me.

"I'm sorry, I should have told you I was going away. But I thought it was better if nobody knew…"

"I understand, love. It's not your fault, it's that idiot. He's to blame, not you. But do you see now what you're up against? This is no joke. That's what I told the officer who was here. It's high time they did something. It's outrageous that they want victims before they take these threats seriously."

"And what did he say?"

"They're not certain yet whether the fire was started deliberately. I said: well, believe me, it was. Maria wasn't even at home. How else would you explain it?"

"I think *he* set the place alight precisely because I wasn't at home. Out of anger. I'm one step ahead of him and he can't stand it."

"Mmm. What next? He'll try to find you. I don't think he'll give up quite so easily."

I didn't think so either. If he was an acquaintance, he wouldn't have much trouble tracking me down.

Outside the sun broke through the grey clouds and the cold northerly wind had died down. Slowly but surely the seagulls started screeching again. Wolf and Merel were waiting by the door, wearing their winter coats and rubber boots, their faces hidden behind thick woollen scarves. I put on my sister's boots and her lambskin coat, because I hadn't brought a coat that was warm enough for this harsh coastal climate. To be honest, I was afraid to venture out onto the wide open beach without any kind of protection, but the children couldn't wait to let off steam and to feed bread crusts to the mangy llamas in Parnassia Park. We were safe. He didn't know we were here. Not yet anyway. I didn't want to become a prisoner of my own fear. I wanted to stand up to him and show him that I would carry on, live my life my way, and that whatever his tactics he would never bring me to my knees.

Wolf almost stumbled over his little legs as he ran down the dune towards the greyish brown sea and the quivering masses of pale-green foam. Merel followed, taking small steps, her hands in her pockets. Very self-conscious. Only last year she had been bursting with childlike energy, losing herself completely in her games, but after a recent growth spurt her gangly limbs had started getting in the way. It moved me to see her knees knocking together and I thought about myself at her age, about my insecurity and my growing pains. Twenty years ago I had been just as awkward as my daughter was now, playing here, on the same beach, by the same sea. I could only hope that she didn't feel as lonely as I had back then. I used to hang around here day in day out, away from my parents. I had wandered along these dunes so many times, through wind and rain and in sweltering heat, always in the knowledge that I was walking along the edge of the Netherlands.

Merel and Wolf didn't seem to mind the cold. With red cheeks and runny noses, they were busy lugging stuff that had washed ashore: jerrycans, a wooden pallet, a length of thick orange rope, a piece of filthy tarpaulin and a large barrel. They were building a raft. Wolf sat down on it, and scanned the sea with his hand over his eyes. Merel stirred a blue plastic bowl with a twig, sprinkled in some sand and made soup. She was completely absorbed in her role as a pirate. It could be hours before they got cold and started begging for ice cream or chips.

I sat down at the bottom of the dune. The cold rose up from the damp sand, triggering painful cramps in my womb that reminded me of my lost child and everything else I had lost in the past few weeks: my house, my relationship, my security, everything. Was it mere chance, bad luck, or had I brought it upon myself?

I looked at my children, at Wolf, running to meet the wind with his arms spread wide, and at Merel, pretending to eat a bunch of seaweed as though it were a tropical fruit. None of this mattered to them. Whatever happened, they would carry on playing. Children are so good at living, so flexible and strong. They bump their heads, have a quick cry and move on. They need nothing except love.

Shortly after they were born, I vowed to give them all my love. I was brimming with emotion, cried over the nails on their little toes, carried them close to my heart for months and just couldn't get enough of their sweet smell. Their soft bellies; the way they relaxed when they drank from my breast; how they opened their fists and closed their eyes – it made me tender, so much so that in the end I could barely sing without getting a lump in my throat. I had to step back before I disappeared completely, swallowed up by motherhood. I had to get back on stage, back into the studio, because I couldn't afford to become dependent on Steve, or later on Geert. Fortunately I was still lucid enough to realize that. It was no mean feat to detach myself and leave my crying baby in the arms of a childminder and to go on stage pretending to be a tough woman, my throbbing breasts and wobbly belly strapped into a tight bodysuit. But once I had taken that step, the second time a little easier than the first, I realized I could still do it, still stir up a crowd. Once I felt my energy levels surge again, fuelled by a thumping bass, my tenderness slowly dried up. I had no more time for sentiment – music had priority over my children. Sometimes I even saw them as a burden, just another obstacle on my way to a breakthrough and fame. But it never happened and who better to blame than my children? The thought that motherhood had got in the way of my career was more agreeable than the notion that I might not be good enough.

Here on the beach, shivering with cold, I fell in love with my children all over again. They were so beautiful and strong, so sweet and small. I was wrong to think that I had lost everything. I had everything that mattered.


## 22


Detective Inspector Van Dijk was the kind of man who commanded instant respect. He was just shy of forty, but his severe, bristly haircut and his pale, worried face made him

106

look middle-aged. As he pumped my hand he very nearly squashed my bones. No, he'd had no trouble finding the house; in fact it had been quite easy, you couldn't miss it, the way Duinzicht towered over the rest of the village. This was quite different from Amsterdam. Quiet, certainly, but also rather remote and isolated. Not his cup of tea. He loved the city with all its hustle and bustle. But the summers here must be wonderful, with the beach and everything. While I made tea, he filled the silence with platitudes. He must have been on a course: put the victim at ease with some twaddle until the person in question indicates he/she is ready for interrogation.

Wolf and Merel hung in front of the television, too tired to look up and say hello to Van Dijk. He tried to have a bit of a chat with them, but only garnered some annoyed looks. When Merel asked him to step aside because he was blocking her view of the screen, he gave up and sat down on the chair opposite Ans' lounger, in which I sat. I sent the children upstairs with the promise of a bag of sweets, and they left amid a good deal of complaining.

I poured the tea and handed a cup to Van Dijk, who put it down beside him. He took a notebook from his inside pocket, pulled up his trouser legs and leaned towards me.

"Right, Ms Vos, you must have been quite shocked to hear that your house burned down…"

"Yes, that's putting it mildly." I took a cigarette and he immediately whipped out his lighter. I leaned forward, lit my cigarette and inhaled deeply. When I sat up, I caught him looking at my breasts.

"After the fire it was determined that I should take charge of the investigation. My colleague, Wittebrood, has told me about your visit to the station and your telephone conversation following the incident with De Korte, the undertaker. Now, since my colleague hasn't recorded all of your previous statements yet, I thought it might be a good idea if you told me the whole story again."

I told him about the threatening letters, the rat, the pictures of the aborted babies, the whole business of the undertaker turning up at my house and that it had freaked me out so much I had wasted no time and had taken the children and fled my own home. Van Dijk jotted everything down, glancing up occasionally and nodding sympathetically.

"Extraordinary. I'm afraid we're dealing with a rather complicated issue here. You say you don't know who's behind all this…"

I shook my head. "That's what's making me so paranoid. I feel as if I can't trust a soul. It could be anyone. But then I think: nobody in my immediate surroundings has any reason to hate me so much."

"You're not living with the father of your children?"

"No. My relationship with Wolf's father has just ended and I haven't seen Merel's father for a long, long time. Although having said that, he recently moved back to Amsterdam…"

"Were you the one to end the relationship with Wolf's father?"

"Yes. But he's not behind this. He's got every reason to be angry with me, but he's also a big softie. He would never resort to violence or threaten me."

"Why, if I may ask, did you end the relationship?"

I stared at the charred logs in the fireplace. Rain began to beat against the windows again, got heavier and then turned into a furious rattle of hail. I realized that everything I said about Geert would weigh against him. Sweet, skinny, crazy Geert. I thought of his hands; his long, bony fingers around my buttocks and breasts; the greed with which he grabbed hold of my body.

108

"He was depressed. I just couldn't take it any more. He refused to seek help and started drinking more and more. In the end he had become impossible to live with. I felt he was sucking me dry. I had no choice but to end the relationship, before he dragged me and the children down with him."

"So you're saying that your ex-partner was mentally unstable. That he drank. You had an abortion… I'm assuming it was his child?" I nodded. "Was this abortion a joint decision?"

"No. I didn't tell him until after I'd had the termination. I knew he would have wanted to keep the child… He really lost it. He was throwing all sorts of stuff around the room."

"You just said he'd never resort to violence."

"That wasn't violence. He felt powerless, frustrated, that's all."

"And you received the first letter…"

"Four days later."

"Would you mind giving me those letters?"

I blushed. "Well, you see, the problem is… I'm afraid they got burnt. I'd left the letters in my house in Amsterdam. I'd hidden them from the children and when I left it didn't occur to me to take them with me."

Van Dijk frowned. I could tell by the look on his face that he thought I was a bit weird. "That's a shame indeed, Ms Vos, those letters were our only evidence. But I presume you did show them to Mr Wittebrood?"

"Yes."

He made a note and then turned back to an earlier page.

"I'll be honest with you. We have nothing that might help us any further. This morning I received a print-out of all of De Korte's incoming calls and it turns out that the report of your death was phoned through with a mobile registered in your name. And the fire at your house on Vondelkerkstraat wasn't started deliberately, but was almost certainly caused by shoddily installed kitchen lights. When they burned out the kitchen cabinets caught fire. Besides, it looks as if the gas may have been left on, which caused an explosion. This in turn destroyed potential evidence. In other words, we have nothing. Except an official complaint from De Korte against you."

## 23

After Van Dijk had gone, a myriad of thoughts tumbled through my head. Fire. Kitchen cabinets. Burning lights. Had I left the lights on? I was certain I had not. But then again, I was no longer certain about anything. Someone had been in my house. Had used my mobile phone. That night, when I had been afraid to go out into the corridor and Merel and Wolf had been in bed with me, he had been downstairs. He had called the undertaker. Not only did he want to kill me, he wanted everyone to take me for a lunatic. That was his strategy.

Cold sweat trickled down my back and the tea I had drunk repeated on me. I pressed my fists into my stomach and bent over in an attempt to get a grip on myself. The whole band had seen the rat. Geert had read the letters. Wittebrood had read the letters. I wasn't mad. But Van Dijk didn't believe me, I could see it in his eyes. He thought I was pathetic, perhaps even mentally unstable and so eager for attention I had conjured up a stalker. He must have delved into my past and discovered that my mother had been a paranoid schizophrenic who thought we wanted to poison her and therefore tried to kill my father.

If only I knew what to do. If only I knew why he had it in for me. If only I knew *who* had it in for me. It had to be someone who knew me. I could no longer rule out Geert. He had a key to my house. He knew my mother's history. He had installed the kitchen lights.

Suddenly I thought of Martin and his desire to have children. Martin, who had settled the inheritance. He, too, knew everything about me and my sister. He had invested part of my inheritance in shares, for my children. He was in trouble. If he got rid of me, my sister would inherit my house and my belongings and she would gain custody of Wolf and Merel. Geert would challenge it, of course, but with his lifestyle he wouldn't stand a chance.

Or Steve. It had all started the moment he suddenly reappeared. But what motive did he have? No, I could definitely cross him off my list of suspects. Steve was too lazy and too egocentric for this kind of thing.

This had to stop. I had a sneaking suspicion that this was exactly what my stalker had in mind: I would turn against all those I loved and become increasingly isolated. He was the one who was crazy, not me. He wanted to show me how close he could get and that he was the one pulling the strings. I couldn't escape his clutches, nobody would believe me and not even the police could protect me.

Ans came home in a bad mood. She kicked off her shoes in the hallway, hung up her wet coat, put on her slippers and shuffled into the living room, complaining profusely.

"Fucking traffic. It's doing my head in. And this foul weather. Ugh!" She flopped down into her chair, swivelled once and closed her eyes. "I'm shattered." Her long hair was plastered to her face. While she sat slumped in her chair, I noticed that she looked like Dad. Her jaw line was stronger

111

than mine and she had a sharper nose. Her skin was smooth and so thin it was almost transparent, which was something she had inherited from our mother. I was also much curvier than she was.

"Can I have a cigarette?" she asked, still with her eyes closed. I wanted to talk to her, tell her what new catastrophe had befallen me today. But I sensed that we were miles apart again. I felt like the little sister who got in the way. What's more, I was afraid that when she heard the story, she might think Van Dijk was right. It might remind her of what had happened to our mother.

Ans walked over to the window and looked at the dunes, her hands wrapped around her waist.

"You wouldn't believe some of the shit I hear," she started saying, almost to herself. "Today I saw three mothers with their children. One's on drugs and takes her frustrations out on her four-year-old girl, the other allowed her boyfriend to abuse her thirteen-year-old daughter, while the third got plastered and caused a fatal car accident with three small children in the back. And yet all three claim to love their children and beg me to reinstate custody. I can actually smell the booze on their breath! These children are all doomed. I look at the brats and I see no life, no emotions, nothing in their eyes. They're completely vacant."

I joined her.

"Sounds awful. I'm amazed that you never tire of looking after others. You were like that as a child... Don't you ever get fed up?"

Ans shrugged. "No, never. If there's anyone out there who knows how unhappy these children are, it's me. I know exactly how they feel. I know how mothers can manipulate and use their children. I'm just the person to help. Not that it makes any difference – the years of neglect and abuse have

112

already left their mark. But if I can give them a sense of security, the sense that there's someone who cares, even for just a moment, I've achieved my goal."

Together we looked at the swaying beach grass and the clouds that were swept over the sea. I never understood why Ans chose to wallow in our painful childhood by staying here and working with damaged children.

"Anyway," she sighed. "How are things here? Who came to see you? I saw the teacups in the kitchen…"

"Someone from the police."

She raised her eyebrows. "They caught him?"

"No. Quite the opposite. It's only getting worse. My house burned down last night."

There was a tremor in my voice as I spoke. Ans gasped.

"Good grief," she whispered. "I can't believe it. That's terrible. How on earth…"

I sat down on the sofa.

"I'm scared," I said and poured myself a glass of white wine. Ans came and stood in front of me, lifted my chin up and looked me straight in the eye. "There's no need to be afraid. You're here with me and I'm looking after you. I'll take a week off work and I'll take care of everything. Just leave it all to me. You need a rest."

Wolf came in, crawled onto my lap and showered my face with kisses.

"Don't be sad now, Mummy," he said in his sweetest little voice. I laughed and held him tight.

"No. You're right. It's time for some fun." I tickled his round tummy until he was purring with delight.

"Was it started deliberately?" Ans asked, as she went round the room, picking the children's toys off the floor.

"They're not sure yet. The police claim the fire started when the light bulbs that Geert installed underneath the

113

kitchen cabinets burned a hole through the hardboard. The gas oven was on as well. And then the whole shebang exploded. But I'm sure I switched the light off when I left. Anyway, I never leave the kitchen lights on during the day. He must have been in the house and he must have known that those bulbs could burn through the cabinets. I don't see how else it could have happened."

"For Christ's sake, where did Geert get the idea to install that kind of light bulb underneath the cabinets? What an idiot. Surely everybody knows that's asking for trouble."

"He thought the fluorescent tubes were too cold and ugly when we were sitting in the kitchen in the evening. So one Sunday he replaced them with bulbs."

"When was this?"

"I'm not sure... About a month ago, I think."

"Shortly before you split up?"

"Yes."

"You didn't put the house in his name, did you?"

"No. I didn't want to. He acknowledged Wolf, but other than that there are no formal ties between us."

"But he wanted to?"

"He thought I didn't trust him. He wanted us to share everything. A joint bank account, a house in joint ownership, marriage."

"But why didn't you want to?"

"It's my house. It's the only thing Mum and Dad left me. I don't know, just a hunch..."

I didn't really want to tell her about his dark moods. I didn't want her to see me as "a case", as a woman who keeps falling for the wrong men. I had spent years defending Geert and didn't fancy hearing her say: "See? Told you so!" But I couldn't get round it. I wanted to be honest with her. However sticky my situation was right now, it did have an

114

upside: we had found each other again. And so I told her about Geert's sleepless nights, his panic attacks, his alcohol abuse. I explained that he hadn't always been like this, on the contrary, in the early days of our relationship he had been attentive and sweet. I had no idea why it had all gone pear-shaped, why he was so depressed and anxious, and for a long time I had blamed myself and had done everything in my power to convince him of my love. Except, that is, to have joint ownership of the house.

Ans kept still. When I was done, she only said that Geert was right. I hadn't loved him enough. If I had really loved him, I would have married him and shared my house with him.


We cooked together. Ans chopped garlic and parsley, while I shredded lettuce, cut tomatoes and whisked together a dressing from olive oil, salt and lemon juice. She fried mushrooms and cubes of bacon and added them to the pasta along with some egg and cheese. I put on a Billie Holiday CD and sang along quietly.

Merel barged into the kitchen and started criticizing my "boring old farts" music. We put dinner on the table just as Merel switched the radio on, frantically turning the knobs in search of something more modern. I told her to turn it off because we wanted to have a quiet meal. But Merel didn't fancy any quiet, she jumped around the table, showed off her dance steps and when she found that nobody paid her any attention she started pulling Wolf from his chair. He ended up on the floor in floods of tears and I started screaming at Merel, who yelled back that it wasn't her fault, until finally Ans unplugged the stereo and politely asked us to sit down. The children sat down in a huff, their arms crossed, determined not to touch their plates. My blood boiled.

"Guys, your mother's feeling a little tired and sad. Please try and be nice to her, OK?" Ans said and spooned the steaming pasta onto our plates. Merel glared at me, her black eyebrows set in an exaggerated frown.

"Well, what about me? I'm feeling sad too you know. She only ever thinks of herself. That's why we're here in the first place, and I don't have any girlfriends and I'm not allowed to listen to my music. And now our house is gone too. If you think I'm going to move in here, well forget it, I won't!"

"Me neither!" Wolf joined in so we wouldn't forget about him. I couldn't think of anything else to say or do to defuse this crisis. Or at least make sure the children suffered as little as possible. I'd had it. I had nothing more to give, except more snot and tears.

Ans gave my hand a little squeeze. "Nobody is forcing you to move in here. You're just staying here a little while till your house has been done up. Just think of it as a holiday."

"But what about Santa?" Wolf asked. "What if he comes to our house and we're not there. And the house isn't there either. How's he supposed to give us our presents?"

"I'm sure Santa will figure it out. You mother and I have already told him you're here."

Merel started crying.

"Bullshit. I'm going to miss Zoë's party…" She flung herself into my lap and sobbed. I stroked her curls and promised it would all be fine. At that point my phone rang. "Geert", it said on the display.

"Maria! What the hell is going on? Why don't you answer the phone? Where are you?"

I could hear his voice tremble.

"I'm sorry, Geert. I should have called…"

"Should have called? Our house burned down! Why do

you think I left a hundred messages on your voicemail! Jesus, I'm worried! Doesn't that mean anything to you?"

"I'm sorry…"

"But how come? How come the whole place went up in flames?"

"Remember those light bulbs you replaced?"

"No way, that's impossible."

"And the gas was on…"

"Impossible, I can't believe it… Did you leave the gas on?"

"No. I switched the lights off before I left and I'm sure the gas wasn't on."

"So whose version of events is this?"

"The police's. They were here this afternoon."

"Shit." I heard him sigh, clear his throat, sniffle. He didn't say anything for a while and I could picture him sitting slumped by the phone, with his head down, eyes closed, cigarette in his right hand, receiver in his left, one elbow resting on his knee. The gloomy strains of Nick Cave in the background hinted at his state of mind.

"Do you reckon it was *him*?"

"Yes."

"I have to talk to you. I want to see you. And Wolf and Merel as well. Please, say yes. Don't freeze me out, Maria."

His pleading voice touched me and I just didn't have the heart to turn him down.

"I don't know, Geert, I'm not sure if that's a good idea."

"You don't think I'm involved, do you?"

"The police do."

"There's only one person who could have put that idea in their heads and that's you."

I wanted to talk to him too, although I knew it wasn't the sensible thing to do. Ans shook her head and looked at me as if I was putting the noose around my neck.

"We could meet somewhere."

"Where are you?"

"None of your business. Let's meet at Central Station in Amsterdam."

"OK, OK. I'll be there tomorrow. In restaurant 'First Class'. Around midday. Can I speak to Wolf for a minute?"

It hurt me to say no, but I knew it wouldn't be long before Wolf let the cat out of the bag.

I rang off and turned to Ans. She was seething and beckoned me over to the hallway with a nod of her head. I followed her, like a naughty child anticipating a ticking-off.

She stood in the hallway with her arms crossed.

"Have you gone completely insane?!" she snapped at me. "What were you thinking? Less than a frigging hour ago you were telling me what an idiot he is! And now you're meeting up with him. He's our prime suspect! He's playing a game with you, but don't think I'll stand by and watch…"

"What do you mean?"

She planted her hands on her hips and sighed. "If you go out and meet him, I don't want you back here. Then you're on your own."

I very nearly exploded and felt an uncontrollable urge to wipe that condescending smirk off her face. "Get a grip, Ans! I'm an adult! You can't tell me what to do. It's not fair!"

"No, I can't tell you what to do, but I have limits too. And this is too much. I want to help, you're welcome to hide here and rest, but not if you get all pally again with the person doing this to you. Think about your children for once!"

"But it's not Geert! He's not capable of pulling such a stunt. I just know it."

"Maria, please… don't be so naive."

She walked off in a huff back to the kitchen, where she clapped her hands.

118

"Right, little ones. Aunt Ans is going to tuck you in. I know a wonderful story and I'll tell it to you if you're good and put on your pyjamas right now."

She didn't come back down again. I cleared the table, did the washing-up, made coffee, lit some candles in the living room, put some logs on the fire and waited for her to return so I could tell her why I trusted Geert, but she left me to my own devices.

In the end, I switched on the television and watched some stupid reality show about six young people sharing a luxury villa in Spain, hopping in and out of each others' beds and dying to let the whole world know about it. "*It's all just a game,*" an annoyingly self-assured young man laughed. He infuriated me. Everything infuriated me. The guy playing dirty tricks on his female housemates in front of the camera. The people wanting to watch this. The world's progressive loutishness. The fact that mind games appeared to have become a form of public entertainment. My dour and dogmatic sister, who always knew best. But most of all, I was furious with myself.

24

I couldn't sleep. I was so worked up that my muscles resisted all relaxation. I decided to have another cigarette on the balcony, with the duvet wrapped around me. The wind had died down and the sky was littered with stars. As a child I used to see at least one shooting star a week from this balcony. Ans never did and it exasperated her. But I happened to be patient enough to spend hours staring up at the tiny lights, trying to figure out what it really meant: infinity. She was too busy making sure her shoes were all lined up and her dolls were sitting up straight.

I missed my house. My living room with the old, red arm-chair that I liked to sit in with my legs swung across the worn armrest. My music. Ann Peebles. Softly I sang 'Steal Away' to myself. *I have to see you somehow, wooh, not tomorrow, but right now.*

It only made me gloomier. I pined for my life in Amsterdam. Cycling through the city and buying my groceries at Albert Cuyp market. Rehearsing with the band, bickering with Martin and finishing up at some bar for a drink. Frying my own chips for the children. Let's face it, I had quite a nice life. I enjoyed playing with the band a couple of times a week, earning money as a voice-over and having the rest of the time off to be with the children. I simply lived my life, without giving it too much thought. And overnight it had all been taken away from me. I hadn't even had the time to mourn my lost child and my lost love. What did he want from me? And why? Was Ans right and should I be afraid of Geert? Had I ever been afraid of him?

Yes, once, not even all that long ago. In a fit of jealousy he had swept the teapot off the table and hurled a plate at my head. He'd had too much to drink and when he came home I was on the phone, talking to Martin. We were laughing about something silly and he thought we were making fun of him. At that moment I was afraid of him. It had been the last straw. I knew then that we couldn't go on like this and that I had to make a decision.

I shivered, despite the duvet, and went back inside. Merel and Wolf were sleeping side by side, peaceful and trusting. I sat on the edge of their bed and caressed Wolf's warm, soft cheeks. They looked so vulnerable, so tender, so innocent. Perhaps Ans was right. Perhaps it would be better to stay away from Geert for the time being.

\* \* \*

It was now half-past two in the morning and I had spent the past hour dithering about whether or not to do it. But I had to. I wouldn't sleep a wink until I had spoken to her. I couldn't bear the thought of her being angry with me. She would understand why I woke her up.

My entire body was in the clutches of fear and I could only release it by talking to someone. I needed to know that I wasn't alone, that she hadn't turned against me once and for all.

I walked down the stairs on my bare feet, which had grown so cold I could barely feel them. In front of her bedroom door I paused. What was all this about? I was a grown-up woman, yet here I was, running to my big sister like some frightened little kid. What was wrong with me? I began to tremble and sob, my knees gave way and I slid down the wall and onto the floor. I was afraid to knock on her door, to admit how scared I was and ask her to comfort me.

The bed creaked and I heard footsteps on the wooden floor. The door opened. I could tell from her face that she hadn't slept either.

"Maria, what's wrong?"

"I'm sorry. For waking you up, I mean. But I couldn't sleep. I don't want us to fight."

"Come in and sit down. It's OK. I wasn't asleep."

I sat down next to her on the bed.

"Here, have a sip."

She handed me a glass of water and draped her dressing gown around my shoulders. I looked at the photos on her bedside table. One showed the pair of them on a sunny day on the beach. Ans, in a red bathing suit, leaned against Martin's bronzed body. She smiled, he looked serious. His blonde hair was slicked back, he frowned and squinted his eyes to keep out the sun. There was something devilish about

121

him. I had never noticed it before, but in that picture his face reminded me of a hawk, with the sharp nose, heavy brows and deep furrows on either side of his mouth.

The other photo was a family portrait. My father proud and beaming behind my mother, who had a vague smile on her face and a sleeping baby in her arms. Our baby brother. On either side of our mother stood Ans and I. Ans, about ten years old and all arms and legs, wore a frilly pink frock and stared solemnly into the camera, whereas I was a chubby toddler in a naff white dress, holding my father's hand and smiling shyly. The photograph must have been taken twenty-five years ago. In 1976. The time of bell-bottoms, brown and orange velvet, platform shoes and sideburns. But not in our family. We wore kitschy dresses made of cheap, synthetic materials that my mother knocked up on her sewing machine.

"I shouldn't have lost my temper like that. I'm sorry."

Ans put her hand on my knee, which jerked under her touch. "You're very tense," she said and slipped behind me. She bared my shoulders and started massaging them gently.

"You're all knotted up. Relax your arms. And your neck. You've got quite a lot on your shoulders, I know."

Her thumbs traced small circles in my neck and slowly moved down to my shoulder blades. She finished with a powerful rub along my vertebrae. It only made me feel worse. I hated this kind of intimacy between women, sisters or no sisters. But I didn't dare ask her to stop.

"I thought you'd come back down again for a chat," I began.

"It was all getting a bit too much. But tell me, Maria, don't you agree it's a bad idea to meet up with Geert?"

She tugged at my skin, which hurt. I shook her off and pulled the dressing gown back over my shoulders.

"Can I smoke in here?"

122

"All right then. But go and stand by the door, please." She got up to open the balcony doors and indicated that she wanted a cigarette as well.

"It's not Geert. I don't know why I'm so sure, but I don't think it's someone I know personally. He's a psychopath who gets a kick out of scaring women... Not so long ago I read in the paper that some idiot is stalking one of the Spice Girls. It's something like that. Some sad individual who thinks he and I have a 'special' bond, who fantasizes about me..."

Ans looked at me sympathetically. "I think that's what you want to believe. But let's be honest, you're not a Spice Girl. You're not on TV, your private life isn't plastered all over the tabloids. Of course it's dreadful to think that you're being threatened by someone you used to love and trust. But you shouldn't lose touch with reality. Day in day out I meet women who are abused and threatened by their former partners. Men who go berserk when their wife or girlfriend decides to leave them. Even intelligent, successful men, dentists, artists, managers, men in all shapes and sizes, who can't stomach the fact that their woman would rather be on her own or with someone else. Geert is and remains the most likely culprit..."

"But then why does he call me? Why's he in such a state himself?"

"Perhaps he's sorry. It's quite common. First these blokes batter their girlfriend and then they start blubbing because they didn't mean to do it. Then a day later they're at it again. These are men with two faces, who cannot keep their emotions on an even keel. On the one hand they hate their wife or girlfriend, on the other they adore her. They want to kill her, but love her at the same time."

I thought of the fights Geert and I had had over the past six months. At night when we came back home after a gig and he accused me of flirting with someone in the audience or the band. On one occasion he had become so irate after I had been chatting to a guy who had put his hand on my bum that he slammed his fist into the linen cupboard and broke his wrist. He hadn't been able to play for six weeks.

But he had never hurt me. He tormented himself more than anyone.

My feet got cold. I walked over to the bed and sat down with my feet tucked under my legs. Tiny silver specks appeared before my eyes. When I shook my head more specks appeared, like snowflakes.

"You're tired, aren't you?" Ans took two pillows and plumped them up behind my back. "You're exhausted. Why don't you relax, Maria. You're safe here. I'll stay with you."

I sank back into the pillows, which felt like falling into a big mountain of feathers, falling and falling, with white down whirling all around me and Ans' words reaching me from a great distance.

"Go to sleep now."

The children. I didn't want to leave the children. I tried to get up, but I couldn't. I was floating and had lost all strength. Somewhere amid all the feathers were Merel and Wolf. Then I found myself swimming through dark, icy water. I heard my children calling out and thrashing about in the water since they couldn't swim, but I couldn't find them because the water turned black.

## 25

The bed was drenched. I woke up shivering in a clammy, cold bathrobe, with my hair stuck to my face. There was something wrong with my head. A throbbing and smarting just above my left temple. I touched my forehead and felt something sticky. Blood. There was blood everywhere. Not just on my head, but on my hands, on my pillow, in my hair. I tried to scream, but my throat was sore, as if I had been screaming for hours on end. When I looked at my hands I noticed that my nails were broken. My fingertips were red and raw.

Ans' bedroom was a complete mess. Her pastel-pink linen curtains were in tatters, a crystal decanter lay in pieces on the floor, the reading lights on either side of the bed had toppled and her clothes were scattered all over the carpet. The white plaster wall at the head of the bed was streaked with blood.

What on earth had happened here? All I remembered was falling asleep and having the most dreadful dreams all night. That's all. My heart was thumping so hard against my ribcage it frightened me. It felt like a train tearing through my body. A panic train. I wanted to get out of this room, out of this house, as far away as possible. I hurled myself at the door, which was locked, and began yanking at it and hammering on it with my fists. I was on the verge of hysteria. I yelled Ans' name, begging her to come and help me – if she was still here.

Nobody came. I was locked up. The throbbing in my head worsened, my knees buckled and I slid along the doorpost and onto the floor. I touched the wound above my temple. It was swollen and even the slightest touch made me wince. I held on to the washbasin beside the door, hauled myself up and looked in the mirror. The sight of my injured head and the frantic look in my eyes made me start. On the left of my forehead was a large gaping wound, fringed by clotted blood. My left eye was red and swollen. My entire face was streaked with blood, my hair was sticky with it. The face staring at me from the mirror was that of a lunatic. And I noticed dried-up foam around my mouth.

I shivered. I took a washcloth from the crooked rattan shelf beside the washbasin and turned on the tap. Cold, clear water. I let it run over my wrists and my hands, rinsed the taste of blood from my mouth and dabbed at my face. Meanwhile I breathed in as deeply as possible, and out again forcefully, in an attempt to get myself back under control.

The children, they were all that mattered now. I had to pull myself together and plan my escape. Where were they? It was eerily quiet in the house. Perhaps they were gone. Perhaps he had taken them. And what about Ans? Where was she? She had been with me when I fell asleep. This was her room. I was afraid to think what might have happened to her.

I looked at the door and saw a tuft of blonde hair stuck to a large bloodstain on the doorpost. My hair. Or Ans'. Probably mine. I must have banged my head against the wood. I gently tried the door again. It swung open straight away.

The sound of muffled voices drifted from the living room. A male and a female voice. Ans and someone else. I crept down the stairs. What time was it? I tiptoed to the kitchen and checked the clock. Ten past two. Had I slept that long? I cocked my ears in an effort to hear the children, but I couldn't hear a thing. There were no wellies under the coat stand, no crayons on the kitchen table. The place looked immaculate, like a commercial for cleaning products. The wooden table gleamed, the kitchen cabinets sparkled and the floor smelled of floor polish. Who was that man talking to my sister? Martin?

Ans was in her chair, sitting opposite a scruffy, middle-aged man in a brown suede jacket. Both looked startled when

I entered. My sister jumped up, rushed towards me and started fussing over me like a nurse. She patted me tenderly on the back.

"How are you? Please sit down. This is Victor. Victor, you've met Maria…"

He gave me a limp, dry hand. He had big bags under his eyes and at least three days' worth of stubble. His grey, frizzy hair stood on end and lent him the air of an absent-minded professor.

"Hello, Maria. How are you feeling now?"

I shifted my gaze from my sister to Victor. Something about them struck me. They seemed guarded.

"Where are the children?"

"They're playing in their room. I just went and bought some toys with them. Wolf was missing his Lego…"

"I'll go and have a look." I turned round, but Ans stopped me.

"Trust me, Maria, they're upstairs. They're safe. Sit down. If they were to see you like this…"

I looked down at my bloodstained bathrobe and my grazed fingers.

"What's going on? What happened?"

The look in my sister's eyes terrified me. She looked at me as if I wasn't in my right mind. She ushered me to the sofa and forced me gently down onto the seat.

"Do you have no recollection of last night?" Victor asked. He scrutinized me, his eyes all screwed up. It was intimidating, creepy really, to have him stare at me like I was some kind of talking monkey.

"Who's he? What's he doing here?"

"You're right. My apologies. Let me introduce myself properly. I'm a psychiatrist at Riagg, the regional institute for mental welfare, and one of Ans' colleagues. We often work as a team. Ans supervises problem families, while I assess the parents' mental health. Your sister called me last night, or early this morning to be precise, and asked me to come over."

Ans started nervously stroking the palm of my hand.

"You were extremely distraught. You came to my room, around half-past two, in floods of tears. I shouldn't have lost my temper with you. But anyway, we had a bit of a chat, about Geert and everything you've been through recently, and just when you seemed to have calmed down a bit you suddenly wanted to wake the children. When I tried to stop you, you went berserk. Completely out of control. I mean, physically. You trashed the room. You attacked me. I fled the room and locked the door. Then I called Victor. When he got here you were banging your head against the doorpost. You'd ripped open your hands. Merel and Wolf were crying in the corridor. Victor gave you some sedatives."

I tried to light a cigarette, but my body was shaking so badly that I dropped the lighter. Victor picked it up off the floor and gave me a light.

Things were starting to fall into place. I knew what was going on here. It was absolutely vital now that I kept a grip on myself. My every word, my every movement was being monitored. I wanted the fog in my head to lift so I could think clearly.

"I need to eat something," was all I could utter.

"I'll make you a sandwich. Cheese, no butter, right?"

I nodded.

"No recollection whatsoever?" Victor crossed his legs and rubbed his worn corduroy trousers. He wore yellow socks. There was a hole in the sole of his left shoe.

"No. I had dreams. About my children. I heard them screaming. Like they were drowning. But I couldn't find them, it was too dark."

128

"I see." He leaned over, took his half-finished cigar from the ashtray on the table and lit it with his Zippo. The smell of lighter fluid prickled my nose.

"Your sister is extremely worried about you. She's told me a few things about your situation and I'm afraid her concerns are justified. You've been through a lot in the past few weeks... I'm not sure I know what to do. Normally I have patients who show symptoms of psychosis committed. But Ans won't hear of it."

"I'm not psychotic."

"Perhaps not. It's hard for me to judge. But last night you certainly posed a threat to those around you..."

"I don't know if Ans told you this, but I'm here because someone's threatening me."

"And do you have any idea who that might be?"

"No. Except that it's someone who knows a lot about me. Who hates me with a passion and thinks I'm a whore. I think he may have given me some kind of drug..."

"How could he have done that?"

"How would I know!? That's for the police to figure out. Take a blood sample, take some samples of my food and drink."

"Right. I'm afraid the police don't have time for that sort of thing."

"They've got plenty of time, but they think I'm crazy, like you."

"I don't think you're crazy at all. I think it's all become a bit too much. You just need someone to talk to and perhaps some medication to help you relax a little. That's all."

I got up. Suddenly I felt completely drained.

"How do you think someone could have drugged you here in the house?"

Victor folded his hands behind his head and leaned back, his squishy lips wrapped around his wet cigar. I looked at him and thought to myself that I would never, ever lie down on his couch. He was the kind of man I loathed. A smug social worker. He only did this job because it made him feel virtuous. I wanted him to leave and never come back. I didn't answer his question, because I knew he would only find me more unhinged, but it did plant an idea in my head. There was only one person who had access to this house. One man who knew everything about my past. It all fell into place now.

I listened to Victor's psychological drivel, promised him that I would take my medication and feigned gratitude when he stressed that I could call him day and night. He would be back in three days' time to see how I was and whether the medication had taken effect.

Ans promised Victor that she would stay with me. We shook hands and Victor gave me a friendly pat on the back. Ans hugged me and I promised her that I'd take it easy. For the first time in weeks I knew exactly what to do.

## 26

"Are you better now, Mum?" Wolf clambered onto my lap and looked at me wide-eyed.

"Sure, sweetie. Mummy just had a bad dream. The fire had given Mummy such a shock…"

"Me too. I dreamed that the fire chased me, and then Merel woke me up and said that someone was trying to kill you, and that you weren't in our room any more. And then we heard you crying and calling us. And then I started crying too and so did Merel. And then Aunt Ans came and took us to that man in the room."

Merel stared intently at the television screen.

"I'm so sorry about everything. But it will be fine, I promise. Mummy loves you. A lot." I rubbed my nose against his cheeks. They smelled of milk and peanut butter.

"I love you too, Mummy. And Daddy too." He planted a kiss on my lips, squirmed out of my embrace and jumped onto the sofa next to Merel.

In the bathroom I inspected my body. My arms were full of scratches and red weals. A purplish blue lump the shape of an egg covered my left eye and made me look like an alien from *Star Trek*.

In fact, I looked like my mother. That haunted look, the trembling hands. I'd had foam around my mouth. So had she, shortly before her first spell in hospital.

That stifling evening in August, my father was working on the beach. The orange sun hung low over the sea, the dunes glowed in the evening light and the holiday-makers were sitting on the sand with bottles of wine, waiting for a glorious sunset. I was five years old and had been told by Ans to fetch Dad quickly. Ans would stay with Mum, who had barricaded herself in the scullery. She had sat there all day on a stool, muttering to herself and polishing boxes full of cutlery. I had been avoiding her for months. She scared me, the way she would suddenly grab my braids and pull me into the kitchen, where she would rap me over the knuckles because I had a stain on my dress or dirty fingernails, or else take me onto her lap, lovingly stroke my head and tell me how pretty I was and that it was a shame, such a shame that Daddy was trying to destroy us all. I would run as fast as my legs would take me to Dad on the beach. I felt safe with him. He was big and strong and gentle.

That's what I thought then. I have since come to realize that he was a wimp, closing his eyes to his wife's illness and letting his eldest daughter deal with the fall-out. But at the time I adored him, the way he would lift deck chairs high above his head with his strong brown arms, as if it was nothing. He could dive straight into the cold sea, build beach pavilions, rescue reckless German tourists from the waves. He was my hero.

I had heard an enormous bang, followed by a rattling sound and the most desperate wailing. A moment later Ans ran up to me, looking flushed and panicky.

"Fetch Dad. Now."

"Why? What's wrong?"

"Nothing. Just do it. Go!"

I ran across the wooden duckboards, against the stream of sauntering, sunburnt tourists, and called my dad. I ran onto the beach to his blue hut, where he was laughing and drinking beer with a fat man.

"Dad, Dad, come quick! There was a big bang. I think something's happened to Mum."

He sped away in his swimming trunks, with me hot on his heels. Half the sun had disappeared into the sea. The sand was warm.

The door to the guesthouse scullery was closed. I was sent away. I heard my mother shrieking and throwing things around the room, while my father tried to soothe her. Ans came out, charged up the stairs and returned with a glass of water and a small white box. All without a word. I asked her what was wrong. "Go away," came her reply.

My mother was carried up to her room by my father. She lay in his arms like a rag doll. Her face was blotchy and bloated. She shivered. There was a white substance around her mouth. Foam. She looked straight through me. It looked as though she was wearing a mask.

Ans and I were allowed to go out and buy chips. We ate our food in silence, on a bench in the square.

"What happened?"

"Nothing. Mum's tired. She's going to sleep now."

At night I was woken up by voices outside. Screams. Ans and I pushed aside our curtains and saw guests running around barefoot in their pyjamas. Dad stormed in and told us to get out quick. Some guests took us under their wing and together we ran hysterically away from the guesthouse. From a safe distance we looked at Duinzicht. An ambulance, fire engine and police car all drove past with wailing sirens. "What is it?" I asked a woman who had wrapped her arms around me. "Gas," she said. "A gas leak. It was a narrow escape. The whole place could have gone up in the air."

Mum was admitted to the psychiatric clinic in Santpoort. Connie, a sweet young woman, moved in with us, to help out in the guesthouse. It was a lovely time. We talked during meals. The guests loved her. So did Dad and I. On Sundays we would go and visit Mum. She would sit there like a zombie on a grubby, green upholstered chair, fidgeting with her skirt. She started smoking in Santpoort. One cigarette after the other. She smoked them down to the filter. Six months later, Mum came back home and we said goodbye to Connie. We were in tears.

I got in the shower. The hot water stung my wounds, but it was a pleasant feeling. The pain cleared my head. I wouldn't let him get to me. I washed my hair with Ans' coconut shampoo and the whole bathroom instantly smelled of Steve, who used to rub every inch of his body with coconut oil. He would sit on a white plastic stool, naked, and inspect his toes, cut his toenails and then massage his entire body with the fragrant oil, his toes, his shins, his thighs, until he glistened all over. Then he would stand in front of the mirror, still naked, and admire himself.

Memories. Of my mother scrubbing me while I bit my lip, trying not to cry as the soap got into my eyes. The images floated through my head like soap bubbles and burst just as easily.

I put on my jeans, which no longer fit me snugly but sagged around my hips, pulled my black sweater over my head and carefully brushed my hair. My mother had never known what was wrong with her. She had rejected all help and therapy, refused to take her medication and always insisted that we were trying to get rid of her. My father was seeing someone else. We were all plotting against her. Nobody would listen to her. I looked out the window at a swooping seagull, and with a jolt I realized that she may have been right. I had never made the slightest effort to understand her. I immediately suppressed this thought. She had been unmistakably paranoid. She had tried to beat my father to death. I didn't have a single pleasant memory of her.

## 27

I decided not to tell Ans that I suspected her husband. She would only think I had lost it completely.

I found her in the living room, playing a board game with the children.

"Look who's here. Would you like some tea?"

"I'll get it, thanks."

I poured myself a cup and joined the others. "I'm sorry. About last night. It's odd… I quite honestly can't remember a thing."

Ans turned to me, scowled and shook her head. She put a finger to her lips and nodded in the direction of the children. She got up, patted Merel and Wolf on the head and announced she was going to make some fresh tea. I followed her into the kitchen.

"You shouldn't talk about these things in front of the children," she began. "They're still in a state of shock because of last night. You should talk to them about everyday things, rebuild their trust."

"Like you never told me anything when we were young, is that what you mean? And still don't tell me anything? Just keep mum about problems, so you can pretend they don't exist?"

"There's no need to attack *me*, Maria. I'm not the patient here," she hissed at me through her teeth.

"I'm not attacking you. I just don't want you to interfere in my children's upbringing. We are open with one another. When they ask me a question, they get an honest answer. That's why they trust me."

"You're burdening them with your problems and the responsibility is too much for them. They're scared." She pursed her lips. "I have no choice but to step in."

She picked up the kettle and held it under the tap. Then she turned the gas on and banged the kettle down on the stove. I lit a cigarette. Step in. Over my dead body. But I held back, for I knew there was no point arguing with her. She would clam up and give me the silent treatment and I was allergic to that.

"Tell me honestly: do you think I've concocted this whole story?"

"What you see and feel is your truth. I don't think you'd go around fabricating things."

She pulled a chair out from under the table and sat down with a sigh.

"With plenty of rest and proper support... I want to help you, Maria. Victor can help you. Nobody else needs to know about this..."

"So you don't believe I received those letters..."

"I believe what I see. And last night I saw you go berserk. You were a far cry from the Maria I know..."

"I'm not like Mum."

Ans put the teapot on the tray.

"No, of course you're not. Besides, these are different times. We know so much more these days. We have better drugs. Today's therapies are more effective. You've been through a lot, Maria, enough to confuse anyone. Have faith in Victor."

"Ans, I'm your sister, not your patient."

"Client."

"Spare me your social worker spiel. I'll take the frigging pills, I'll talk to Victor, but I don't want you to treat me like one of your 'clients'."

"Don't get all worked up. I'll pop by the pharmacy later to pick up your medication, and I'll take the children along to give you a bit of a break."

We drank our tea in a tense silence. The tinkling of my teaspoon, the rattling china cups, Ans' discreet slurping, all these delicate sounds were almost intolerable. I was relieved when she got up to leave. She urged me to lie down for a while. Rest, rest and yet more rest, that's what I needed. Only rest would restore me back to health. I promised I would go to bed.

I watched them drive off in her black Volkswagen Golf and felt a pang when I saw my children join her so readily. They had become quite attached to her within a matter of days.

## 28

Her office was adjacent to the kitchen, at the front of the house, and from her desk she had a view of the dunes. Her pens were neatly lined up on the walnut desktop. An eraser, a pencil sharpener and four marker pens formed a still life beside a pile of colourful folders. Otherwise her desk was empty.

The right wall was dominated by an enormous bookcase filled with specialist literature. Thousands of books, arranged by subject. Four shelves on children and pedagogy. A section dedicated to medical and psychiatric reference books. Row upon row of feminist literature. Marilyn French, Anja Meulenbelt, the Cinderella complex, all that 1970s rubbish that other women had long since dumped at a charity shop. All misery known to man was gathered on these bookshelves here.

On the wall by the window hung a photograph of Martin, tanned and smiling in an orange life-jacket. I took it off the wall and looked at his face. A face I thought I knew, with bushy eyebrows and that strange, pointed hawk nose. I remembered looking at a photograph of him last night, thinking there was something of the devil in him. I couldn't see it now. He was just good old Martin, laughing after a sun-soaked sailing trip. The Martin I trusted, who managed my savings and who did my tax returns without ever asking a penny for it.

At first glance, he and my sister seemed ill-matched. One would expect to see him alongside a lively, down-to-earth woman, who also liked sailing, playing golf and driving around in convertibles. Ans wasn't interested in any of those things. Her favourite pastime was tidying up. Organizing. Categorizing. Restoring order. In her own home and in the lives of others. She used to do that as a child when she would line up her shoes beside her bed and then with a ruler check if they were completely straight. If not, she couldn't sleep.

Where might she keep the keys? Not in an old, dented soup bowl like I did. Perhaps she didn't even have a key to Martin's office. Perhaps he had locked away his secrets in the knowledge that in his absence Ans would be snooping around. It suddenly struck me that Ans had taken the news of his disappearance rather calmly. As if she thought it was normal that he had just upped and left. What had really happened between them? More than she let on, that was obvious. Ans never talked about herself. She had been brought up on reticence.

"*What's wrong with Mum?*"

"*Nothing.*"

"*Why's she always angry?*"

"*Don't know.*"

"*Where's Dad?*"

"*Outside.*"

"*What are you doing?*"

"*None of your business.*"

So it didn't come as a surprise to me that all of her drawers were locked. The key to her desk drawer must be on her bunch of keys. Which she always carried with her. What if she lost it? Impossible, Ans never lost anything. But it could be stolen of course. And in that case she would need a spare key. Somewhere in this enormous house there had to be a spare key.

I checked to see if she might have attached the key to the underside of the desk or chair with a piece of Sellotape, like Dad used to do. No luck.

I was on the floor, with my head underneath her desk, when I heard footsteps. Someone was prowling around the

138

house. And I was alone. I inched a bit further under the desk. I made myself as small as possible, with my head between my knees and my legs pulled up, and tried to breathe as quietly as possible.

What on earth was I doing here? What if it was Ans and she came in and found me here in her office, hiding under her desk? It would only strengthen her belief that I had lost it completely. Or perhaps it was the postman. Or a Jehovah's Witness. I got cramp in my neck, sitting there with my head pressed against the table top, hearing the footsteps continue hesitantly. I was well on my way to becoming paranoid. The doorbell rang. Twice. Short, long. The piercing sound of the bell got my heart racing and I broke out in a cold sweat. I thought of my singing instructor, Mrs Hupke. *Relax your muscles, one by one, really loosen up. Breathe in, hold, let your belly go all slack, clench, and pffffff, out with the stress. Clear space. Space in your abdomen, in all your cavities, in your head. Straighten your back, tilt your pelvis forward, lower your shoulders.*

I crawled out from under the desk and out of the room, over to the window in the hallway. I would peep from behind the curtain to see who was on the doorstep.

The man was already on his way back to the silver-coloured Audi parked in the drive. He seemed to be about my age. He looked attractive from the back. Slender, with medium-length brown hair, jeans and a dark-brown leather jacket. He looked back one more time at the door and the upstairs windows, as if he was looking for someone and knew this person to be in the house, even though he didn't answer the door.

My curiosity proved stronger than my fear and I ran to the front door to call the man. I managed to make myself heard over the wind and he turned round.

139

"Ah, so there is someone after all." He walked back, his hand extended.

Estate agent, salesman, insurance agent, accountant, it flashed through my mind. He had that aura of confidence, that particular brand of optimism.

"Harry Menninga, good afternoon."

I showed him my bandaged fingers and he abruptly withdrew his hand. His gaze briefly flitted over my black eye and the large plaster above it.

"Say, is Martin home by any chance?"

When I answered in the negative, his self-confidence wavered briefly. He took a pair of black sunglasses from his hair, fiddled with their hinges for a bit and then stuck the right hinge between his teeth. The sea wind blew straight through my jumper and I pulled the collar up to try and protect myself from the cold and from Harry Menninga.

"I see. And you are…"

"Ans' sister. I'm staying here. Can I take a message?"

"Well… I'd like to speak to Martin, but I can't seem to get hold of him. Not on his mobile and not by email. Ans keeps telling me he's gone away on business for a couple of days, but then I should be able to reach him on his mobile…"

I offered him some coffee. I wanted to trust him. He knew Martin. He wouldn't hurt me. I decided not to be afraid, but while I carried two cups of coffee into the living room my hands shook so badly I spilt coffee on the beige carpet. Harry took the cups from me, while I went to fetch a cloth to rub off the stain.

"Green soap," he yelled after me. "Whatever you do, don't use all-purpose cleaner. It only makes it worse."

While I rubbed off the stain, Harry sat on the edge of the sofa, pouring the coffee on the saucers back into the cups.

"If you don't mind me asking, what happened to you?"

140

I covered the bruised half of my face with my hand. I had forgotten that I looked awful.

"Nothing to worry about, just a little accident."

Harry frowned, but fortunately didn't ask any further.

"Are you a friend of Martin's?" I asked him.

'Yeah, you might say that. Friend and colleague. I'm an estate agent. Martin and I used to work together at ZHV. I've since set up my own business and now we're helping each other out. We refer clients to one another, that kind of thing. Martin takes care of my finances. And we sail together. Two weeks ago, we'd arranged to go to a football match, Ajax–Feyenoord, but he never showed up. Ans said he was ill. A few days later we had a meeting with a mutual client, and again he didn't show. Turns out he's temporarily transferred his business to this prick at ZHV. Without consulting me! I was furious. But now… it just doesn't add up. It looks as if he's disappeared off the face of the earth."

I took a gulp of lukewarm coffee and offered him a cigarette, which he accepted gratefully.

"Actually, I quit," he smiled. "But I always think to myself: as long as I don't buy them myself…"

"Sounds familiar. You guys will end up bankrupting me."

He gave me a light with his promotional lighter and we both inhaled as if our lives depended on it.

"Anyhow, I guess Ans is at work? Does she have any idea where he is?"

"I don't know if I should tell you this, but… He's not well. He's had a burn-out and left. He's in Spain now. He called Ans from Madrid and asked her to hand over his business to ZHV."

"Burn-out? That doesn't sound like Martin… gosh. He's really made a mess of it…"

A strange kind of tension flitted across Harry's face. He was furious, but tried very hard to hide it from me. He tapped his foot impatiently.

"Listen, I have to find him. It's absolutely imperative. What time are you expecting Ans back?"

"I don't know. Any minute, or perhaps she'll be another hour or so."

He sighed.

"Did he take his mobile? Did he leave an address or a phone number?"

"No, not as far as I know. But you'd have to ask Ans."

"Never mind. So he called? Perhaps we could trace the number…"

He stubbed out his cigarette with what looked like a trembling hand. Here we were, two neurotics side by side. This guy knew something about Martin, I could feel it. But how could I get it out of him? To my mind, all estate agents are seasoned liars. "I could try and trace the number and call you when I've got it…"

"Let's try it now."

"Whoa, it's not that easy. Perhaps it's in Ans' diary. Or perhaps she wrote it down somewhere else. What's the rush? What's going on here?"

I poured him some more coffee. He rested his head in his hands and massaged his temples. "A business thing. If I don't get hold of him soon, we'll have a disaster on our hands. Perhaps we already have."

"But I thought he'd handed over his business? Can't they help you at ZHV?"

Beads of sweat appeared on his upper lip. Harry seemed to be getting more nervous and more furious by the minute. "What a dickhead. No, ZHV doesn't know about this. This is private. Shit. It just doesn't make sense…"

He was close to boiling point. Whatever he and Martin were up to, it was rapidly dawning on him that he was in deep trouble. He picked at his eyebrows.

"Burn-out, my arse." He sounded completely worked up. "I'm sorry."

"Listen, Martin and I are dabbling in shares. We both invested a bit of money that we weren't using anyway and we made a handsome profit. Martin was doing better than me, on the Internet, the Nasdaq, so in the end I gave him my money to invest for me. And now he's gone. That arsehole!" He was about to slam his fist on the table when he realized that it wasn't quite the done thing. His hand hovered over the table for a second, before it came to settle on his thigh.

"He said we had to take out a loan. We had such a great portfolio, it was all going so well, that if we borrowed a little money to buy some extra shares we'd make a killing. And I trusted him. I transferred the money to our investment account, I don't know, about two weeks ago… And the next day he didn't show up. He just made off with it! God knows how many other people he duped…"

At those words, a shiver ran down my spine. Martin needed money. My house in Amsterdam would make him a tidy sum.

Harry got up.

"I have to go. Save what I can. Talk to the bank. They're constantly on the phone anyway."

"Perhaps you should go to the police…"

"Are you mad? They won't leave a stone unturned. My reputation would suffer. No, I'll have to track him down myself. Something happened, I'm sure of it. I simply can't believe he'd screw me…"

"Does Ans know about this? I mean, about you dabbling with money that's hers too?"

143

"No, I'm afraid not. And something that strikes me as very odd now: shortly before he disappeared he asked me to value this property, but Ans wasn't to know, he didn't want to cause any concern… Martin's a friend, we must find out what's really going on. He must be given a chance to…"

Harry was speaking to himself rather than to me.

I followed him to the door, where he gave me his card. He gave me an awkward pat on the back and frowned. "Let's keep this between the two of us for the time being, OK?"

He looked up at the damp, grey walls of Duinzicht, and cast a final, professional eye over the fortress of my pathetic past. "You'll call me about that number, OK?" He brandished his car keys and put his sunglasses on, even though the sky was grey and it could start raining any minute. "Ciao."

He zapped at his Audi. His rear lights winked back, just as agitated as he was. He got in, his mind already on other things, and drove off with screaming tyres.

## 29

Money. Was there a more banal motive to drive a person insane, or murder them?

Money didn't interest me in the slightest. Besides, I was comfortable enough to not really have to worry about it. I had inherited money. My parents had worked themselves to the bone, lived frugally and left us a small fortune. It meant I could live in my own home yet still dedicate myself wholly to music. I could get by on the little money I earned singing.

I found it simply unimaginable that money could be so important that you would harm or even kill a person for it. Love, jealousy, obsessive infatuation, all-consuming anger,

144

fair enough, but money? To live for money, to work with it, it all seemed incredibly dull.

"Tell me, what's the thrill of investing?" I had asked Harry. He called it an exhilarating game, a bit like gambling, and the thrill lay in winning, seeing the share prices rise, selling at just the right moment, putting the cash back in and making yet more money. Playing the large multinationals at their own game. It made him feel powerful, like he too pulled some weight. It was difficult to quit.

But he had, because he lacked the confidence. He either waited too long, or not long enough, he had been a coward and it had cost him dearly. But Martin, Martin was hard as nails. He was brave enough to take risks.

But now he had disappeared, taking his friend's money and perhaps Ans' as well. Should I tell her? No, not yet. I wanted some proof first. And Harry was the person who could help me obtain it.

Ans and the children arrived home with carrier bags full of groceries. Ans handed me a small white bag with medicines. "You're not allowed to drink when you take them," she said and made her way to the kitchen with a bag of fruit under her arm. Wolf and Merel followed her eagerly.

"Are we going to make hot chocolate now? And bake cookies? Are you joining us, Mum? We're making gingerbread!" Wolf tugged at my hand. I trailed after them, but felt a little redundant, as if I was under a gigantic bell jar, cut off from everyone else. I could see them, and they could see me, but we couldn't communicate.

Ans put her keys on the table, next to the groceries. Merel and Wolf rummaged in the bags, beside themselves with enthusiasm, and showed me all the treats they had been allowed to buy.

145

"Look, Mum, chocolate pudding! And mini Twix bars! Mum, look!"

I wasn't looking. I was keeping an eye on the keys, an enormous bunch on a small chain with an orange life buoy. Ans snatched them off the table and walked over to a small painting on the wall. She opened it and hung the keys on a hook, next to some other keys, each with its own colour buoy. The painting turned out to be a key cabinet.

"What a funny little cabinet," I said and took a closer look: a naive, kitschy picture of a farm, with a farmer and his wife sitting on a bench in front of two large stable doors. The stable doors opened with a tiny wooden doorknob. Only Ans would put up such a silly little thing and then actually use it too.

"Martin brought it back from Switzerland. He saw it in this guesthouse where he was staying and thought it was so quaint he asked if he could buy it. Turns out the manageress made them herself, together with her husband."

"How cute. What was Martin doing in Switzerland?"

"Skiing. Here, take this. Make yourself comfortable in the living room. I'll keep the children occupied."

She handed me a mug of warm tea that reeked of piss.

"St John's wort. It has a calming and anti-depressant effect."

"Thanks." I took a mouthful. It didn't taste of anything. But now I knew where she kept the keys and it made me feel almost euphoric. In Martin's office I would find answers, I was convinced.

Rini was the first to see the flames. I was in her kitchen sipping a glass of wine when suddenly she yelled that my house was on fire. We dashed out, yelling hysterically. Flames shot out of my kitchen and I screamed: "The children! My children are sleeping up there!" I wanted to go in, go upstairs, but I was

146

completely paralysed. I turned round, but Rini had vanished and I stood there all alone, staring at my burning house. I wanted to cry, but the tears wouldn't come. The anguish was too great, the fear too intense. I felt a terrible pain in my belly, as if I was giving birth, as if the children that had come out of my womb were crawling back in. I looked down and saw that I really was pregnant, my belly was big and round and taut. All of a sudden, my mother appeared in front of me and regarded me with contempt. "You asked for it," she said, "you can't welcome one child and not the other."

She left again and I wanted to go after her, but I still couldn't move.

I didn't feel a thing when the baby slid out of me, fell onto the floor and cried. I looked up and realized there was no fire. Merel and Wolf came out of the house and happily greeted their new brother. Merel picked him up and showered the baby in kisses.

Then I woke up. I was bathed in sweat and my mouth was sticky and dry. The intense sorrow I had felt in my dream weighed heavily on me. I felt as if I was under water. The sluggish flow of blood through my veins sounded like the sea. I went under again, back to the nightmare I knew was only a dream, but couldn't wake from.

Someone shook me by the shoulder and stroked my forehead.

"Wake up," Ans said softly. "Are you all right?"

When I shook my head my brains sloshed against my skull. I tried to get up, but my muscles were like jelly.

"Just lie down and rest," she said and covered me with an itchy woollen blanket.

I was lying on the sofa. I could smell the fire in the hearth. It was probably quite late in the evening, as I couldn't hear the children any more. Gentle piano music filled the room. I had been completely out of it. I closed my eyes and listened to the minimalist piano strains that lent the room the air of a funeral parlour.

It felt as if I was already dead. Life was slowly oozing out of me, and every day I felt emptier and weaker. What on earth was wrong with me?

I asked Ans for water. She brought me some and then some more. I drank as if my life depended on it, while she sat beside me with her hands in her lap, gazing at me like I was a retard.

"What's wrong with me?" I asked her. She told me the storm in my head would abate in due course, provided I had plenty of rest. She claimed it was the medication that knocked me out. I couldn't remember taking any medication.

"I want to go out."

Ans didn't think this was a good idea. She thought I was too unstable to go out on my own.

"I'm not going anywhere, I just want to get some fresh air. I've been cooped up inside all day."

Suddenly I couldn't bear to be in the house a minute longer. The tinkling piano music sounded like someone was banging together two cymbals right next to my ear. Ans suggested we go for a stroll together, but I didn't want the children to be left on their own. I needed to think and I couldn't do that with her around.

## 30

I got swept along by the wind on legs of jelly, while trying to light a cigarette at the same time. Thoughts surfaced, bobbed around for a bit and then disappeared again. For a moment I couldn't remember what I was doing outside, in the dark, or what had happened today. I took a deep breath and touched my wound. The pain that shot through me was almost pleasurable. I was still capable of sensation.

In the car park, my grimy white Golf stood next to Ans' gleaming black one. My small, valiant, indefatigable car. The last of my earthly possessions. I would wash it tomorrow. Now I had the time for this kind of thing. I would rub the faded paintwork with wax, touch up the rust patches, scrape the bird droppings off the windows. I would throw out all the empty coke cans, remove the dirty socks and stale bread crusts and vacuum the sand and crumbs from between the seats. Tomorrow my trusty Golf would be just as immaculate as Ans'.

I loved my car, even though it was old and occasionally temperamental, refusing service at the most untimely moments.

The door was open. Apparently I hadn't locked it properly. I sat behind the wheel and breathed in the musty, humid smell. I switched on the radio and took a Red Hot Chili Peppers CD from the glove compartment. It was cold and my fingers hurt when I slipped the CD into the player. Green fluorescent figures appeared on the display. The time: 03:30. It was almost morning. Had I been asleep on the sofa for that long? I reached in my coat pocket to check the time on my mobile, but I must have left it inside. Shit. What time had it been when I felt unwell and lay down for a nap? Not much later than half-past five in the afternoon. That meant I had been out of it for nearly ten hours.

Ans had been awake when I woke up. That too was odd. Had she been beside me on the sofa until half-past three? I bit my hand. I appeared to have lost all sense of time. I had lost touch with this world. I was caught in a twilight zone. For

149

the first time I began to seriously doubt myself. What if they were right and I really was confused?

Panting, I hurried back inside, hung up my coat and walked into the room where Ans was reading.

"What time is it?"

"It's late. Very late. We should go to bed." Ans put down her book and stretched her arms and legs.

"What time?" I was out of breath even though I had barely exerted myself. Ans got up.

"Half-past three, if not later. You slept for ages…"

"And why are you still up?"

"I was afraid to let you out of my sight, sweetheart. Victor told me to keep an eye on you and check whether the medication wasn't making you too drowsy or leaving you too agitated. Come, I'll take you upstairs."

She put her arm around my waist and pushed me gently but determinedly towards the staircase. I freed myself from her grip.

"I can go to bed on my own, thanks," I snapped.

Ans smiled her angelic nurse's smile. "Have it your way. But make sure you take your medicines. They're on your bedside table."

I climbed the stairs, but halfway up I slumped. All of a sudden, I couldn't move another inch. I was so tired I could have slept right there on the staircase, with my head resting on the soft velvet runner.

Ans tugged at my arm.

"Come on now, just a few more steps. We're nearly there." She hoisted me up, wrapped my right arm around her shoulders and dragged me the rest of the way. She talked to me like you would to a toddler learning to walk. At the top of the stairs, she leaned me against the wall, opened the door and switched on the light.

150

"Right, here we are. If you put your pyjamas on, I'll fetch you a glass of water."

This wasn't the room I had slept in before. The children weren't here. I hadn't seen them since half-past five in the afternoon. I opened the wardrobe and found all my clothes neatly on hangers. On the shelves were my T-shirts, underwear and socks, all carefully folded and smelling of lavender. Ans had moved me to a different room. Or I had moved myself. I couldn't remember which. I couldn't remember what day of the week it was, what month or what I had done today. I looked at my hand and saw blood. There were teeth marks just below my thumb. I had bitten myself.

Ans cleaned the wound with alcohol. She shook her head. "What's wrong with you? You can't go around biting yourself."

I asked her where the children were. In her room, she said. The children didn't mind. They realized their mother was ill.

I wanted to see them.

"You should go to sleep," she said, tearing a piece of sticking plaster from the roll with her teeth.

"They're safe, trust me. We'd better not wake them up now. They'd only get upset."

She handed me a glass of water and a yellow capsule.

"Here you are. It'll help you sleep so you'll be on top form again tomorrow."

I refused to take the pill. I was so tired, I would sleep without that rubbish. I felt confused and drained enough and I reckoned the medication would only make it worse.

Ans didn't argue with me.

"Have a sip of water then. It's good for you."

I took the glass but it slipped from my hands. Ans offered to fetch me another one, but I told her not to bother. I had

151

to go to the bathroom anyway. Reluctantly, she cleared off, but not before reminding me that my medication was in the medicine cabinet, on the left-hand side. Just in case.

Steve and I had been living together in Amsterdam for six months when my mother finally managed to end her life. Six days before Christmas she lay down on her bed, in her Sunday best, and swallowed every single pill in the house. There were quite a few. Seresta to calm down, lithium for depression, Tegretol in the event of an epileptic fit, Haldol in case of psychotic episodes. In the bathroom stood a big, white, metal cabinet full of drugs to keep my mother in check. The cabinet was always locked, except on that fateful Sunday. My father was working on the beach. Ans was studying in her room. Neither of them had seen or heard anything. They had no idea how Mum had managed to get hold of the key. Had someone forgotten to remove it from the lock? Had Mum known where the key was?

It made me feel sick. Not so much the loss of my mother – I had lost her a long time ago – but the futility of her life and finally her death. We had closed our eyes and averted our gaze, stuffed her full of pills just to be rid of her. Might a good psychiatrist have helped her? Might we have helped her, if we had actually listened to her? Everything she said, we dismissed as the ravings of a lunatic, a mental patient who made our lives miserable, without whom we would be much better off. How had Dad managed to put up with her for so long?

"She was a good woman," he said after the funeral. "May she rest in peace, free from the illness that tormented her."

What else could he have done? Have her locked away in an asylum? File for divorce and condemn her to roaming the streets? He had done what he thought was best. He had stayed with her for better and for worse, just as he had promised.

But let's face it, he had been a wimp. He had never really bothered. He had fled the house whenever he could and left her to run the guesthouse. And when she couldn't take it any more, the cabinet full of dope appeared and my mother became an automaton.

She hadn't left a note. As far as I could remember, she had never told us she loved us. The locket she wore when Ans found her held a photograph of Stephan, our dead brother. The loss of Stephan, my father said, was something she never came to terms with. Now at long last she would be reunited with him. In the twelve years since Stephan's death, it was the first time Dad had mentioned his name.

Her funeral. Such a dismal affair. It was warm for the time of year, and we were sweltering in our black, woollen suits. There were just a few of us. Ans, Dad, Steve, a couple of neighbours and staff. A small, lonely family. No granddads and grandmas, aunts and uncles. My mother had been a bastard child. My father was the son of two people who had never expected to have any children. Steve's family wanted to come, but I managed to talk them out of it. Imagine the clash: his big, vibrant, boisterous family versus my small, dull and parochial one.

Ans spoke. She said that Mum had finally found the peace she had been craving for years. She had left us with a great many questions and we would miss her. We would look after Dad and the guesthouse. Not me, I thought to myself. More than ever, I felt the urge to leave all this behind, get out of this oppressive dump, as far away as possible. My life was about to begin and nobody could stop me. I would live. I would be someone, and when I died my friends would cry and dance on my grave. Nobody shed a tear for my mother. Including me. I was furious. She had allowed her life to be a failure.

There was coffee and cake at the reception afterwards. Ans flitted tirelessly among the whispering mourners, hugged them, fetched coffee for Dad, shook clammy hands, her heels clacking on the linoleum. I couldn't bear to watch her play the ministering angel, the heart and soul of our family.

"That sister of yours is so strong and sweet. I take my hat off to her! Your dad must be so pleased she's going to run Duinzicht."

Nobody said a word to Steve. Dressed in a white suit, he sat bolt upright in a black plastic chair. His shaven head shone with coconut oil. I knew the neighbours were gossiping about us: "nail in her coffin", or something along those lines. After the reception, in the boiling car in the car park, I unzipped his trousers, pulled down his black, silk boxer shorts and without any foreplay took him straight inside me. Steve laughed his roaring laugh. "*Oh baby, you're crazy*," he moaned.

31

I had four voicemails and two text messages. Geert had phoned. He was furious with me for not turning up. "*I know where you are, Maria. You're at your sister's! I've had enough, I'm coming over right now!*"

His aggressive tone frightened me. And the fact that he was on his way even more so. Ans wouldn't be impressed.

The second voicemail was from Steve. "*Hi baby, why won't you call me back? Listen, I've got good news. And I need you. Call me back, please.*"

And again: "*Listen baby, since you won't call me back: I'm competing in the National Song Contest.*" He roared with laughter. "*And I want you to join me. On backing vocals. This is it, Maria, your big break! I hope you've got a reason now to call me back. Bye.*"

154

The Song Contest. Steve made me laugh. He had been back for less than a month and he was already fixing things. I had always regarded the Song Contest as the beginning of the end. But since my career had never really got off the ground… It was a chance, a small one, but still. I would be on television and meet some of the players in the music industry. I would be able to charge higher fees for gigs. And imagine if we won and were selected to go to the Eurovision Song Contest – we'd be talking international exposure. It would be huge.

For the first time in ages I felt a glimmer of hope. I hadn't thought about my future for weeks, except in terms of fleeing and surviving, but now I had something to focus on, the big break I had been dreaming of for so long. I could look forward again. Whatever happened, I would join Steve at the Song Contest.

The final voicemail came from Van Dijk: "*We have a few more questions for you in connection with the inquiry into the fire at your home. Could you please contact us at your earliest convenience? End of message.*"

One of the text messages was from Rini, who wanted to know if we were OK. The second was from someone called Petra. My mother's name. It had to be from *him*.

"*You can run, but you can't escape your destiny.*"

From: Petra

Number: (unknown)

I shivered as if someone had just emptied a bucket of iced water over my head. My destiny. What was my destiny? Was I meant to go insane, like my mother? Would he find me and kill me? No way! My destiny was to go on stage with Steve and perform at the Song Contest.

At least now I had some evidence that these threats were not just a figment of my imagination. I saved the message to show to Ans and Victor, and to Van Dijk. It would be a start.

I would go to Amsterdam today, to talk to Van Dijk and to have a look at my house. Perhaps I would call Geert and Steve. I had wasted enough time dozing on the sofa.

I couldn't convince Ans that I would be fine on my own. She insisted on coming along. I wasn't allowed to drive with my medication and she thought police questioning would prove too much of a mental strain for me.

"I can't let you go. I'm responsible for you. It took all my powers of persuasion to talk Victor out of having you committed. What if you have an accident!? What if you get confused during police questioning? I won't be there to protect you! Or to stop them committing you! Let me call Van Dijk and ask him to come here…"

"I won't have a fit, Ans. I just want to see what state my house is in. I need to do *something*. If you call them, or come along, they'll definitely think I'm barmy. I'm fine, trust me. And I've stopped taking those pills. They made me feel like a zombie. My hands started trembling and I felt tired and apathetic all the time. I'm sick of lying on the sofa, dead to the world. I'm going and I'll be back again in one piece tonight."

She couldn't stop me. I was determined to go. Without a word, Ans poured coffee into a small thermos flask and handed it to me.

"Be careful. Call me when you get there."

"I will, I promise. And will you please look after my children?"

"Of course."

Merel stamped her feet, demanding I take her with me. She wanted to go to Amsterdam to see her room and to meet up with her best friend. Ans managed to calm her down with the promise of a surprise. I put on my coat, grabbed my bag and donned a pair of sunglasses. Then I hugged Wolf, cuddled my angry daughter and left the house.

How wonderful it was to be driving again, seeing the sun, however pale and wintry, hearing my own music. *With the birds I share this lonely view.*

It felt like crawling out of a dark and damp dungeon. The fear had gone. The key to his office was in my bag. I had retrieved it from the cabinet when Ans had left the kitchen briefly.

I put on my work CD. Songs by The Supremes, Dusty Springfield, Aretha Franklin, Ann Peebles, Gloria Gaynor. 'I Will Survive'. It was a guaranteed hit with the female crowd, both young and old, students and supermarket check-out girls alike.

*Did you think I'd crumble,*
*Did you think I'd lay down and die,*
*Oh no, not I,*
*I will survive.*

I sang along with Gloria. At first my voice was barely audible, fragile and even broke a few times, but gradually it got deeper and deeper until finally it came from deep down in my belly. As I sang at the top of my voice all the tension left my body.

*Go on now, go,*
*Walk out the door,*
*Just turn around now,*
*'Cause you're not welcome any more.*

157

It had been my *Get Over Steve* song.

I whizzed along the motorway and felt like I was flying. I was singing in my own video. I was good. Bloody good.

The streets of Amsterdam. People. The trams clanging. It made me nervous. The more familiar the neighbourhood, the clammier my hands became. I passed the bakery where I used to buy fresh croissants and multi-grain bread rolls every morning. The greengrocer selling the fresh vegetable stir-fry mixes. The twenty-four-hour snack bar, just the place for chips after a gig. I saw mothers taking Wolf's classmates home on their bikes.

When I turned into my street, my muscles tightened; in fact, my whole body seemed to seize up. There were no parking spaces. Mine was occupied by a brand-new, shiny black Saab.

I got out of the car and looked at the fence in front of my house. The kitchen window was boarded up. The red bricks were blackened and the dark-green window frames had burnt to a cinder. On the first floor, the window of Wolf and Merel's bedroom was open. Their curtains, sky-blue with a little moon motif, fluttered in the wind. It was a pitiful sight. My bedroom window, right next to theirs, was boarded up as well.

The wisteria had come off the wall and swayed lifeless and forlorn in the wind.

I uttered a deep sigh and put my hand on the cold steel fence. A note had been stuck to the front door: "*Please deliver the mail to no. 11. Thank you.*"

That must have been Rini. I swallowed my tears and lit a cigarette.

"It looks worse than it is," said Van Dijk as he got out of the black Saab. He held out his hand. "Good afternoon, Ms Vos. The upper floors are still intact, just a little water damage."

I showed him my injured fingers and didn't shake his hand.

"Oh, I'm sorry, what happened?"

158

"A little mishap," I replied.

"I see. You seem to be rather accident-prone of late."

"Can I go in?"

"Sure. Your shoes will get dirty, though. The kitchen's still water-logged."

"I don't mind. I want to have a look."

He undid the chain lock, pushed the fence aside and led the way up the steps to the door. He also had a key to the new padlock on the front door. The hallway was filled with at least an inch of murky water. Van Dijk wore rubber boots. I saw he had exceptionally large feet. He took a torch from his inside pocket. I had to take my sunglasses off in order to see anything, and when I did his gaze fell on my left eye, which was still black and swollen.

The staircase had been reduced to little more than a charred frame. The walls were black and here and there the plaster was coming off. The framed pictures of Geert and me on stage had gone. All that remained were some melted, warped bits of plastic. There was no trace of the coat stand or the row of wellies underneath it, while only the bare frames of the children's bikes were left on the wall. The house looked like the kind you see in a war zone.

We walked through to the kitchen. The doorway was propped up by a steel post. What was left of the kitchen cabinets was coming off the wall and all the doors had been blown off. My kitchen table, the wooden chairs, everything had gone, melted, ripped apart, charred, turned to black cinders drifting in the water. Merel's Barbie house was a filthy lump of pink plastic. There was a large gaping hole where the French doors had once been. My ironing board, with its legs up, lay in the garden.

I had done the ironing two nights before we left. I had made tea. Merel had sat at the table, playing with her Barbie

159

dolls. Wolf had been watching television. The kitchen lights had been on throughout.

Van Dijk pointed at the crooked, half-burnt shelves above the tap, protruding from the blackened tiles. "We suspect that this is where it started. See, the bottom shelf is almost completely gone, that's where the lights burned through. And above it is the shelf where you kept your cleaning products. The bottles exploded."

"No, the cleaning products were in the cabinet under the sink. Up there I kept the olive oil, ketchup, vinegar, soy sauce, that kind of thing. And on the shelf above were jars of sugar, pasta, rice."

"Perhaps you made a mistake and inadvertently put a bottle of methylated spirits up there instead of under the sink. We also found the remains of a can of lighter fluid."

That would have been Geert's. He used it to fill his Zippo. But I thought he kept it in his desk drawer?

"We've already questioned your ex. He says he may have accidentally put the can in the kitchen cabinet…"

Without waiting for a response, Van Dijk waded through the black sludge to the place where my gas cooker and oven had once stood. Everything had been blown away. The wall, the floor, the cooker hood.

"…which brings us to our biggest mystery. The oven exploded like a kind of bomb. We can only assume that either the gas hadn't been switched off or there was a leak. We don't think a lot of gas escaped, or else the kitchen would have filled up and this house wouldn't be here any more. Nor, I suspect, would your neighbours' house."

I could no longer bear to see my house in ruins and breathe in the pungent, sulphurous smell of fire. I needed fresh air urgently. I turned round to go too quickly, and saw stars. Van Dijk grabbed me by the elbow.

160

"Are you all right, Ms Vos? Let's go outside." Gently he escorted me out, his right hand around my waist, his left firmly clutching my arm. I swallowed my bitter saliva.

Back outside the light hurt my eyes. Van Dijk was still supporting me. He opened the passenger door of his Saab and eased me onto the seat.

"You're very pale. Try holding your head between your knees. There you are. I'm going to lock up. Will you be OK?"

I nodded, with my head dangling between my knees. I would be fine. Except that my black eye started throbbing with all the blood flowing to my head. I looked at my boots. The black sludge had ruined them. A shiver ran down my spine when Van Dijk shut the squeaking fence again.

He sat down behind the wheel and offered to give me a ride to the police station. He didn't think I was in a fit state to drive myself. I could only nod. Before he drove off he handed me a plastic bag. "In case you need to throw up." We drove to the police station. Mariah Carey's voice filled the car. *All I want for Christmas is you.*

"Would you mind changing the channel?" I asked, and he immediately started fiddling with the dial. *It'll be lonely this Christmas, lonely and cold.*

"I'm afraid there's no escaping it," he laughed sheepishly. "I can imagine you're not too keen on hearing Christmas songs right now."

He switched off the radio.

"Right. No more warbling. Better?"

I nodded. Van Dijk probably thought I was a poor wretch, a single mother without a roof over her head, with Christmas just around the corner.

\* \* \*

Next to the reception desk stood a large Christmas tree, decorated with red ribbons, red lights and red baubles. "Nice," I muttered. Van Dijk replied that he thought it was all a bit over the top too.

It jarred. Criminals, victims, plastic chairs, coffee vending machines and a Christmas tree. It made the station look even bleaker. I could easily imagine some criminal who had been brought in here wanting to hurl that tree across the lobby. I felt a similar urge. We made our way to an interview room. It was dark, drab and windowless and reeked of nicotine and stale sweat.

"At least I can smoke in here," I said and flung my coat over a chair. Van Dijk put two cups of coffee and an ashtray on the table and sat down opposite me. He took a folder from his bag and placed it in front of him.

"Well, Ms Vos. My colleagues and I are at a bit of a loss as far as this case is concerned. You claim you're being threatened by a stranger, and some of your friends have indeed confirmed this, but other than that we have no solid evidence whatsoever. We have the phone call to the undertakers, but it turns out it was made with your own mobile phone. And we've been unable to track down the person who dropped off that parcel at the Leiden student society. It was a young man on a moped, who kept his helmet on when he handed it over. The letters you received were lost in the fire. And the fire was probably caused by your own negligence."

I sat with my head in my hands. "He's really clever and manipulative. He's making it look as if I'm insane. As if I'm doing all this to myself."

"You mean to say that *he* made that call on your mobile?"

"Yes. He forced his way into my house that night and called the undertakers. I remember waking up and feeling terrified. I sensed someone creeping around the house. And

162

now I'm almost certain who's behind all this. I can't prove it, but I suspect it's my brother-in-law Martin. Martin Bijlsma. He's got a key to my house. And he has a motive. I think he's having financial difficulties. He knows that if he gets rid of me, my sister will inherit everything. And that he will be the one managing the lot."

"Hang on a minute. You're saying it's your brother-in-law? The husband of the sister you're staying with?"

"That's right. He's disappeared. My sister hasn't seen him for two weeks. She says he's in Spain, trying to recover from a burn-out. Strange, don't you think? I reckon he's not in Spain at all. I reckon he's still knocking around here, trying to drive me insane. Look. I received this text message this morning."

I handed Van Dijk my mobile phone. He read the message and frowned.

"I'm afraid it doesn't prove a thing. Anyone can send this kind of message. It was sent via the Internet. We'll never trace it. Why do you think your brother-in-law is having financial difficulties?"

"I spoke to a colleague of his. A certain Harry Menninga. Martin invested his money for him and now it's all gone."

Van Dijk stuck a pen in his mouth and twirled it round between his teeth.

"And you believe your brother-in-law is capable of threatening a relative and committing arson in order to solve his financial problems?"

"He's the only one I know who has a motive. Besides, he's disappeared off the face of the earth, with a couple of hundred grand belonging to his best friend. At the very least, it proves he doesn't mind hurting his wife, or his friend…"

"I don't know, Ms Vos. I really don't know what to make of all this. I've spoken to your sister and *she* told me her husband is away on business. She also told me about your mother…"

163

I pricked up my ears. Ans had been here? That bitch, why hadn't she told me?

"What did you talk about?"

"Your sister didn't have a bad word to say about you. I phoned but you were asleep and she didn't want to disturb you. I asked her to tell you to call me back and she said she'd rather not bother you with this. The next day she came to the station. She wanted to know if there'd been any further developments and if there was anything she could do to help you."

"And she told you that I've lost my marbles."

"No. But she did say that you're having a hard time and that we should leave you alone for a bit. I told her I'd prefer to judge that for myself."

"I see. And that's what you're doing right now."

"Listen, there's the undertaker. He has brought a charge against you. It means that the only evidence in this case incriminates *you*. And the fire appears to have been caused by negligence, on *your* part. Sure, your ex-boyfriend claims to have read the threatening letters, but I never saw them. And now you maintain that your brother-in-law has hatched this rather convoluted plot to get rid of you. I would like to believe you, but I really don't see how I can."

I took my cigarettes, had one last sip of coffee, got up and headed for the door. "Fine, don't believe me. But then there's no point in me wasting any more time here…"

"Look, Ms Vos, you must understand that we're in a difficult position too. We're having to cope with a serious staff shortage. We've got no leads in this case. We've got nothing! Except a fire and you're not being very forthcoming on that either…"

"Let me tell you something, Mr Van Dijk. Until two weeks ago I had a life. In my own house, with my two children.

Now that's gone and everybody thinks I'm crazy enough to coordinate a campaign of threats against myself! Whatever else I say will only confirm your preconceived notions. I think I'd better end this conversation. Good afternoon."

The sun was still out, but not for much longer. Dark snow clouds were gathering. I took my purse from my handbag and dug out Harry Menninga's card. I dialled his number on my mobile. He answered immediately.

"Menninga."

"Hello, this is Maria Vos, remember me, we spoke about Martin the other day?"

"Ah! I've been trying to get hold of you. Hang on a second…"

He must have been talking to somebody because I heard him mutter something before going outside.

"Have you got the number?"

"No. And to be honest I don't know how to get hold of it either. I'm calling about something else. I'm planning to have a look around Martin's office tomorrow evening. Would you like to come along?"

"I think that's commonly known as breaking and entering. Does Ans know about this?"

"No. And I'd rather keep it that way."

"And what do you want me to do?"

"How about finding out what's happened to your money? I don't know the first thing about computers…"

"OK, count me in. What time do you need me?"

"Let's meet at half-past nine at Neptune, you know, the restaurant on the square."

"I'll find it. See you then. Ciao."

## 32

Geert was early. He was sitting, or slouching rather, at the bar. The minute I walked in I recognized him from his posture, the ribs poking through his jumper and his mass of brown curls.

I hadn't been in the Cell for at least ten years, but nothing had changed. It still had the same psychedelic mural, the same smell of marijuana. Weed-smoking adolescents around a corner table, solitary beer drinkers at the bar, some arty types with bloated, red faces. Not what you'd call a cheery place. Janis Joplin was still worshipped in these parts.

I put my hand on Geert's fragile back and he turned round. He looked at me with his big, sad brown eyes, smiled and wrapped his arms around me. When he kissed me, hard and desperate, his stubble scratched my cheeks. Then he held me tight, buried his nose in my hair and breathed in. "I'm so glad to see you, Maria."

We ordered beer. Geert looked at my chafed fingers and caressed the wound above my eye. He looked dreadful too. The skin around his eyes was a dullish brown, he hadn't shaved for at least two days and the collar of his white T-shirt was grimy.

"I really freaked out yesterday. You didn't show up, but instead I found the police on my doorstep. For a moment I thought you'd turned me in. Fuck! I lost my house too, you know! And you, and the kids! The grilling they gave me, you'd think it was me who set the bloody place alight. That I'm the joker harassing you."

We both stared into space. The bar-keeper raised our empty glasses to ask if we wanted more. We nodded. Janis Joplin was followed by Pink Floyd.

"Be honest, please. Do you think it's me?"

"Would I be sitting here with you if I did?"

"Probably not."

"Do you think I'm doing all this to myself?"

"Why? Is that what they're thinking?"

"That phone call to the undertaker was traced back to my mobile. My gas oven was on when the fire started. All the evidence went up in flames. And my mother has a psychiatric record stretching from here to Timbuktu. Even my sister thinks I've lost my marbles."

"Why would you do a thing like that?"

'How would I know? To attract attention. These things happen. Some people pretend to have terminal cancer just to get some attention. I must confess I'm beginning to doubt myself. Yesterday I woke up drenched in blood, but I couldn't remember what had happened… I nod off at all hours and I'm a complete nervous wreck. Something's wrong, I do know that."

"You come across as fairly normal to me. Of course you're not feeling great, what do you expect? These past few weeks have been pretty eventful."

I smiled at him.

"How do you know if you're not right in the head? I keep asking myself that question. You just don't know. That's what scares me. My mother didn't know. She genuinely thought my father was trying to kill her and that the whole world was conspiring against her. A German tourist once saved her from drowning. She had walked into the sea in her nightgown, in the middle of winter. Had she done that before, the man asked my father when he brought her home. Of course not, my dad replied, whereas she had been released from hospital less than a month ago. He wrapped her in a towel, put her to bed and made some coffee for the German. Later he got the gin out and they ended up getting completely plastered

167

together. The following morning my mother was back in the kitchen making us breakfast. As if nothing ever happened. She couldn't remember a thing. When Dad came down he asked for some bacon and eggs, sat down and read the paper."

"What are you trying to say?"

"It's possible to be completely nuts without realizing it."

"I've known you for six years, Maria. You're a tough woman. You had an awful time growing up in this parochial dump, but you fought your way out... You're neither crazy nor depressed, nor will you ever be. You're not the type. I should know."

He ran his hand through his hair. The ashes from his roll-up fell into his beer. "Shit." He rubbed the corners of his eyes. He was tired. And drunk. I was sorely tempted to stay here beside him and carry on drinking till it got darker and the music louder. But I couldn't. It was snowing. I was driving. And besides, I wanted to get back to the children. I rummaged in my bag for my purse.

"I'll get it," Geert said and left some money on the bar. He struggled into his leather jacket and walked to the exit.

"What do we do now?" He watched the snow whirling down.

"You don't have to do anything." I stuck my hands under my arms to keep them warm. "I think I know who's doing this to me."

He looked at me, stunned.

"Now she's telling me!" He got his tobacco pouch from his inside pocket and started rolling a cigarette. "Who? Tell me!"

"Martin. He's in trouble. He needs money. If he gets rid of me, the two of them will inherit the house. It's worth a fortune now."

168

Geert burst out laughing.

"I'm sorry. Martin, you say? That oaf? I find that hard to believe. Besides, what are you doing under his roof then?"

"He's gone. He left two weeks ago. He claims to be in Spain, recovering from burn-out."

An annoyed youth squeezed past us into the warm pub.

Geert exhaled forcefully. "I don't know. He always seemed OK to me. He called me, you know. About two weeks ago. Thereabouts. He was very friendly. It was you he wanted to talk to, but he couldn't get hold of you."

"What else did he say? What did he want from me?" I took a drag from Geert's cigarette.

"He didn't say. I was really upset at the time. He called just after that fight we had, remember, about the abortion. I was so angry…"

"No! You told him! Shit! That's it. You see? He knew about my abortion!"

We said goodbye. Geert said he wanted to see the children as soon as possible. He was spending the weekend in a guesthouse in the village and I could get in touch day and night.

"What about the band?" I asked him.

He shook his head. "Not now. There's all kinds of shit going on, but never mind that. I'll fill you in later."

I promised to phone him. He begged me to be careful. "I love you," he whispered, and hugged me tight. I couldn't say a word.

I drove back slowly along a snow-covered road. The gardens of the villas along Eeuwigelaan were decorated with Christmas lights. Behind the big bay windows were families: parents sipping wine from big-bellied glasses and children drawing pictures in front of snug fireplaces. That, at any rate, was the picture I'd had as a child, riding pillion on my dad's bicycle, heading into the village.

We were on our way to the Christmas market at my school. I had made two angels out of gold-coloured cardboard, real angel's hair and glitter, and I was so proud of them I begged my father to come along. He had never been to my school. Parents' evenings, open days, Easter and Christmas markets, spring and autumn fairs – they were all wasted on my parents. They were busy, and besides, it was all a load of nonsense. You went to school to learn things, not to have non-stop parties. When they were young, school wasn't a fun place at all. And they had to go on Saturdays too. Letters from our teacher, asking parents to lend a hand with arts and crafts activities, Christmas celebrations, school trips or the big clean-up before the summer holidays, were promptly chucked out by my mother. It was all very well for mothers with nothing better to do, but she was busy. Besides, they paid enough tax. The school ought to use it to hire a proper cleaner instead of organizing expensive school trips.

But on this one occasion, when I begged him in tears to come and look at my angels, my father gave in. My mother was still at Duin en Bosch, the mental hospital. Connie, our home care assistant, would help Ans put up the Christmas decorations in the guesthouse.

"Don't be such a spoilsport," she smiled at my father, and suddenly he said: "All right then. Let's go!" Connie smiled and pinched my cheek.

We went by bike. It was snowing. I was perfectly happy. It would be a white Christmas, with my angels in our tree, with Connie, and we wouldn't have to tiptoe around Mum. I danced around in the snow. Dad took his bike from the

170

shed, covered the luggage carrier with a towel and hoisted me onto it.

"There you are. A comfy seat. Hold on tight."

He mounted his bike. I wrapped my arms around his waist and buried my hands in his pockets. I rested my head against his brown velvet coat. We slid along the white snow-covered cycling path, past the dunes and the villas with their fireplaces and Christmas trees out in the garden and on through the illuminated village.

When we got to the school, my father and I entered hand in hand. We were given hot chocolate and one of the teachers, Miss Clara, came to say hello to my father. I was proud of him.

"This is my dad," I said to the girls in my class. I steered him towards the stall with the angels. He loved them. The booth was manned by another teacher, Miss Marijke, who gave us a slice of Christmas cake.

"You have a very creative daughter, Mr Vos," she told him. He laughed.

"She takes after her dad."

He put his hand on my neck. I blushed. He bought my angels for one guilder. Miss Marijke carefully slid them into a plastic carrier bag and handed them to my father.

We cycled back. The bag swung from his steering wheel. More snow had fallen, so much that we couldn't cycle up the dune. When we continued on foot, the snow crunched under our feet. On top of the dune, my father dropped his bike. He picked up a handful of snow and threw a snowball at me. We pelted each other with snowballs until we fell about laughing. My father put his arm around me and I laid my head on his chest. "We're going to have a lovely Christmas, Maria," he said. We both looked up at the snow falling from the pitch-black sky. It was as if we were floating through space.

That evening I told Ans. She turned her back on me. "You always have more fun," she snapped.

33

Victor flung open the door. "Ah, Maria, there you are, at last. Your sister was extremely worried." A sickly sweet smell hit me in the face. Victor took my coat.

"Where is she?" Something was wrong here. I could feel it.

"Out looking for you. We'd better give her a call to say you're back in one piece." He ushered me into the living room. There, next to the fireplace, stood a huge Christmas tree, decorated with cornflower-blue baubles and cornflower-blue ribbons. The lights, also blue, emitted a cool blue light.

"What about the children? Where are they?"

"They're in bed, sound asleep."

Merel was still awake. She jumped up when she heard me.

"Mum! You're back!" I sat down on her bed. We hugged. "Where were you, Mum? I thought you were ill. You're not supposed to stay out that long. And then it started snowing. Aunt Ans called the police…"

I kissed her soft cheeks.

"I had an appointment in Amsterdam. And I had to see Geert. He wanted to speak to me. He misses the two of you."

"Did you see the room? The Christmas tree? Wolf and I decorated it, together with Aunt Ans. And the Christmas wreaths, did you see those? We spent the whole afternoon putting them together. And look…" Merel jumped out of bed. She was wearing a pair of pyjamas I had never seen before. White flannel, with a holly pattern.

"Where did you get those pyjamas?"

"Aunt Ans gave them to me." She walked to Wolf's bedside table and switched on a light. Our little crib, surrounded by candles. Small plaster statuettes of Joseph and Mary – broken and glued back together again a hundred times – an ox, an ass, four sheep and the manger with baby Jesus. Merel kneeled and looked reverently at the scene. She stroked Joseph and Mary and very gently picked the baby from the manger.

"This is Jesus, the son of God. Christmas is all about him, not about Father Christmas. It's his birth we're celebrating."

"He's been dead for ages." Wolf, his curly hair dishevelled, sat up straight and rubbed his eyes. He scrambled over to us.

"Hi Mum. I thought you were dead too."

I lifted him onto my lap. "Where did you get that idea?"

"Ans said so. To that man."

"Victor," Merel snarled.

"Yeah. She said: 'What if she's run into a tree?'"

I tucked them in. Wolf stuck his thumb in his mouth and fell asleep instantly. Merel asked if it was OK to leave the lights of the crib on. I said yes.

"Mum?" Merel said, as I was about to close the door behind me. "What's wrong with you?"

"Nothing's wrong with me. I was a little tired. And I'd had a bit of a shock. That's all. I'm better now."

"Ans says you're ill. And that we shouldn't bother you."

"Nonsense, the two of you never get in the way."

"But your Mum was always ill, wasn't she?"

"I'm not always ill. And tomorrow we'll go out and do lots of fun things."

"OK. A promise is a promise!" Merel wagged her finger at me and gave me a stern look.

"I promise. Go to sleep now."

Downstairs I heard Ans come back home.

She lunged at me when I entered the room. "Where in God's name have you been!?" Her mother superior act got on my nerves. She had managed to suppress it for quite some time, but now she showed her true colours again.

"You know what, it's none of your business. Anyway, you know where I've been! I went to see your friends at the police station!"

Ans glared at me. "What do you mean 'your friends'?"

"Well, didn't you pop in to see them the other day? To tell them what a nutcase I am?"

I lit a cigarette. Ans walked over to the coffee table and slammed the coffee cups and mugs down on the tray.

"I never said that. I asked them to leave you alone for a while. Then they asked me a couple of questions, that's all."

"But why didn't you tell me?"

"I didn't want to bother you." She left the room with the tray.

"Maria, can't you see that Ans was worried? You were out all day. Besides, you didn't take your medication this morning…" Victor turned to me and put a fatherly hand on mine.

"What are you doing here anyway?"

"Ans phoned me. She was rather upset. I came over straight away. To be honest, I felt a bit guilty too. If anything happens to you, I'll be to blame as well, given that I agreed to treat you at home."

"Victor, listen, I don't need any pills. I feel well again today, for the first time in ages. Without that junk. I had a look at my house, spoke to my ex and was questioned by the police. I got through all that without medication."

"Do you still feel threatened?"

174

"I *am* being threatened. Look." I showed him the text message on my mobile.

"Petra. You see? That was my mother's name. I don't know what he's up to, but I won't let him get away with it. I'm fighting back. Whatever you and my sister say."

Ans came back in. She had recovered her composure. With her hair in a neat ponytail and her make-up touched up, she smiled at me. "My apologies, Maria, but you must understand. I was really rather worried, especially when it started snowing. I thought you might be back around three. The children and I had decorated the room, put up the Christmas tree and prepared some nice food. We wanted to surprise you. And still you didn't show. Merel tried to call you, but your phone was switched off."

"Impossible. It was on all day…"

"You could have called us. That's not asking too much, is it?"

Of course not. Why hadn't I thought of that? I had left Amsterdam, still preoccupied with the day's events: seeing my ruined house, the awkward interview with Van Dijk, not to mention my reunion with Geert…

"I'm a grown woman, Ans. I don't owe you an explanation."

"True. But you've got a responsibility towards your children."

Victor handed me my phone back. Surprised, Ans looked first at him and then at me. I gave her my mobile.

"He's been in touch again."

She read the message. Then she looked at Victor. He returned her worried gaze and shrugged.

Ans put the phone on the table. "I'm not an expert, but don't you think it's possible that someone sent it by mistake? Something along the lines of 'sorry, wrong number'?"

"Good God, what does it take for the two of you to believe me? How can this be a mistake? 'Petra', my mother's name? 'You can run, but you can't escape your destiny.' A mistake?"

"But sweetheart, Petra is such a common name. And that sentence could mean all kinds of things. It doesn't sound all that threatening to me."

"It's what you feel that matters," Victor suggested. "We believe you, Maria. Ans is just trying to reassure you. Your fears are real. This is your truth."

"Piss off with your 'this is your truth'. I'm going to make myself an egg sandwich and then I'm going to bed. Without pills. Goodnight."

They didn't stop me. I felt their gaze on me as I walked out of the room. The second I closed the door, they would start whispering. About me. About how soon they could get me locked up. Whatever happened now, I mustn't lose my composure.

The bacon sizzled in the pan. I cracked open an egg, poured boiling water in a mug and put in a bag of Earl Grey tea. I put two slices of bread on a plate and picked up the newspaper.

When I looked up I saw Victor observing me from the doorway.

"Your egg's burning," he said and pointed at the stove.

I turned off the gas, slid the fried egg onto my bread, sat down at the table and opened the newspaper. I wanted him to sod off. Victor took a chair and sat down across the table from me.

"Why are you so uncooperative?" he whispered, trying to catch my eye.

I returned his gaze and stared straight into his heavy-lidded brown eyes, before turning to my egg again. I pierced it with the tip of my knife. The yolk trickled across the egg white. I cut the bread into quarters.

"Why don't you go home?" I took a bite. It could do with a bit more salt.

"I would like to know how you are."

"Fine."

"Maria, listen. We are really very worried about you. And not without reason, I'm afraid to say. Why do you refuse to take your medication?"

"Because there's nothing wrong with me."

"I think there is. So does Ans. And so do the police. Ans and I are keen to stop you from sliding deeper into trouble."

A drop of sweat trickled down from my armpit. It was very important now that I remained calm. He wanted to have me committed. Separate me from my children. It was out of my hands.

"What do you think is wrong with me?"

"Hard to say. We'd need to have a proper talk. But I do believe you're experiencing psychotic episodes. And you're feeling threatened. Let me put it this way: your body is in a constant state of alert. And this creates so much stress that you're no longer capable of breaking this negative spiral."

"But I *am* being threatened. If not by him, then by the two of you."

"We're only trying to help."

"You'd help me by believing me."

"We believe you, Maria, we really do. I know how awful you must feel."

"If you have me committed, my enemy will have won."

"Who do you think your 'enemy' is?"

"I know who he is, but I can't tell you. First I need some proof. I'll need a couple of days to get it."

"It would be best if you came with me of your own free will."

"What if I don't?"

"We could have you sectioned."

"Meaning?"

"Have you detained under the mental health act."

"You'll never pull it off. I'm not a risk to the public, am I?"

"The police suspect you set fire to your own home."

"That's a load of rubbish. I wasn't even around during the blaze."

"Somebody left the gas on."

"Somebody's playing games with me." I pushed my plate away. What I really wanted to do was hurl it across the kitchen and shove Victor's cigar down his throat. My head started buzzing. Whatever happened, I had to stay with my children. "And what if I promise that from now on I'll be a good girl and take my medication?"

"I'm afraid I won't fall for that again."

"You've got it all figured out, haven't you? If I don't come along, my sister will sign the papers and the men in white coats will come and take me away…"

Victor fidgeted with his earlobe. "We only want what's best for you. Your children are safe here. Ans dotes on them. She'll look after them until you've recovered."

I had to let go of them. It was the only way. I had my back to the wall. They were safe with Ans. "OK. I'll come along. But please give me some time to say goodbye to the children and pack my things…"

"Very well, dear. It's for the best, trust me. Here, take this before you go."

He took a tablet from his pocket and pressed it into my hand.

"Dissolve it in water, it's better for your stomach."

My hands were trembling. I took a glass, filled it with water and dropped in the pill. I stirred until it had completely dissolved. Then I poured it down my throat.

"Excellent. I'll call Ans and ask her to help you pack."

"That's OK. I'll do it myself."

He left the kitchen. In the hallway I heard him type in a number on his mobile phone. I had no time to lose.

## 34

I stuck my index finger down my throat, as far down as possible. That should do the trick. It used to, when I was young and I'd had too much to drink and the night was still young. My eyes filled with tears. I retched, but failed to throw up. I had to concentrate now. Concentrate on vomiting. I kneeled down and hung my head over the toilet seat. I stuck two fingers even further down and held them there. My throat seized up. I retched again and again and then finally a wave of bitter, warm liquid came out. I puked my guts out, until I knew my system had been purged of any traces of Victor's pill.

The children were asleep. The warm Christmas lighting illuminated their serene faces. Wolf's mouth was half open and his thumb had slid down to the corner of his mouth. Merel lay curled up under her duvet with her back to the door, her hair stuck to her face.

I sat down beside her and planted a kiss on her cheek. She smelled of gingerbread and sleep. Merel groaned in her sleep and turned her head away. "Bye, my sweet Merel. I love you. Everything will be fine." I laid my cheek against hers and breathed in her wonderful smell again. I didn't want to leave her, simply walk out of her life, like her father had done. I would be back. As soon as possible.

I walked over to Wolf's bed. When I sat down by his side, he rolled onto his back and raised both hands over his head. I stroked his curly hair and his solemn little face. "Bye, Wolfie." I kissed him on the mouth. "Bye, Mummy," he mumbled and turned over again.

The bedroom door opened a little. Victor peered in. "Are you ready, Maria?"

I shook my head.

"Come along now. Ans will take good care of them. Quiet, we mustn't wake them."

I got up and walked to the door.

Victor led me to the staircase and patted me on the back in some half-hearted attempt at comforting me.

"Wait," I said halfway down the stairs. "I need one more thing."

"Ans will get it, just tell me what it is," Victor replied, while ushering me down.

"No. I know where it is. I need it. It's a picture of the children."

Victor sighed. "I'll get it if you tell me where to find it."

I turned round and walked back up again.

"Listen. I'm cooperating, I took that pill of yours and I'm not planning to top myself or anything. I don't want you or Ans rummaging through my stuff. It's in a little box full of old things with sentimental value. Just let me get it, will you?"

"All right then. I'll wait downstairs."

The door to the hallway was slammed shut. Ans asked Victor what was keeping me. As soon as I was out of sight, I dashed into my bedroom, snatched my grey woollen jumper off the chair, grabbed my bag from the bed and opened the balcony doors. Now wasn't the time to think, or the time to be afraid. I clambered over the wooden railing and jumped.

With a heavy thud, I landed in the frozen sand. For a moment my head was swimming and I worried that I had ingested some traces of that pill after all. My left ankle was incredibly sore. Still, I leapt to my feet and started running. I ran as fast as I could down the dune and onto the beach, where it was dark. Nobody would see me there. It was freezing cold outside and it was still snowing.

I stumbled and rolled down through the snow. I heard Victor and Ans calling out my name. I scrambled to my feet, clutched my bag and jumper under my arm and ran to the shoreline where the sand was harder. Victor would come after me. I had to make for the dark as fast as possible – head northwards, away from civilization.

It was strangely quiet on the beach. The sea murmured softly, there was no wind and snowflakes came whirling down from a pitch-black sky. All I could hear was my own wheezing. My lungs were on fire. I didn't know how much longer I could keep this up. Two weeks of chain-smoking had made quick work of the little stamina I'd had. But I carried on regardless, ignoring the pain. I knew Victor would give up before me. He was older, fatter and smoked just as much as me. Just a little further, just a little bit further and I'd be rid of him.

My feet got wet, water penetrated my boots. My heart was pounding. From afar I heard Victor frantically calling out my name and telling me there was no need to be afraid.

I couldn't go on. My eyes were watering, so I could barely see a thing, and my feet were wet and numb with cold. I fell, scrambled to my feet again and stumbled towards the shadowy dunes. I was outside Victor's range of vision now.

If I managed to climb the dune and reach the forest I would be safe.

I kept stumbling in the loose sand. I clambered up the dune on hands and feet, hoisted myself up on the beach grass, ripped my jeans and thigh on barbed wire, tasted sand. But I couldn't rest until I reached the trees.

When I got to the top I set off on a trot again. I ran through wild rose bushes and thistle towards the tall pine trees. My mouth was dry and my blood roared through my veins with such force that I feared my head might explode. Completely out of breath I reached the edge of the forest, where it was pitch dark. I couldn't hear Victor any more.

## 35

It was so quiet in the forest I could hear my blood whooshing in my ears. The snow was luminous, so at least I could see something. I leaned against a large pine tree, panting, and blew into my frozen hands. I was soaked through with sweat and snow and felt something warm trickle down my leg. Blood.

I couldn't move another inch, the pain was too severe. There was a terrible throbbing in my left ankle. I sat down on my jumper and dug cigarettes and a lighter out of my bag. But my hands trembled and tingled so badly I couldn't light my cigarette. I cursed. This was madness. What on earth was I doing here? And what was I to do now? A cold chill ran down my spine. If I stayed here I would freeze to death. And then my children would grow up thinking that their mother had indeed been psychotic. They would become just as lonely and angry as Ans and I had been, incapable of having proper relationships, incapable of trusting either each other or anyone else.

An odd little squeaky sound, a sob, escaped my throat. All my strength appeared to be draining from me and I became scared. Scared stiff. I was scared that something would happen to Wolf or Merel in my absence. What if one of them fell ill or had an accident? They would be in pain or, worse, die and I would never again feel their warm, live bodies in my arms. What was I thinking, leaving them in the lurch like this?

I kept fidgeting with my lighter. I was dying for a little light and warmth and I needed a cigarette to calm down. I would quit. As soon as all this was over and everything was back to normal, one way or another, I would never touch a cigarette again. I would do it for Merel and Wolf.

Finally I managed to produce a little flame. I shielded it with my hand until the wind extinguished it. What next? I had to call someone. Geert. But what could Geert do for me? He would only fly into a rage and have a go at Ans. And I had to admit that deep down I was still a little wary of him. There was only one man I could call.

With frozen fingers I dug my phone out of my bag and switched it on.

"You have three voicemail messages," it said on the illuminated display. Two messages from Ans, one from an unknown mobile number. I dialled my voicemail.

"Network not found."

I wiped my runny nose on my sleeve and struggled to my feet. The pain that shot through my leg was so intense that my eyes filled with tears. God damn it! You could use your phone in the Himalayas and God knows where else, but walk into a forest in this overcrowded country and there will be a network problem. I limped around for a bit, not knowing which way to go. There were no lights anywhere, no signs of life. I headed back towards the dunes and tried to call again. This time it worked.

183

"*Maria, please, come back. It's cold out there…* (Victor muttered something in the background) *We can talk about it.*"

And again.

"*Maria, I hope you can hear me. Please don't do anything rash. Think of the children. Come back. Please.*"

Then it was Victor's turn. "*Maria, wherever you are, we only want to help. If you're afraid, or confused, or whatever, please call me, or call the crisis helpline: 0800 050…*"

I hung up and tried to find Harry Menninga's card.

Four times I typed in the wrong number. My fingers were virtually frozen by now and I was so cold in my soaking wet clothes that my teeth started chattering. I shook my arms and legs in a bid to get warmer, but it made no difference whatsoever. If Harry didn't answer I would have to continue on foot.

He answered. He must have been down the pub, because he barked his name and then yelled to hang on a minute. I heard him squeeze past talking and laughing people and go outside. The party sounds died down and we could finally have a conversation.

"Harry speaking…"

My jaw muscles were so numb I could barely speak.

"Who is this?"

"Hi, it's Maria."

"Ah, Maria. Weren't we supposed to meet tomorrow evening?"

I didn't want to burst out crying. "I need your help. I have a bit of a problem, I'm in the middle of a forest…"

"In a forest? What's going on? What are you doing? It's minus ten out there!"

"It's a long story, I'll tell you later, OK. I'm not quite sure where I am. Could you come and pick me up somewhere?"

"How, if you don't even know where you are?"

"I reckon I'm somewhere between Bergen and Bergen aan Zee."

"Are you close to a cycle path?"

"No. Not as far as I can see, anyway. All I can see are dunes further off."

"OK, don't worry. Let me think. Hang on. Can you see some kind of tower on top of those dunes?"

I peered into the distance. I couldn't see a thing.

"Turn round. Are you at the bottom of a hill, or on top of one?"

I looked round. Behind me the forest did seem to be on somewhat of an incline.

That's it. All of a sudden, I knew where I was. On top of this hill here was Bio Recreation. The cycle path and coastal road should be close by. Somewhere to my left.

"I know! I'm standing just below Bio Recreation."

"OK, listen. I'm heading there now. Meanwhile you make your way to that road. I'll park and leave my lights on so you should be able to find me. If not, call me."

"I need to be certain it's you. I don't feel safe."

"Call me when you see me. I'll flash my indicators."

"Fine. But if you see another car, keep going! In that case, you call me!"

"Agreed. I'll be there in ten minutes."

My teeth wouldn't stop chattering, despite the warm fug spread by the car heating. When Harry saw my bleeding thigh, he swore under his breath and handed me a box of tissues. I dabbed at the wound, a substantial gash that really needed stitching.

"I think that requires a visit to A&E," Harry said, while he started the car and accelerated excessively. Simply Red blasted out of the loudspeakers.

"No, that's out of the question." I tried to lean on my right buttock to avoid bleeding all over his leather seat.

"Why? What happened?"

I could only shake my head.

As we drove, I watched the lights and snow-covered landscape go by. My children were asleep. I had promised to do something fun with them tomorrow. They would wake around seven and run straight to my bedroom. They would be looking for me, yelling my name, until Ans broke the news that I wasn't there. They would bombard her with questions. Where had Mummy gone? Why? When would she be back? But Mummy promised...

If there was anyone who could give them all the right answers, it was Ans. She was great with the kids. The thought was as reassuring as it was painful.

## 36

Harry pointed at the sofa and said: "Sit down," but I didn't dare. I was covered in mud, seawater and blood and couldn't possibly sit on his pristine white sofa. I shivered and stuck my hands under my armpits.

"Could I have a shower perhaps?" I asked. He laughed a little sheepishly.

"Of course. Forgive me, I'm so stupid. You must be half-frozen. Look, here's the bathroom."

He slid aside a wooden panel and ushered me in. I stepped inside a small, concrete space, just as minimalist as his living room. He opened a large mirror cabinet and showed me the towels and his bathrobe. I could wear it after my shower if I wanted to. He would try and find me some clean clothes.

186

The warm water made my skin tingle. I rinsed the sand from my hair and scrubbed my arms and legs, which were covered in scratches from my encounters with the thorns and thistles. The gash in my left thigh was still bleeding, while my ankle was swelling up and turning black and blue. I rotated my shoulders and noticed that the muscles were quite sore. I would be incredibly stiff in the morning.

I turned off the shower and grabbed the soft, grey towel. It smelled of musk. Harry had paid attention to every single detail. Everything in his home was colour-coordinated. In search of a toothbrush I opened the cabinet above the washbasin to find a grey cup with a grey toothbrush and a grey tube of toothpaste, all from the Body Shop. Even his deodorant stick and the box of painkillers were grey. I could think of only one other man who was just as obsessed with his appearance and lifestyle: Steve. All the other men I had ever met didn't care a fig about these things. They slept on a mattress on the floor next to the stereo, until one day they hooked up with a girl who suggested they might want to try a bed. But that was a different scene. They were all musicians. Harry was an estate agent. Details mattered to him.

He knocked on the door and, while politely averting his head so as not to embarrass me, handed me a sweatshirt, jogging bottoms and Nike socks. I covered the wound on my leg with a sterile gauze dressing I found in the medicine cabinet and slipped into his soft leisure outfit. Now I could sit down on his immaculate sofa.

The living room was filled with the aroma of fresh espresso. Harry came in with two cups and handed me one.

"Here you are. You're certainly looking much better than before. Would you like anything with your coffee? I've got whisky, brandy, Armagnac, Sambuca, Tia Maria, Amaretto…"

187

"Armagnac, please."

He got two large brandy glasses from a cabinet beside the sofa and poured two generous measures of Armagnac. I took my glass, held it under my nose and breathed in the smell of the expensive alcohol. Just what I needed. If it didn't give me such bad hangovers I would drink the stuff every day.

I took a gulp and relished the burning sensation on my tongue and in my throat. Harry lit two Marlboros and handed me one.

"Are you ready to tell me what happened?"

He sat down opposite me. I hesitated briefly. I didn't want him to doubt my sanity too, like everybody else. But once I got talking, I couldn't stop. I wanted to trust him, even if I didn't have any reason to. I wanted him to save me from this god-awful mess.

While I spoke, he poured more Armagnac, lit cigarettes, spread pungent brie on slices of warm, crispy baguette and put new CDs on. Every now and then he asked a question, nodded and rubbed his chin. When I finished, he leaned back and sighed.

"Goodness," he muttered and for a moment I feared he might reach for the phone and call the crisis centre.

"I know it sounds bizarre. I'm finding it hard to believe myself. There have been times when I too thought I was going insane. But the threatening letters I received were real. My ex saw them too."

Harry looked into my eyes, as if they might reveal whether or not I was telling the truth.

"You know, when nobody believes you, you start doubting yourself. It's very odd, the way it works. It's not up to them to prove I've lost my marbles, but up to me to prove I haven't. But how do you prove such a thing? And meanwhile I'm in danger. My children are in danger. And I'm powerless."

He got up and started pacing up and down the room, staring at his feet. I took another sip. Harry still didn't say a word and his brooding look and Miles Davis' trumpeting began to get on my nerves. It occurred to me that I'd had hardly anything to eat all day and I was slowly getting legless. I asked him for a glass of water. He went to the kitchen and came back with a large glass of water full of clinking ice cubes. I drained it.

"Well," Harry began. "I believe you. I don't know why, seeing as I hardly know you. It's just a hunch. But I just can't believe Martin would go to such extremes. I can't bear the thought."

He sat down beside me. He tapped his foot to the rhythm of the music. I fished the ice cubes out of my glass and put them on my sore ankle, which had turned a deep shade of purple.

"That's looking pretty bad. May I?" He took my foot, ever so gently, put it on his lap and then very carefully peeled off my sock. He asked me to wriggle my toes. I could, though it hurt. He wrapped his hands around my ankle and very gently turned it first left and then right. I groaned with pain.

"I'd say it's bruised. Not broken. I'll get you an ice pack. And I reckon I've got a bandage somewhere. Just a second."

He put my foot on a pillow. All of a sudden I felt an irrepressible urge to kiss him. He believed me. And now he was looking after me.

Harry bandaged my ankle and applied the ice pack.

"Sit back and relax," he said and plumped up a few pillows. I leaned back.

"I'm glad you called me. We can help each other. So what's the latest on the key to Martin's office?"

I pointed at my mud-spattered bag. He picked it up and handed it to me. I rummaged through the lipsticks, lighters and crumbs until I found the key with the blue buoy. I hadn't lost it.

"Super," Harry said and gave us both a refill.

We clinked glasses. I asked if he didn't have anything better than Miles Davis. He said good old Miles was the best, but if I insisted... What did I fancy hearing? Something that went with drinking too much Armagnac, in the dead of night, on a stranger's sofa.

"I would never have guessed you were a mother." He looked at me.

"Why not?"

"You're such a cool woman. The mothers I know all wear comfortable clothes and sensible shoes. They're always cranky and in a hurry, ferrying their whining brats to and fro." He chuckled at his own definition of motherhood.

"They're the good mothers. They sacrifice their own needs to give their kids a good, sheltered upbringing. I'm the kind of decadent, chaotic mother who wants to see and do everything and ends up sending the children to school in their pyjama bottoms because she forgot to do the laundry the night before."

"I bet you're a great mother."

"I don't know. I love my children. I think love is the most important thing you can give a child. I enjoy spending time with them, playing, singing and dancing. I'd much rather horse around with them than do a big pile of ironing, or make sure they're tucked up in bed on time. Sometimes, when the weather's atrocious, I keep them home from school and then the three of us will watch *ET* in bed. Of course I know it's not done. The children have to go to school. And they have to go to bed on time. Learn to keep their room tidy. Eat broccoli. Have a shower every day. Play a sport..."

190

"I bet your children have much more fun than those kids who get carted around all day by their stressed-out mothers, the kind who get into a fit whenever their brats refuse to drink their milk."

"Says the perfect estate agent, with his minimalist house, his impeccably ironed shirts, his immaculate white sofa and his designer toothbrush. I get the impression you're a bit of a neat freak."

"True. I can't stand clutter. I can't think or relax with clutter around. Besides, I love tidying up. I can really lose myself in cleaning my house. I'll throw open the windows, put some nice music on…"

We smiled at each other. His head touched my leg. He stayed in that position, his head virtually in my lap, a smile on his face, his eyes fixed on mine. I broke out in a cold sweat. Neither of us knew what to say. But it was a done deal. From the moment his head touched my leg, there had been no way back. He asked if he could kiss me and I nodded. We kissed. His warm hands slid under my sweatshirt and caressed my back, then slowly made their way down towards my buttocks, which he held gently and tentatively as if he expected to be stopped any moment. I didn't stop him. I pulled my hands through his hair, brushed my lips against his and then our tongues met. We kissed with our eyes open. I wanted to see as well as feel that I wasn't alone.

Harry pulled the sweatshirt over my head and looked at my small breasts. He touched them, caressed my nipples, sucked them and kissed me again, greedier this time. He whispered my name and kissed my eyelids, while I unbuttoned his shirt, took it off and stroked his smooth, muscular chest. He licked my ear and via my neck found his way down to my breasts, my stomach, my navel. I felt shivers down my spine as he pulled down my jogging bottoms and buried his head between my legs.

191

I gently drew him back up again. I didn't want him to disappear, I wanted to see his eyes and feel his body on top of mine. The pain had gone. I unbuttoned his jeans, admired his taut, warm belly and slid my hand into his boxer shorts. He groaned and searched for my mouth. Then he jumped up and tugged at his jeans. All of a sudden we were in a hurry, a great hurry, as if we didn't have a second to lose. We wanted to go deeper and harder, disappear into one another, and so we clung together desperately, like animals, sucking, squeezing and scratching, and when he entered me, something inside me broke. I sobbed and wailed, tears streaming down my face.

"Am I hurting you?" he whispered, shocked. I shook my head and smiled at him. I stroked his eyebrows, his nose, his lips. He licked my tears away and brushed the hair from my face. We laughed. He pushed deeper, pressed his groin against mine and stopped moving. Leaning on his arms, he towered above me, tried to catch my eye and started thrusting again. "I'm coming," he groaned, while I massaged his buttocks and said that was fine.

## 37

Harry was asleep. He lay cuddled up against me, with his hand on my belly, snoring softly. I was awake. A splitting headache and a full bladder were to blame. I rolled out of Harry's embrace and sat down on the edge of the bed. My entire body ached and my ankle had swollen up even more. I hopped naked across the cold stone floor to the bathroom to find some paracetamol.

I looked in the mirror. My face was bloated with booze, my mascara smudgy, the wound above my eye was framed by a purplish yellow bruise and my hair stood on end, like a bale of straw. Harry must have been very drunk indeed. And what about me? What had come over me? Why did I always throw myself into the arms of the first half-decent guy to come along, like some lonely little girl? I loathed myself. Now was the time to think clearly, to concentrate on getting my life back on track.

I sat down on the loo and buried my face in my hands. I shivered with cold, but it felt good, it sobered me up, allowed me to think straight. I touched my lips, which still throbbed from our passionate kisses.

It was getting light outside. I reckoned it must be around eight o'clock by now. It had stopped snowing. I thought about my children, who had probably been awake for about an hour. The thought that they were worried about me, not to mention angry and afraid, was almost unbearable.

I rummaged through my bag for my cigarettes. There was one left in the packet. I found my lighter and the key to Martin's office. I clasped it, kissed it and sighed. "Please let us find something. Anything." My voice was hoarse after all the booze and cigarettes and lack of sleep.

"Are you talking to yourself?" Harry sat up in bed. He yawned and stretched.

"Good morning to you too. I was talking to Martin's key. You see, I really am bonkers."

"Yes, I got a taste of that last night. The way you carried on, I thought to myself: mad as a hatter that one." He laughed and got out of bed. He draped the duvet around his shoulders, walked over to where I was sitting and took me in his arms.

"You're frozen. How long have you been sitting here?" I laid my head on his warm chest. He smelled fresh, even after a night like this. We sat there, wrapped in the duvet, rocking to and fro.

193

Under the shower I rinsed off the traces of our lovemaking. I washed my face, shaved my legs and armpits with Harry's razor, cut my toenails and vigorously rubbed my thighs with his massage glove. I would have liked to spend hours fussing over my body in this simple, steamed-up space. Plucking eyebrows, squeezing blackheads, cleaning ears, filing nails, pushing back cuticles, removing calluses. Now I understood why, after a spat, Steve would lock himself in the bathroom for hours on end. There was something comforting about fiddling with your toenails. It was a pleasant way of putting off your problems, in the hope that things would somehow work themselves out beyond the walls of this humid, timeless space. But meanwhile my longing for my children sat in my stomach like a brick.

Harry, dressed in his grey bathrobe, had just finished boiling some eggs. He was whistling. His cheeriness got on my nerves. I sat down at the table without saying a word and felt sweaty, despite my lengthy ablutions. He put breakfast on the table: a pot of tea, a basket of fresh rolls, two eggs in grey egg-cups and two glasses of fresh orange juice. I drained mine in one gulp and felt the sour stuff burn in my throat.

"Do you have any coffee?" I asked and he jumped up again to make some.

"Cappuccino or espresso?"

"A double espresso, please."

I couldn't eat a thing. Without thinking I started rummaging in my bag for some cigarettes, until I remembered that I had smoked my last one earlier.

"I don't suppose you've got any cigarettes?"

"Actually, I do. There should be a packet in the cupboard somewhere. Camel. I'll get it."

When he came back I lit one straight away. I took one drag and started coughing like an old, asthmatic tramp.

194

"Sounds awful."

"I'm sorry. I *feel* awful. And I'm rigid with nerves. If it was up to me, we'd be going to Martin's office right now."

Harry checked the station clock in the kitchen and chewed his food pensively.

"It's nine o'clock now. Let's try and come up with a plan."

A plan. Suddenly the whole thing seemed pointless. How were we supposed to sneak into Martin's office without being seen? And what if we did? Where were we supposed to look? What were we supposed to look for? Suppose we didn't find anything. Or Ans caught us red-handed. If that happened, I would be done for. I would be in the loony bin tomorrow.

"It'll be all right, Maria. Have faith. I know my way around Martin's accounts, there is no way he can embezzle a fortune without leaving a trace. Trust me." Harry poured himself some more tea.

"Perhaps he destroyed all the evidence. Or put it in a safe."

"He's got a PC, right? We're bound to find something on there."

"But don't you think it will be protected with a password?"

"A password is never an issue. It won't be his date of birth, he's not that stupid, but it's got to be a word he'll remember but others won't easily guess. And I reckon I know it..."

Harry put his elbows on the table and looked away from me. He started fidgeting with the cellophane wrapper of the Camels.

"What do you think it is?"

"I reckon Martin's got a girlfriend. While I was trying to track him down, I picked up rumours that things weren't going so well between him and Ans and that he had been spotted with a blonde. Nobody could tell me anything more, but then last night, just before you phoned, a female colleague of his said her name was Annabel. I reckon that's his password."

"You're telling me now?"

I got up and hobbled over to the window. "If we're going tonight, we'll have to do something about that ankle of mine."

Harry offered to rub it with a painkilling ointment and then bandage it again. Some painkillers, and I would be fine. If not, he would go on his own.

"No. I'm coming along. Come what may. This is my problem too."

I sat down on the window sill and looked out at a typical Sunday in Alkmaar. The snow in the street had turned to sludge and the ice on the canal was covered by a thin layer of water. It looked as if the thaw had already set in. Winters in the Netherlands were never long-lived.

So Martin had a girlfriend. Perhaps he was planning a fresh start with her. That's why he had asked Harry to evaluate Duinzicht. If that were true, Ans and my children were in danger too.

"I suspect," Harry said, "that he did a runner. He was working on something, making a killing, and after I'd given him the money he asked for, things went pear-shaped. He didn't have the time to tie up all the loose ends."

"Perhaps he's dead. Killed by his greedy Annabel…"

"Impossible. That's to say, when he made off with my money he was still alive. And that's when he started stalking you."

Harry frowned at me. He looked tired. In this light I could see that he'd had acne as a child. It explained his huge collection of skincare products. He took my hand. "I'm wondering... Where does Ans figure in all this? Does she really not know what's going on, or is she just not telling you?"

"Ans isn't much of a talker. She'd much rather meddle in other people's problems than her own. Her life is supposed to look perfect. I suspect she knows more about Martin, but she'll never tell me. It's clear that her marriage is in serious trouble, but again, she won't say a word."

"Do you trust her?"

His question surprised me. "She's my sister! Do you think I'd leave my children with someone I didn't trust? We're not very close, but when it comes down to it..."

"OK. I just think it's odd that she doesn't let you in on her problems with Martin. It sounds like the sort of thing you'd discuss with your sister."

"We never discuss anything. Never have done either. We used to help each other, when we were little, but we never talked. And later, after I'd left home, we grew apart. She felt abandoned by me, and I was annoyed by her sanctimonious behaviour, by the fact that she always knew best. She tried to mother me and I hated it."

"But when you had to leave Amsterdam, she was the one you turned to."

"I didn't have anyone else."

"Don't you have any girlfriends?"

I shook my head. "Not really. Not outside Amsterdam anyway."

"No old school friends?"

"No. Let's give it a break, OK? Let's talk business. What's the plan for tonight?"

## 38

It was dark and Bergen aan Zee seemed deserted. Only a few dog-walkers had ventured out, their heads down against the wind. Most of the snow had gone. Harry and I were sitting in his car, waiting for Ans to leave the house. It was getting chilly and we tried to ease the cold and tension by smoking. She kept us waiting.

I had phoned her thirty minutes ago to say that I was in a motel in Akersloot, about a twenty-minute drive from here, and that I was at my wits' end. She wanted to come and get me straight away. I told her that if she brought Victor along, I'd leg it at once. She had to come alone. I trusted her and only her. Nobody else. She promised. She would arrange a babysitter for the children. I could hear Wolf and Merel in the background and asked to speak to them, but Ans said she didn't think that was such a great idea. She had finally managed to calm them down and hearing my voice would only upset them. I hung up and threw the phone on the back seat.

My hands had grown numb with cold. Harry suggested a coffee at the hotel where we had parked. "We can see her from the window. Come on, otherwise we'll get so chilled we won't be able to move."

We got out of the car and walked into the hotel. The bar was dark and stuffy, as though it never saw any sun. The place smelled of stale coffee, cigar smoke and biscuits. The fat waitress sighed and climbed down from her bar stool when she spotted her sole customers. Harry ordered two coffees while I found a seat beside a large window with a view of Ans' front door.

We sat and stared without a word. The waitress slammed down two cups with half the coffee sloshed onto the saucers and slipped the bill under the pathetic little Christmas flower arrangement. She offered to light the red candle, but Harry said it was OK, it gave him a headache. She shrugged and sauntered back to the bar, back to her smouldering cigarette.

Harry checked his watch and looked at me.

"She really ought to get going if she wants to be in Akersloot by half-past eight."

"Perhaps she's not going at all, perhaps she's unleashed Victor and Van Dijk on me."

"Would she do that? I can't believe we didn't think of that…"

"I don't know, Harry. I reckon she'll go. I mean, if she's serious about helping me. I made it pretty clear…"

"Perhaps she thinks you're trying to lure her away from the children. Phone her. Ask her if she's on her way. Here, take my phone. I've got no caller ID."

"What am I supposed to say?"

"Anything. Just get her out of the house."

"Why don't we just wait for them to go to bed?"

"What are you afraid of? Your sister?"

He dangled his phone in front me. I took it and typed in her number. My hands got all clammy.

Ans sounded slightly winded when she answered the phone.

"It's me… I'm waiting for you…" I said with a catch in my voice. So much the better: I was supposed to sound confused.

"I can't get away. I've got a little problem here."

"But you have to come. I can't hack it much longer…"

"I'm trying. But Wolf is sick and he doesn't want me to go. And I can't saddle the babysitter with a crying child…"

"Oh my God, what's wrong?"

Harry gave a start. He pushed a beer mat and a pen towards me. I wrote down: *Wolf sick!*

"He's nauseous. He's throwing up and running a temperature. He keeps asking for you."

Harry scribbled something on the beer mat and pushed it back to me:

*Rubbish! Trying to lure you back!*

"Will you please come and get me?"

"Can't you get a taxi? I'll pay…"

"No, Ans, I'm sorry. They won't let me go. I'm broke. I'm scared!"

"You're drunk."

"This man here says he's going to call the police…"

I began to whimper and my nose started running. I wasn't pretending either. My child was sick and I felt light years away from him. It actually hurt me physically. As if my heart was being wrenched from my body.

"Let me talk to that man…"

I handed the phone to Harry and tried to get a grip on myself. Wolf wasn't sick. It was just a trick.

Harry sounded extremely condescending. "Your sister has insufficient funds and is unable to settle her account… No, I can't phone a taxi and we refuse to do any more on credit. Experience tells us that unpaid bills and all associated charges are rarely settled… No, you listen to me, this is your problem. If you don't come and collect her and settle the bill within the next hour, I shall have to call the police… No… Good. I shall see you shortly. Good evening."

He looked pretty pleased with himself as he snapped his mobile shut.

I shivered, despite the blanket of fug in the bar.

"Look," Harry said. "There she is."

200

Ans, huddled up in her coat, rushed over to her car. A second later she drove off with screaming tires down the dune and past our window. It was half-past eight. We had just under an hour before she would be back, fuming.

## 39

The sticker saying THIS PROPERTY IS PROTECTED BY ATRON SECURITY SYSTEMS had only been stuck on the door in a bid to deter burglars. Inside there was no sign of a security system. Martin's office had been done up like one of those old-fashioned gentlemen's studies, with dark wood panelling, classic dark-green wallpaper and the odd small painting.

In the middle of the room stood a large, antique desk with a green leather insert and on top of it a flat-screen display, a wireless, ergonomic keyboard and a large pile of unopened mail. His black leather Filofax was flipped open. The wall was lined with cabinets made of the same dark wood as the panelling and full of files and hanging folders. The top shelf was reserved for books.

Harry sat down behind the desk and switched the computer on. The thing started buzzing and beeping and a few seconds later asked for a password. Harry typed in the name of Martin's reputed girlfriend: Annabel. Then he pressed "enter". The response was an angry "ping". "*Invalid password.*"

"No problem, no problem," Harry muttered, more to himself than to me. He brushed my hand from his shoulder.

"Do you mind? Leave me to it. I'll manage, trust me."

He tapped away at the keyboard and kept eliciting the same angry response. Meanwhile I leafed through the mail. A golfing magazine, large envelopes from banks and insurance companies, letters from the taxman, evaluation reports, annual accounts from big corporations, flyers and brochures, drawings of planned projects – all information that was of no use to me whatsoever. I opened the blue envelopes from the taxman and saw that Martin paid his tax by direct debit. His bank statements showed a positive balance.

His securities statements made no sense to me at all, so I put them aside for Harry. All I could deduce from them was that he had over half a million in his investor's account and that until Monday, 30 October he had been actively buying shares.

"Yes!" Harry exclaimed when the computer produced a wave of synthesizer noise. "I'm in. 'Belle', it was just 'Bellc', not 'Annabel'. Hah!"

I checked the clock. We had been here fifteen minutes.

The money that Harry had transferred to Martin's account on 23 October had been received on 25 October and had been immediately diverted to another investment account. It was all properly documented on statements that were kept in a folder. I could comb through other folders, but I reckoned it would be pointless. Martin kept his dirty business out of his books. I had a feeling we were looking in the wrong place.

I combed through his desk drawers, but found nothing besides staples, a box of biros, paper clips, stacks of pictures of his sailboat and a golfing trip with some buddies, six packs of Sultana biscuits and in the right-hand bottom drawer a bottle of Bushmill's sixteen-year-old single malt Irish whiskey and a bottle of Augier Frères Cognac from 1906 with two brandy and two whiskey glasses. I also came across a small wallet with pictures from a golfing trip with some colleagues and recognized Harry in a hideous red-and-yellow striped polo shirt and a red baseball cap on his head.

Harry's frantic mouse clicking yielded just as little. All of Martin's online transactions looked squeaky clean. No foreign bank accounts, no exorbitant expenditures, no mysterious emails or chat sessions. Harry swore.

"Nothing. He invested my money in American IT shares and bonds and they rocketed. He earned me loads of money. The problem is, I can't touch any of it without him. Damn!"

"Didn't you sign a contract?"

I picked up Martin's diary and started leafing through it.

"He'd take care of it. That Monday, 30 October, we were going to finalize it all. And then he didn't show."

Harry found thirty-seven files in Martin's recycle bin. It was five past nine. We had ten more minutes.

There were dozens of business cards on the inside cover of his diary. I flicked through them, but none of the names rang any bells. Notaries, lawyers, restaurant owners and a card for an auberge in France. I put the latter to one side, along with his emergency breakdown card and his two credit cards. Strange that he hadn't taken them with him.

"Perhaps he took another one," Harry said. "Aren't there any credit-card statements in the mail?" He pulled the pile towards him and started flicking through it. He found two envelopes.

Stuck between the last few pages of Martin's diary was a transparent plastic wallet with a punch card and an appointment card for the Alkmaar Medical Centre. This past year he'd had five appointments at the gynaecology clinic. I removed the wallet from the diary and showed it to Harry.

"What's a man doing at a gynaecologist?"

Harry was staring at Martin's American Express statement.

"This is the statement for the credit card he must be carrying right now. He used it for only a single transaction.

On 27 October he filled up at a Shell station. He hasn't taken any cash out either since 28 October. Did he take a coffer full of black money or something? What's he living on, I don't get it. Here, have a look at his phone bill for November. He hasn't made any more calls on his mobile."

I checked the time. We had to get going. Harry stuffed the statements into his pocket and I put the wallet with the appointment card into my bag.

"I've got a very bad feeling about this," Harry whispered. "He seems to have disappeared off the face of the earth. Something's not right."

He quickly switched off the desk lamp and signalled for me to hurry. I was about to follow him to the door when I felt a searing pain in my ankle and my leg gave out from under me. I fell over and when I tried to scramble to my feet I knocked over Martin's wastebasket. It was full of crumpled-up paper and slit-open envelopes. My eye fell on a torn A4 sheet, with just a single line at the top: "http://www.mttu.com/abort-gallery/index.html page 3 of 3."

This looked familiar. It had been the line at the top of the aborted baby pictures he had sent me. I stuffed the piece of paper into my pocket and hobbled to the door. But before I had a chance to register that Harry looked very peculiar indeed, splayed on the ground outside, I felt a dull blow on my neck. I saw stars and fell to the floor.

# 40

A dog barked in the distance. I tried to open my eyes, but couldn't. It felt as if my eyelids had been glued shut with superglue. I was parched. A bright light shone in my face, but I couldn't avert my head. My hands were strapped to either side of a bed, as were my feet. I was trapped in an immobile body. I couldn't see, feel or do anything other than slide into an uneasy sleep. Every now and then, a silent, spiteful shadow glided across the room. Rough hands put a stinging ointment on my face and bandaged my neck so tightly I could barely breathe. Later someone cut the bandage with a pair of scissors, shaved my head and hoisted my buttocks up. I lay there shivering for hours, with my bare bottom over a bedpan, until I thought my back would break. I let it all go, not knowing whether any of this was really happening.

After this treatment he jabbed a needle into my arm. It had me falling off the tallest tower blocks, into the deepest oceans, soaring through the sky and plunging into bottomless depths. Or my children would be tortured in front of my eyes, hanged or pushed under water, while I struggled to break free, open my eyes and yell, but no sound came out. My body was bound and rigid.

Other times he gave me pills that made me retch and almost suffocated me. Once he hit me because I pushed them out of my mouth with my swollen tongue. He stuffed the tablets back in again, rammed them down my throat and kept me unconscious that way. There were times when I thought I had died and gone to hell. Or perhaps I had ended up in the isolation cell of an asylum.

I had lost all sense of time and place. Light followed dark, the icy cold the clammy heat. But at one point the pain in my head began to ebb away and I gradually regained some control over my thoughts. My first lucid thought was: why doesn't he just kill me? Why does he lock me up, strap me to the bed and drug me? What's his plan? Then, very slowly, it began to dawn on me that as long as he kept me alive I had a chance. But I had to remain lucid.

More and more often I managed to hide the pills under my tongue without him noticing. As soon as he left, I spat them out, as far from the bed as possible. The drawback was that the pain increased. The pain of lying immobile in bed, the pain in my neck, the pain in my muscles and bones, which creaked and squeaked at the slightest movement. Not to mention the hunger. The hunger and thirst were acutely painful.

When I touched them I discovered that the ropes that tied me to the bed were strips of cotton material, improvised chains. The bed, however, felt like a proper hospital bed. I turned my head and managed to move my stiff neck a little, inch down a bit and peer from under the blindfold. The light shining in my face turned out to be the sun coming through a tiny window high up on my left. There were bars in front of the window. That's all I could see.

Again I heard a dog bark, a high-pitched yapping. Why did I keep hearing dogs? Was there a kennel close by? Or a vet? I focused on the noises outside. Every so often a car passed by. I heard them brake. Car doors were slammed shut. And then came the barking. Excited barking. It could only mean one thing: I was still in Bergen aan Zee. People came here from far and wide to walk their dogs on the beach.

For a moment, this realization plunged me into despair. Merel and Wolf couldn't be very far. Oh my God, my children! They must think I had abandoned them. I could picture them, dressed in their pyjamas, sitting on the sofa beside Ans, who stroked their hair and comforted them, who had taken my place. My sister would know how to deal with their traumatized souls. I flexed my arm muscles and as I tried to wriggle out of the chains I managed to create a little more room for manoeuvre. I found a small screw under the edge of the bed and rubbed my wrist against it, ignoring the pain.

Then I heard footsteps. Light footsteps, hurrying down a staircase, approaching rapidly. The door rattled, a key was put in the lock. I smelled fried garlic. It was too late to slip the blindfold back over my eyes. I looked and saw a figure in jeans and black polo neck. A female figure, smelling of perfume. She walked towards me, and when she bent over me, her hair tickled my face. Her nails scratched my forehead as she pulled the blindfold off.

Ans smiled at me and put her hand on my forehead as though she wanted to feel if I was still running a temperature. "Well, well," she said, "our patient is coming along nicely."

# 41

For a moment I thought I was delirious again. I had ingested some traces of those pills after all and this was the effect. A nightmare. My own sister strapping me to this bed.

But I felt her hands glide across my bald head. And I heard her voice. I smelled her flowery perfume. She bent over me and looked into my sore eyes. She dabbed my eye sockets, which felt painful and swollen. Then she took my nose between her thumb and forefinger and jiggled it gently.

"Does this hurt?" she asked, and I nodded as the tears sprang into my eyes.

"You had a nasty tumble. In fact, you're still in a bad state."

She walked back to the door, turned the key and took a pile of bed linen from a red folding chair. We used to have a lot of those on the guesthouse patio.

"I need to change the bed. You've made a stinking mess. I'll untie you and then I want you to sit on that chair for a bit. Do you think you'll manage that?"

I opened my mouth to try and answer, but the only sound that came out was a pathetic little squeak and I started coughing uncontrollably. I had to have some water. My mouth, my throat, my tongue, my lips, they all felt like leather.

Ans held a cup with a straw in front of my mouth, but I realized just in time that I shouldn't drink it. There might be drugs in everything. I wouldn't accept anything from her. I pressed my lips together and fought the urge to take a sip, not even to wet my mouth a little. She pushed the straw against my mouth.

"Come on, Maria, you need to drink. It's just water."

I turned my head and squeaked: "I don't want your water."

She pinched my nose so I couldn't breathe and I had no choice but to open my mouth.

"We'll do it the hard way if that's what you want."

A searing pain shot through my nose, and the next moment she poured the water into my mouth. I nearly choked and coughed it all up again. The water ran down my chin and my neck. Ans flew into a rage. Her nostrils flared, her mouth narrowed to a thin line and she hissed that she'd had enough of always clearing up after me, always being there for everybody, and that it would only take a single phone call, just a single one, and I'd be finished.

She pulled a card from her back pocket and brandished it before my eyes.

"Look, Maria! This is what you did to that fuck buddy of yours! The whole world's looking for you! I'd keep a low profile if I were you…"

She flung the card into my lap.

208

It is with great sadness that we announce the sudden and violent death of our dearly beloved son, grandson, brother and brother-in-law Harry Menninga

This wasn't merely a slap in the face, but an immense blow. Harry was dead.

"I didn't kill him…" I whispered in shock, but I instantly realized that I was at least partly to blame for his death. I had enlisted his help.

"Oh no, of course not. You're innocence personified, aren't you? You wouldn't hurt a fly." She shook her head with pent-up anger.

I cleared my throat. "Why did you tie me up?" The words came out sounding groggy.

"You were hysterical. You were a danger to yourself. You were kicking and scratching and biting. I had no choice."

"You gave me pills and jabs…"

"What do you expect? I had to sedate you, or you would have continued harming yourself."

"And now? You're not afraid I'll have another go at you?"

"You appear to have come back to your senses. It's my task now to patch you up again." My shackles had come off and she helped me sit up. Everything hurt. She pulled the blankets off and untied my ankles. I got a shock when I saw my legs. They looked bony and dry and they were covered in dark bruises. The skin on my legs was flaky and my ankles were purple.

"Try to move them."

I managed to pull up my legs, even though they felt like jelly. Ans put my arm around her shoulder and helped me out of bed. Then my feet touched the concrete floor and I stood upright, if rather shakily. Together we hobbled to the little red chair.

It was cold in the room, all the more so because I only had a T-shirt and a pair of knickers on. I touched my face. It felt knobbly and swollen. There were scabs on my nose and around my eyes.

"Why did you shave my head?!"

"You had lice. It would have taken too long to try and get them out of that big mop of hair of yours."

She unfolded a pillowcase and slipped it over the pillow. That biting stuff I had felt had been anti-lice lotion.

"What about the children? They had lice too?"

"You all did. But nobody has any time. None of you bother doing anything about it. With lice you have to clean everything. *Everything*! Do you understand, Maria? And if that doesn't work, the hair has to come off. There's no other way. But oh no, the little angels must have the latest hair styles, with gel and scrunchies and what have you and if you as much as pick up a comb they start squealing. I wanted to take a nit comb through Merel's hair and she had the nerve to ask: 'What do I get?' What kind of upbringing is that? They expect to be rewarded for doing normal, everyday things."

"But did you?…"

"Of course! Wolf said: 'Oh, scratchies. We get them all the time.' He said they weren't dirty or anything. I said they certainly were and that I knew a way to get rid of them once and for all."

I moaned. I thought of Merel and how proud she was of her gorgeous, thick, shiny black hair. It broke my heart.

Ans ripped the filthy sheets off the bed and pulled a face. I had been lying on a plastic mattress. "It's a good thing I put you in Mother's room. Otherwise I could have kissed goodbye to my mattress."

She wiped the plastic with a cloth. She paced up and down

210

like my mother used to do, impatient, neurotic, like a tiger in a cage.

"Ans, what happened? Why are you keeping me locked up like this?"

"They're looking for you." She jabbed her finger at me. "You killed that guy stone-dead. Right here in front of the house. You bashed his head in with a rock. You're lucky I managed to hide you before the police showed up."

I hugged myself and rocked gently to and fro to keep my emotions in check, to stop myself from losing it. Sweet, handsome Harry. I thought of his smooth olive skin and his tender eyes. His lips, with which he had caressed and kissed me. What had I done? Why had I got him mixed up in all this?

"That's right, Maria, you messed up right royally again."

Ans pulled a fitted sheet over the mattress and smoothed the creases with her hands.

"I didn't do it. I walked out of the house and there he was. And then I got hit over the head. Why would they think it was me?"

"You were seen with him. In the hotel across the street. Your cigarettes were found in his car."

"But what about a motive? Why would I kill a friend?"

"How would I know!? You kept harping on about Martin, claiming Martin was threatening you. And then you talked him into going into the office with you. What happened there remains a mystery to the police, but the fact is you're their only suspect."

"And what do you think?"

"I don't think anything. I think you need to rest." Ans grabbed me under my arms and helped me off the chair.

"Damn it, Ans! What about that bruise on my neck? And those scabs on my nose and around my eyes?"

"You had a nasty tumble. You left me with no alternative but to hit you. You were completely hysterical."

When I yanked myself free, she glared at me.

"I'm the only one you've got, Maria, so you'd better not try anything. You're going back to bed now. I'll bring you some food later and then we'll talk some more."

I lay down on the bed. My head was spinning. She folded the clean, stiff sheets over me and took my hand. "No!" I pulled my hand away. "You're not tying me up again. And I want to see my children!"

"Needs must, Maria. I don't want you to hurt yourself."

"I'm warning you…"

"You're warning me? I don't think so! One wrong move and I'll call the police and you'll never see Merel and Wolf again!"

She was stronger than me. She didn't have much trouble strapping me to the bed again. She pulled a pink pillbox from her pocket, dug out a pill, took the glass of water from the bedside table and held both in front of my mouth. I looked her in the eye and let her put the pill on my tongue. I drank some water through the straw and hid the pill between my teeth and cheek.

Ans tapped my cheek. "Open up."

I refused. She took my jaw between her thumb and middle finger and pinched so hard I had no choice but to open my mouth. She groped around in my mouth, found the pill, shoved it down my throat with her sharp nail and poured in some water. Then she hit me. So hard it left my ear ringing. Now I knew, knew with absolute certainty: my sister was slowly killing me. And she was enjoying it too. That's why she took her time dealing me the final blow.

212

## 42

The pill did its job. I went under again, in clear blue, warm water this time. I swam to the light, to the spot where the sun hit the water. I surfaced and took a breath. The sun was so bright, so blindingly white, that I couldn't open my eyes. I wanted to swim back to the beach, but I couldn't tell which way to go.

All of a sudden, I stood in the middle of Bergen. It was warm and muggy, my T-shirt stuck to my skin and my brow was bathed in sweat. Hordes of people sauntered through the village, eating ice cream and chips. There was some kind of event. A party. There were Chinese lanterns everywhere and I could hear a street organ. The organ grinder walked up to me and rattled his collection box, a deafening noise. He kept following me whichever way I went. I didn't have any money and I was trying to get that across to him when suddenly I noticed it was Martin. He grabbed me by the arm and tried to drag me along, all the while pointing his rattling box ahead of him.

"There they are!" he yelled. "Go after them! Go! What's keeping you, woman!?" I shrank back, tore myself from his grip and hid among the crowd, while I heard him yelling: "I can't believe you still don't get it!"

I elbowed my way through the crowd, frantic with worry. I had lost my children. I had to find them. I called out their names, but couldn't make myself heard over the buzz of the people. There they were, queuing to get chips: Wolf in his red *Dragonball Z* shirt and Merel in a yellow-and-white check dress that my mother had made for Ans. Ans herself stood next to them, holding Wolf's hand. I cried out and Merel turned her head. She looked straight at me. I smiled and reached out my hand, but she didn't recognize me. She turned away and took my sister's other hand. Ans leaned towards her and planted a kiss on her cheek. When a man bumped into me I lost my balance and fell. I clutched at the legs of passers-by to help myself back up, but they all ignored me, trampled me, and when my head hit the cold paving stones I smelled mud and rain and feet kicking me in the stomach and thighs. I made myself small in a bid to protect myself and then everything turned brown and wet.

I woke up in the boot of a car. I lay with my head on a dirty, bristly, damp mat that smelled of soil and sour wine, and got jolted around. My hands had been tied behind my back.

Every time the car hit a bump in the road or turned a corner I heard something slide and scrape across the floor behind me. It was an odd little raspy sound I might never have noticed if my life hadn't depended on it. However weak and drowsy I felt right now, I knew this was a matter of life and death and I needed all my wits about me. I concentrated on the sound, which came and went, and realized it was something that kept rolling back and forth behind my back. It had a clear ring, like glass. It had to be a shard or something which had been left in the car.

Mustering what little strength I had, I wriggled my hands to loosen the chains a little, spread my fingers as wide as possible and waited for the shard to roll past again. Nothing happened. We were driving along a straight stretch of road. I heard it tinkle softly, just above my head, against the side of the car, and for a moment I feared it had got stuck there. I tried to slide up a little by pushing off with my feet, but I couldn't. I was completely wedged in and now the tinkling had stopped too.

I racked my brains for a way of freeing myself, and I tried to imagine what might be in store for me once Ans had parked the car somewhere. She would kill me. She had probably already dug my grave. Next to Martin's. Somewhere nobody would ever look.

I didn't want to die. My will to live had never been stronger. I had to make it through this, protect my children from this woman. I didn't want them to grow up thinking I had been a volatile madwoman who had murdered someone and then taken her own life.

Suddenly the car seemed to swerve off the road and there it was again, the soft tinkling sound. Ans seemed to be driving up a sandy path. I spread my fingers and stretched out my arms as far as I could. The shard rolled a little to the right and I managed to pull it towards me with my fingertips. When I clutched it I felt warm blood trickle into the palms of my hands. It was sharp. Sharp enough to save my life.

I turned the piece of glass to feel its shape: a kind of sickle with a sharp tip. I tried to hook that tip behind the cotton straps and I just about managed it with my cold and stiff fingers, but when I tried to saw I got cramp in my hands. I cursed. I couldn't drop it or I would never find it again, so I had to grit my teeth and go through the pain barrier, even if it meant I couldn't really feel what I was doing. At that point the car started shaking violently, as though we were driving across a road full of potholes. I knocked my head against the wheel housing and my nose started stinging, the way it does when it fills with water. It hurt. Then the car came to an abrupt halt and my head hit the wheel housing again. I only just managed to clutch the shard of glass with my fingertips and wrap my hands around it.

The lid of the boot opened and my sister towered above me in the dark. Now I could see the hatred in her eyes. To think that I had never noticed it before. To think that I had always thought that, despite all the misery, I still had a sister who knew me and loved me, even if she didn't understand me. It had been a fatal mistake.

She bent over me and tugged at my arm. I yielded instantly, because I didn't want to lose my weapon. Groaning with pain, I sat up. The shard cut deeper into the palm of my hand. I swung first one and then the other leg over the edge of the boot and stepped onto the sand. We were in the dunes somewhere, close to the sea. I could hear the waves roaring. Ans had turned onto the cycle path, into the dune nature reserve, and now we were on top of a dune buffeted by a biting north-westerly wind.

She led me to the driver's seat and told me to sit down. She scrutinized my face without looking me in the eye and pulled a pack of paper tissues out of her pocket. She cleaned my face, like I had cleaned Wolf's face a thousand times. She was wearing latex gloves.

All that time I kept trying to catch her eye, but she wouldn't let me. I thought to myself: if only I can catch her eye, if only I can get through to her, touch a chord, remind her of when we were little and lying in bed, terrified, listening to our mother ranting and raving, perhaps then she will let me go.

"Ans," I said softly. "Ans? What are you planning to do to me?"

She didn't reply. She gestured for me to get up again, pulled me away from the door and slammed it shut. She locked the car and took me by the arm.

"Come," she said. "Let's go."

"No," I said. "I'm not going anywhere." I flopped down onto the beach grass and thought to myself: I must gain time. Delay, slow her down. Save energy. Meanwhile I kept sawing at the rope with the shard, not knowing quite what I was cutting.

216

"Finish me off here. Why would I walk for bloody miles? You're going to kill me and I don't understand... I don't understand why, Ans."

She stood beside me. Her wax coat flapped about in the wind. Then I heard an odd little click, under her coat, which freaked me out. It was the click of a handgun. She had released the safety catch and cocked the hammer. She really was going to shoot me right here on the spot...

"Hang on. Ans... Wait. I'm coming..."

Time, I needed more time. I sobbed. Sweat poured out of my armpits and my entire body seized up. I didn't want to die. Even if I only lived another three minutes, those three minutes would be worth the effort.

We walked down the dune. Ans wanted to keep hold of me, but I pulled away. I mustn't lose that shard.

"Is that where Martin is?" I asked her.

Ans sighed. "I'd rather not talk," she said and continued at a brisk pace.

"I'd rather not die. But if I must, I want to know the truth. You owe it to me..."

It was hard to walk and cut at the same time. The sharp tip grazed my lower back.

"I'll tell you why you deserve to die."

She turned round and finally looked me in the eye. Hers were as cold as ice.

"You're a parasite. A vampire. Always have been, since the day you came into this world. You should never have been born... Her body tried to get rid of you. But oh no, she took to her bed and you stayed put. That's when it all started. She was never the same again. She went mad because of you!"

"Jesus, Ans... You know that's not true... Mum never came to terms with Stephan's death..."

217

"No! It goes back much further than that. And you! You couldn't stand to see Mum so sad all the time. Because you had to be the centre of attention. The centre of everything. Always. Still. Any guy who comes along, he's got to look at you. And your job… nothing if not a cry for attention. And you get it too. I just don't understand. Nobody can see through you! Not even Martin. He actually admired you. You managed to juggle it all: singing, raising the children, looking after Geert. Even an abortion!…"

She gave me a violent shove on the shoulder and I tumbled down the dune. The shard fell from my hands. I snatched at it, fumbled for it on the frozen sand, but it was gone…

Ans bent over me and jabbed a finger in my face.

"That was the last straw, Maria! The proverbial last straw. I'd just come home from hospital. Do you know why I was there? Well? Curettage! You know, when they suck a dead child out of your body with a kind of hoover. But you know what I mean, don't you, Maria? You got rid of a living child. You murdered a living child!"

I rubbed my wrists together and tugged at the ropes, which were a bit looser now. Sand chafed my cuts. Then Ans yanked me up and something snapped behind my back. The cotton ropes broke. She pushed me and gave me such a vicious kick in my back I cried out. "Go ahead, scream. It won't make the slightest bit of difference. Nobody will hear you, or come and look for you."

I slipped again and tumbled headlong down the dune. My hands were free. I could make a run for it. Ans would shoot, but in the dark she would have trouble hitting me. And should she hit me, should she shoot me in the back and kill me, she could no longer claim I had taken my own life.

I pushed myself off and rolled down to the beach. I jumped to my feet and was about to run away when, from the corner of my eye, I saw Ans lunging at me. We both ended up in the sand again.

"You bitch! You're free! How did you…"

I lashed out at her, tried to throw sand in her eyes and kick her in the stomach, but she managed to dodge everything. She put her hands around my throat and squeezed so hard I thought my eyes would pop. Then she shoved my face in the sand and I couldn't see any more.

She put the barrel of the gun to my head.

"You fucking bitch!" Screeching hysterically, she sat on my back and yanked my head to one side. I gasped for breath. She slid the barrel to my temple.

"I'm sorry, Ans. I really am. I didn't know. I could have helped. I still can, it's not too late. Please. I know you don't want this."

She yanked at my head again. "You don't deserve it! You and all those other sluts who booze and screw and breed like rabbits and expect others to clear up their mess. It's so unfair! You want everything… You have everything. And still it's not enough. Whereas I… I never asked for much. Except a family. A stab at happiness. I try to get everything right but nobody gives a damn. And you… you only live for yourself and yet you receive love. Everybody loves you. They even love you when you abort their child and throw them out of the house."

She trembled. The barrel of the gun knocked against my temple. I had to try and keep her talking.

"But what about Martin? He loved you…"

"Martin is an arsehole. He dropped me like a ton of bricks. After everything we'd been through together…" Her voice broke. "He wanted children. We talked about it, over and over again. Our home was perfect for a large family. We'd be very different from our own parents. But I kept getting my period, month after month. Do you have any idea how that affects your relationship? No, you don't! You fall pregnant because you're pissed and you don't know any better. You get children you don't even want; I get a dead child. After five rounds of IVF, five rounds of pain and hormone injections, five rounds of getting our hopes up. And then at long last, bingo! I was so happy. Two months. I was puking my guts out, but I couldn't care less. This was our child growing in my belly. I was so happy I didn't even realize what Martin was up to…"

She was panting. Her whole body shuddered. She grabbed my arm and pulled it back. Whatever happened, she mustn't tie me up again. With my hands tied I didn't stand a chance.

"Did you kill him?"

"I didn't mean to. I only wanted him to stay with me. Give our marriage another try. But he'd had enough. He thought I'd changed. I'd become obsessed with having children. He said I had to come to terms with it. We had lost our baby and perhaps it was a sign that it wasn't to be. He thought I should see more of you. 'Maria has children, you can hang out with them,' he said. Hang out, as though that's good enough. Then he told me that he'd spoken to Geert. You were having a tough time too. The two of you had broken up and you'd just had an abortion. A tragic coincidence, he called it. 'Why don't you invite Maria to come and stay with us for a couple of days? It will give you a chance to talk about things and hang out on the beach with the kids.' Hah! So I did, arsehole! Here she is, our strong Maria! And her little lambs are with me. They adore me, you know that?!"

That made me furious. So bloody furious that all my muscles strained, just as she tried to tie some makeshift ropes around my wrists and let her guard down for a second. I pushed my bum up, wrenched my right arm free and struck the hand that held the gun to my head. I turned round and with a primal scream threw her off my back. I felt her nails digging into the flesh of my arm and her knee in my stomach, but I was stronger. I got up and kicked her until she let go. She banged her head on the frozen sand and the gun went off.

We both lay motionless on the beach, stunned by that deafening bang. I was the first to scramble to my feet to see if Ans had hurt herself. I whispered her name and began to worry. She wasn't moving. The wind and the sea were out-roaring each other, an ominous sound, and the moon had now completely disappeared behind the clouds. It began to rain a little, ice-cold drops that brought her round again, but too late – I had already snatched the gun. It was a tiny black thing, smaller and lighter than I had expected. I had never seen a gun before, let alone held one, so I didn't have the faintest idea what to do with it, except aim it at my sister, who was looking at me with blue, trembling lips.

"You'll be making a big mistake if you shoot me," Ans said.

"I'll do it if I have to. I certainly won't let myself be slaughtered by you."

"You're up against it, Maria. Nobody believes you. What do you think will happen if you shoot me? You'll spend the rest of your life in a secure psychiatric unit and Merel and Wolf won't have anyone."

"I won't shoot you. I'm taking you home so you can tell everybody the truth."

"They all think you're mad. Victor spoke to the police and told them everything. Borderline personality disorder. Turned psychotic after an abortion. Thinks everybody's

221

against her. Can't tell fact from fiction and invents a stalker. Criminally insane."

Ans got up and walked towards me.

"Give it to me, Maria, please. Or throw it away, fling it into the sea. You don't really want to kill me. Come here, sweetie, come to me."

I caught a whiff of cigars. He snuck up from behind, grabbed hold of my wrist and put his arm around my waist. Opposite me Ans sank to her knees, wailing uncontrollably.

"It's OK, Maria, let go now. We don't want any more accidents now, do we?" It was Victor.

# 43

Victor wasn't alone. Van Dijk and four other officers were standing close by, on top of the dune. The flashing lights of two police vans and an ambulance cast a sinister glow over the beach grass.

He needn't have overpowered me. I knew it was over and I would have given him the gun without a moment's hesitation. In a way I was relieved that someone had turned up and put an end to our gruelling battle. I would never have shot my sister, and she would never have surrendered. Without intervention we would probably have frozen to death.

Huddled in a scratchy, smelly blanket, with a mug of hot coffee and an acrid-tasting Caballero in my chapped hands, I could only cry. The tears thawed my frozen cheeks and trickled onto my cigarette. There I was, shaking and sobbing, a bald lunatic with bleeding wrists. The very picture of madness.

The paramedic, a young Moroccan lad with a pockmarked face and gentle, brown eyes set off by ridiculously thick, long eyelashes, looked at me with pity. "Madam? Would you come to the ambulance with me? We'll need to have a look at those injuries."

He helped me up and together we shuffled to the yellow vehicle. I felt about eighty-four years old.

"Would you like something to ease the pain?"

He checked my pupils with a kind of pen light. I shook my head.

"Or perhaps something to calm you down?"

"No. I don't want any more pills."

"That's OK, you don't have to, but I imagine you must be in a great deal of pain…"

"I'm not falling for that one again. I know what you're thinking, but I'm not psychotic. I'll cooperate, don't you worry about that, but I'm not swallowing another pill."

"That's fine, madam."

He softly tapped his finger all over my face, asking if it hurt. When he touched my nose, I flinched.

"Ah, I thought so. Your nose is probably broken. You'll have to come along to A&E later. But first I'll clean and bandage your hands." Ever so gently he took both my hands, turned them round, looked at them closely and carefully brushed the sand off.

"They're only cuts. Nothing serious. You won't need any stitches."

His kindness surprised me. Perhaps he was terrified of me, or perhaps he had learned to treat psychos with kid gloves.

A female police officer entered the ambulance, followed by Victor, who looked as though he was the one who had just escaped death. His wind-swept hair made him look like the professor from *Back to the Future*. The officer bent over me and put her hand on my shoulder.

"Ms Vos, do you feel well enough to provide us with a statement later?"

The paramedic objected. "I don't think so. Her nose is broken and I believe she may be undernourished and dehydrated. You'd better wait until tomorrow, in hospital…"

"All right."

The officer half rose and planted her hands on her hips. Handcuffs and a crackling walkie-talkie dangled from her belt.

"I'll come and check in on you tomorrow, Ms Vos, probably with my colleague Van Dijk, whom you've met. We're taking your sister now. You don't need to be afraid any more."

I looked at Victor and then at the officer again. I didn't understand. Was this some kind of trick? My heart started racing.

"Who's looking after the children? They're not all by themselves, are they? Victor? I thought they were with you?"

He crouched down beside me.

"Merel and Wolf are with their father, Maria. They're safe in a hotel here in Bergen, they're asleep and doing just fine. And I owe you an apology. I'm sorry. I'm so terribly sorry. I made a big, a dreadful mistake…"

His cheeks quivered and his voice faltered. For a moment I thought he was going to burst out crying. He nervously pulled his hands through his dishevelled hair and patted my leg. Meanwhile the paramedic bandaged my wrist.

"I don't understand, Victor. What happened? How did you know we were here?"

"It's a long story. But this evening the police excavated Martin's body and during a search of the premises they found the room where you were locked up…"

# 44

I was shocked when I saw them shuffle into the room, two frightened-looking, bald children. Merel and Wolf thought that with my bandaged head and my face full of bruises I looked scary. Geert made up the rear, carrying an enormous bunch of red roses.

Without saying a word, Wolf left a drawing on my bed and then put his fingers in his mouth. He bit his nails and seemed afraid to look at me. I stroked his head and hugged him to my chest. "My sweet, sweet Wolf, I missed you so much."

"Me too, Mum," he stammered and then squirmed from my all-too-tight embrace.

When I reached out for Merel she came forward timidly. She kissed me on the cheek and put her hands gently on my shoulders. "Hi, Mum…" I pulled her close and was almost overcome with grief when I felt her bristly head against my cheek.

"I'm so glad to see you again, my sweeties…"

"Look, Mum," said Wolf as he wriggled one of his upper teeth, which had finally come loose. I was delighted to see how, after a few awkward embraces, it was business as usual. They argued about who could sit on the bed with me. Merel asked if she could watch television; Wolf wanted to make a drawing.

"Did you bring us a present, Mum, because you were away for so long?" Wolf asked and was promptly poked in the ribs by his sister.

"Don't be stupid! Mum is sick, can't you see that!"

Geert sat hunched over on the edge of a folding chair, staring at the floor. His jaw muscles were flexing and I knew he was trying hard to come up with something to say. He didn't know where to start. Neither did I.

"Are you OK?" he croaked and looked at me with pity.

"I'm fine," I replied and smiled at him.

He shook his head.

"It's nothing serious. The drip is to get my fluid levels back to normal, and this bandage here covers the stitches at the back of my head. And my nose is broken. That explains the Mike Tyson look."

He laughed awkwardly and rubbed his eyes. Then he buried his face in his hands. "I thought you were dead, I really did. You'd been reported missing, they found Martin's body... Then I knew. I cursed myself. I thought: how could I have let this happen? Why didn't I go and see Ans? Why am I such a coward?"

"Don't blame yourself, Geert. Nobody could have imagined this." I took his hand and kissed his fingers.

We were interrupted by a cough. Van Dijk and Victor stood in the doorway. They walked in and shook hands with me and Geert. Victor was still in last night's outfit, a scruffy brown corduroy suit with a burgundy red slip-over and a brown check shirt underneath. In his khaki trench coat Van Dijk looked like a stressed-out football coach.

Geert asked the children if they fancied some ice cream, which they did, but they also wanted to stay with me. "I won't ever go away again, kids. You can stay here as long as you like, and when you're leaving, I'm coming with you," I promised both them and myself, whereupon they shuffled out of the room with Geert. I saw Merel reach for his hand, which moved me.

Victor sat down on Geert's chair and Van Dijk sat on the other side of the bed. Victor kept pulling his hands through his hair. "Well..." He made a rather neurotic impression. He rubbed his eyes and glanced up at the ceiling, as though he hoped it might yield the words he wanted to say to me.

"First off, Maria, my apologies. This is the worst error of judgement I've ever made in my entire career as a psychiatrist. I'm devastated. I keep asking myself: how could this have happened? Right before my eyes? How could I have let her use me like that? I'm reconsidering my position. Seriously, you can take it from me…"

A nurse brought some coffee. She offered the men a cup too, which they accepted gratefully. We drank our first sip in silence and I loved the way the hot, fresh coffee warmed me inside.

"You know, I've worked at Riagg for over twenty years. I advise and assess parents with serious personal problems, either with themselves, with each other or with their children. I see junkies, alcoholics, schizophrenics, abused women and children. In the first instance, I try and get them to solve their own problems. It's only when this proves unsuccessful that I recommend admission into a clinic or a custody order, often in consultation with your sister. That's how we got to know each other.

"About a year ago Ans indicated that she was struggling with the pressures of work. She was finding it increasingly difficult to cope with all the misery that comes our way. We talked a lot and developed a bond. You know, as friends and colleagues. I admired her. She told me about your childhood, about your mother tyrannizing the entire family and the fact that nobody ever offered you any help. She told me she became a social worker to help children who were in the same boat. I thought to myself: if there's anybody who can help these children, it's her. She motivated me. However much she struggled sometimes, she always pulled through, she bounced back, despite her problems with Martin, despite the unsuccessful IVF treatments. And this is what she told me: you're the reason I continue doing this job. It's thanks to you that I still enjoy it; you inspire me. I must admit, it was flattering. I liked the fact that she confided in me. I knew she was pregnant. I knew even before her husband that the foetus had died. She called in sick and was off work for quite a while. And during all that time, I was the only one at work with whom she stayed in touch. Having said that, I was surprised that she managed to control her emotions so well. She had lost a child, her husband had left, it couldn't get any worse really, and yet she seemed quite stoical.

"Anyway, that's when you moved in. She didn't mention you very often, but when she did, it was usually for all the wrong reasons. You were the unhinged younger sister with two children by different fathers. You drank, took drugs, neglected your children. You refused all her offers of help. She had already tried a few times to have you placed under a supervision order, but your problems were never quite serious enough. The school that Merel and Wolf attended had no complaints, neighbours said that everything was fine and so did the GP. It bothered her. Things were bound to go wrong, but nobody saw it coming, except Ans.

"I believed her, Maria. You mustn't forget, her stories about your childhood were pretty grim. I didn't know you, but with such a background it seemed entirely plausible that you'd gone off the rails. So when she called me to say that you and the children had moved in for a while, I was actually rather pleased for her. Finally something was afoot. I offered to help."

A sense of unease came over me. Ans had been scheming for ages to try and take my children away from me. The school? My neighbours? None of them had ever told me that I had been the subject of inquiries. And unhinged, me? Just because I didn't have dinner ready at six?

228

"She called in the middle of the night. You were going completely berserk. I was off duty and at first I advised her to call the attendant psychiatrist at the crisis centre. Or the GP. It would be better to handle this via the regular channels. But she didn't want to know. She was terribly upset, crying that you were her sister, her little sister, and that she didn't want you to be sent to an institution. The two of us, we were professionals, we could help you, at home, in a warm and safe environment. It would be better for everyone involved. For the children, for you, for herself. I thought she had a point. We both knew better than anyone what psychiatric units are like. You don't want your loved ones to go through that.

"Now I realize that she needed me to prescribe medication. Of course, I was already prejudiced after hearing her stories. I'm an experienced psychiatrist and yet I allowed myself to be exploited. It got out of hand, spectacularly so…"

He lowered his eyes and squeezed them shut. He sighed and with that sigh every last bit of strength seemed to leave his body. He took the bridge of his nose between his thumb and forefinger, as if it were a button he could press to regain control over himself.

"I called the police when I saw that she'd shaved the children's heads. That's when I knew. That look in her eyes. It was a terrible moment. Dreadful. The realization…"

He shook his head. "All of a sudden I knew what she had in mind. As if deep down I'd known it all along, but had banished those thoughts, those nagging doubts. And then they all came tumbling out. I realized too why I'd helped her carry out this ghastly crusade. It's appalling. She flattered me. I'm a single man, Maria. My patients hate me. You hated me. I'm the one who recommends that children be taken into care, their parents admitted to a psychiatric unit or rehab; I judge and pass sentence. Nobody ever thanks me for it. Not even the children I save from the hands of their abusive fathers."

He rubbed his knees, which must be a bit of a habit, judging by the worn patches on his trousers. He got up.

"My words come too late, I know, and they're nothing but a lame excuse that's of no use to you now. But I hope you believe me when I say I'm sorry. I'm not asking you to forgive me, I just want you to know that I meant no harm by helping your sister. I'm as much a victim as you are."

I suppressed a powerful urge to pat him on the back and tell him not to worry, it was all right.

"I'm sure you meant no harm. But please don't compare yourself with me. Let's not distort the truth."

He avoided my gaze. We said goodbye and shook hands. His was moist and limp.


Van Dijk looked at me and threw his hands in the air. "Mistakes, mistakes, we've all made them. Me too." He got up, stretched his stiff legs and walked over to the window.

"But how did you figure out what was really going on?"

"To be honest, it was pure coincidence. At a certain point a number of strands came together. And then we could no longer ignore it…"

"What kinds of 'strands'?"

"Well, to start with there was Harry Menninga's death. You were the only suspect, but our interviews with his friends and colleagues raised other questions. Where was the money Martin had invested? Where was Martin himself? And of course I still had your story about him in the back of my mind… And then Martin's girlfriend popped up, Annabel. She told us that Martin couldn't have anything to do with Harry's death. He had vanished without a trace the day they had decided to start a new life together. She suspected Ans might be behind it. Martin had told her that Ans was beginning to frighten him. The very same morning Annabel made her statement, we also received some interesting information from an acquaintance of yours, a certain Mrs Wijker."

"Daphne?"

'Yes, Daphne Wijker and her husband Chris. He's a road worker and recently poured a concrete floor at the back of your sister's house. She wanted a patio. Daphne thought it was a bit odd, given all the stories that were doing the rounds in the village about Martin's disappearance and the death of his friend. She also told us that the night before his disappearance she'd seen Martin running naked through the dunes. That's when we decided to search Duinzicht. Ans had vanished by then, with you, as we later learned. We discovered the room where you'd been held. On the basis of that discovery I gave the order to break open the concrete floor. And there we found Martin's body. We immediately raised the alert."

"How did you know we were on the beach?"

"A lad who'd been messing around with fireworks in the area had heard you screaming."

"And what about Merel and Wolf, where were they all this time?"

"Until the morning of the search they were with Ans. When we arrived they were alone in the house. We called their father…"

Wolf came scurrying into the room, holding a large ice-cream cone in front of him. In his other hand he held a silver-coloured balloon in the shape of a heart. *Get well soon* it said in bright letters. "For you! A present from us!"

I thought of Harry, who had never had the pleasure of meeting my children and without whom I might not have survived all this. And of the cycle of lost children: Stephan, Ans' much-wanted and my unwanted child – a spiral that ended with Harry's parents having to bury their son.

## 45

She looked small in the run-down little room with plastic furniture. Small, fragile and scrawny. She certainly didn't look like a murderer. Her hair had been shaved off, like mine. Without make-up she looked older than thirty-five. She was smoking a cigarette with an unsteady hand, like many before her, judging by the burn marks on the green plastic table. We were sitting opposite one another and neither of us knew where to start. Perhaps I shouldn't have come to visit her. I had so much to say, so much to ask, but the woman in front of me wasn't Ans, my sister, but a nervous wreck, who seemed barely capable of speaking, let alone answering my questions.

When I asked her how she was, she flew into a rage.

"What do you think? In this filthy, decrepit dump? What do you think, huh? Bacteria, microbes, filth, everywhere! And I'm surrounded by a bunch of idiots. All day long. Wherever I am, whatever I do, someone's watching me. And you want to know how I am?"

I instantly felt terror grabbing me by the throat again. I couldn't bear to hear her shriek or see the hatred in her eyes. Nothing could happen to me here and yet I didn't feel safe. I got up, gripped by an irresistible urge to run away. Let her rot in here. She hates me. She killed my brother-in-law and the man with whom I might have fallen in love. She deserves no better than this. I had been a hair's breadth from ending up here myself. Or worse. Sod it. I walked back to the door and the guard got up. When I turned round one last time I noticed she was crying. Without a sound. Her shoulders were shaking, her cheeks were quivering and she started banging her fist on the table.

"I didn't mean to," she squeaked, "I didn't mean to. It just… I don't know. It just happened."

Standing where I was, by the door, we were separated by well over six feet and yet it felt as if she had dug her claws into my neck.

"I'm angry. Furious. Do you know what it's like to feel such rage?"

I shook my head. I didn't know what it was like. I asked the guard to open the door.

She started talking. More to herself than to me. "Martin had had enough. That's what he said. It was foolish to carry on like this. It was destroying us both. I kept thinking: he's lying, he's lying, he's lying. And that's what I told him: you're lying, there's more, something else, tell me, tell me the truth! But he just stood there. Piss off! I hurled a vase at his head. I was still bleeding. I was still bleeding from our child. How could he do this to me? I made him tell me the truth. And then he told me you'd had an abortion. He'd wanted to spare me, but I'd given him no choice."

"But you knew he had a girlfriend, right?"

"I had my suspicions. He wanted out. He was going to have a child with someone else and do all the things we'd always dreamed of with someone else. And you'd got rid of a child. He wanted to go to bed. Perhaps we ought to continue our conversation the next day, when we were both a bit calmer…

"I grabbed a candlestick and hit him. He ran away out of the house. It was freezing and he was bleeding. I locked the

233

doors and went upstairs. I was still fuming. It wouldn't go away. It only got worse and worse."

She was shaking so badly now that she couldn't even pull a cigarette from the packet. I was afraid to help her.

"It's the medication."

She buried her face in her hands and started rocking to and fro.

"The next morning I found his body. In front of the French windows, in a pool of blood. I didn't mean to kill him. I dragged him inside, washed him… His body… So white, so dead…

"But you get used to it, you know. A corpse. At first it's a shock and you panic, but at some point… It wasn't Martin any more. It was just a thing, something I had to get rid of as quickly as possible. And the odd thing was, I could think straight. My mind… crystal clear. I knew exactly what to do. The plan, it simply presented itself. So obvious. So brilliant. It unfolded in my head, as though it had been there all along. Every night I'd get a new idea! After Martin's death… Once you've crossed that threshold, I mean, once you've killed a person and buried his corpse and no questions are asked, it turns out to be quite simple. It's only a small step to kill again."

"Did you never stop to think how unhappy Merel and Wolf would be?"

She looked up irritably and I was shocked to see the lack of emotion in her bloodshot eyes.

"Sometimes you must do what's best for the children. They'd much rather stay with parents who beat them to a pulp every day than go to a foster family or a children's home. It's my job to look beyond these emotions."

I hadn't smoked for almost a week, but now I was desperate for a cigarette. I walked back to the table to take one from her packet. She grabbed my wrist and dug her nails into my flesh.

"What do you know about pain, about loneliness!? You were born for happiness, just as I was born for unhappiness. You can't take any credit for that! You attract it, the way I attract misery."

The guard approached us and asked Ans to let go of me.

I took a step back and looked at her. By now I too was shaking with rage, and I got an inkling of the fury that had gripped her for months. "You're my sister, Ans, but more of a stranger to me than anybody else. You weren't born for unhappiness, you chose to be unhappy! You used me as an excuse. You simply chose another path. The path of hatred, suspicion and jealousy."

Ans looked me straight in the eye now. The muscles in her neck were twitching as though she were about to lunge at me. "You! You left us in the lurch. You left me to pick up the pieces! I" – she jabbed a finger at her chest, on the verge of hysteria – "I was the one who looked after him when he started to decline! I was his maidservant! And even then he didn't have an ounce of love to spare! Except when you came to visit, of course, then he'd be over the moon!"

The guard, who had stood between us all this time, put his arm around Ans. "I think it's time to say goodbye now," he said to me. Ans pulled away.

"I'm sorry," I said to her. "But you did have a choice, just like me, but you chose to be invisible. And you just can't expect to be given credit for effacing yourself."

I watched her go, a sad, cowering wreck ushered along by the nurse, and stubbed out my last cigarette.

Thank you Tinekc, Tineke Q., Nicolette, Els, Tom and above all my friend and husband Marcel for your support, inspiration and faith in me.

Thank you Lydia for sharing your knowledge of policing with me.

Thank you Janine for lending me your books about Bergen aan Zee and for sharing your experiences as an ailing little girl at Bio Recreation.

Thank you Mum and Dad for all the stories and memories.

# THE DINNER CLUB

## *Saskia Noort*

**A subversive concoction of greed, lust and violence set in genteel suburbia.**

When Evert dies in his burning villa, everything points to suicide. The other members of the "dinner club", a group of five women who meet regularly and whose husbands do business together, rally around to support Babette, his grieving widow. But events soon spiral out of control. Within weeks a member of the club falls from the balcony of a hotel and dies. Something is poisoning their smug world of flashy 4x4s, coffee mornings and wine-filled evenings and bringing death in its wake. This is a high-spirited, sexy and ingeniously plotted tale about people desperate to hang on to the trappings of success--at any cost.

Imagine *Desperate Housewives* scripted by Patricia Highsmith. That's *The Dinner Club*.

Saskia Noort is a freelance journalist and novelist. Her first thriller, *Back to the Coast*, was published to great acclaim in 2003. *The Dinner Club* followed in 2004 and, with over 400,000 sold, has topped the Dutch bestseller list.

**"*The Dinner Club* is a savage little story of middle-class mayhem in a trendy village near Amsterdam. It's sharp, sexy and a riveting read."** *Sunday Telegraph*

**"Affairs, deceit, manipulation, tax dodges and murder— there's nothing Noort shies away from stirring into the mix, nicely showing off the sinister side of the suburbs."** *Time Out*

£9.99/$14.95
CRIME PAPERBACK ORIGINAL
ISBN 978-1-904738-20-6
**www.bitterlemonpress.com**